EVERSION

EVERSION

Alastair Reynolds

First published in Great Britain in 2022 by Gollancz
an imprint of The Orion Publishing Group Ltd
Carmelite House, 50 Victoria Embankment
London EC4Y 0DZ

An Hachette UK Company

1 3 5 7 9 10 8 6 4 2

A CIP catalogue record for this book is
available from the British Library.

ISBN (Hardback) 978 0 575 09076 7
ISBN (eBook) 978 0 575 09079 8
ISBN (Trade Paperback) 978 0 575 09077 4
ISBN (Audio) 978 1 473 22843 6

Typeset by Input Data Services Ltd, Somerset

Printed and bound in Great Britain by Clays Ltd, Elcograf S.p.A.

www.gollancz.co.uk

For my wife, because.

Physician, heal thyself.

-Luke ch4, v.23

Chapter One

Footsteps rescued me from my nightmare. They were approaching with urgency: hard soles thudding on old, creaking timbers. I came around seated at my writing desk, face pressed to the pages of my manuscript. I lifted my head and pinched at the gummy corners of my eyes. Pince-nez spectacles were before me on the desk, slightly askew where the force of my slumping forehead had borne down on them. I straightened them out, fixed them to my nose, and splashed water on my face from a cork-stoppered earthenware jar.

The footsteps ceased. A knock sounded at the door, followed by the immediate sound of the door being eased ajar.

'Come in, Mortlock,' I said, swivelling in my seat, feigning the impression of being disturbed from innocent business.

The tall, stooping midshipman bent his head and shoulders into the low-ceilinged cabin.

'How did you know it was me, Doctor Coade?'

'You have a manner, Mortlock,' I said pleasantly. 'Everyone has a manner and I remembered yours. Sooner or later, if we are not first shipwrecked, I expect I will know the manner of everyone on this vessel.' I made a show of blotting the manuscript, even though the ink was hours-dry on my last addition. I was in the process of closing the leatherbound covers when my eyes alighted on the little machine-engraved snuff box that was still on the desk, open to reveal its contents. A cold horror of discovery shot through me. 'How is that tooth?' I asked, a touch too hastily.

Mortlock tugged down his scarf to touch the side of his jaw. It was still slightly swollen but a good deal less inflamed than it had been four days ago, when I had dealt with an abscess.

'Much better, doctor, sir, thank you very much.'

'Turn about. Let me see your profile.'

Mortlock did as he was instructed, affording me the precious seconds I needed to spirit the snuff box safely into a drawer. 'Yes,' I said, nodding. 'Yes, very satisfactory. Continue with the tincture I gave you, and you should feel a steady improvement over the coming days.' I looked at him over my spectacles. 'Your company is always welcome, Mortlock. But is there something else besides the abscess?'

'It's the Coronel, sir. He's had a bit of a bump out on deck. Out cold, he was, and now he's back with us but he's striking out, wriggling and cussing in that native tongue of his . . .'

'Spanish, is I believe the term for it. Or at least the form of it endemic in New Spain.' I relaxed slightly, believing that Mortlock had made nothing of the snuff box nor its sudden disappearance. 'What was the nature of the injury?'

'A block came down on his bonce, hard as you like – knocked him clean to the floor.' Mortlock made an emphatic chopping motion. 'We were changing tack, looking for that gap in the cliff, and the Coronel just happened to be in the wrong spot when a rope snapped. There was a bit of blood, but his head hadn't gone all soft as if it had been stoved in, so we thought he'd be all right if we just sat him up and let him have a nip of rum, sir . . .'

I shuddered to think of the poor man's injury being poked

and prodded by men who could barely read, let alone perform a competent diagnosis. 'Bring him to me immediately, Mortlock.'

'What is it, do you reckon?'

'I dare not speculate. But if he has suffered concussion, even in the absence of a skull fracture, there may be elevated intra-cerebral pressure.' I reached beneath the desk for one of several elegant boxes which I had brought with me. 'All haste now, Mortlock!' I continued, raising my voice spiritedly. 'And be so kind as to communicate to Mister Murgatroyd, or Captain Van Vught himself, that it would be extremely helpful if the ship were to maintain a constant heading for the next half an hour.'

'The Master might grumble about that, doctor, if it slows down our search.'

I nodded sombrely. 'He is bound to. But I shall remind him that it is his man-at-arms that I shall be striving to save.'

Mortlock departed, his footsteps ringing away. I sat still for a moment, collecting myself, and reflecting on that irony that I had first hidden one pretty box and then disclosed another. Both were finely-made things; both in their way vital to my work. The box I had concealed contained opium snuff, self-administered with the intention of dulling myself into dreamless oblivion. The other held a French-made trephination brace of impeccable manufacture, but which I had never had cause to use on a living subject.

I feared – no, hoped – that this state of affairs was about to change.

'Are you ready for this, Silas?' I asked myself aloud. 'Your first real test, on this voyage? Your first real test, of any sort?'

I opened the lid on the trephination brace, imagining the college examiners casting their doubtful gazes upon my hesitant efforts. Stern-faced men in black, men with London manners, veterans of troubled voyages and bloody engagements, men for whom cutting and sawing was as effortless as breathing, men

to whom screams were merely the peculiar music of their profession. What hubris was it that made me think that I could
ever join their ranks? I was a West Countryman without connections: a poor, provincial surgeon out of Plymouth (but of
Cornish blood, as I reminded all who would listen), forty-four
(and therefore long past the age at which most surgeons made
their first voyage), a mere Assistant Surgeon (yet the only surgeon of any kind) on a fifth-rate sloop under a Dutch captain.
The captain was kind, but his ship was old, his crew tired, their
provisions threadbare, and the terms of our charter questionable
in the extreme.

This was how I meant to make my way?

The gleaming parts of the trephination brace waited in
snug recesses of purple felt. The metalwork was engraved,
the handles of ebony. Such beautiful artistry, for such brutal
ends. My fingers quivered as I reached to extract the drill-like
components.

Suppressing a spasm of shame, I retrieved the snuff box and
took a hasty pinch in order to settle my nerves and banish the
last traces of the nightmare. It was a habit that was becoming all
too familiar, especially as we ventured further north along the
Norwegian coast. Matters had worsened since leaving Bergen,
with the nightmare repeating itself with increasing regularity. I
had been taking more and more snuff to counter its effects, with
diminishing success.

The nightmares were like nothing I had endured before setting foot on *Demeter*. In them I found myself staggering along a
barely-lit stone passage, clad in hood or mask or helmet, gripped
by the terrible intimation that I myself was dead, merely a sham-
bling corpse, with empty sockets and grinning jaw. I could not
identify the cause of these torments, other than to speculate that
being confined for long hours in my cabin, with only books,
potions and surgical instruments for company, my mind had

become unhealthily focussed on the thin membrane which separates the living from the dead.

My one hope lay in the failure – or should I say abandonment – of our expedition. Perhaps, as we scoured endless dismal miles of Norwegian coastline, looking for a glimpse of something that only one man truly believed to exist – and he not exactly the most sober or reliable among our number – and as the days grew colder, the seas rougher, the ice more abundant, the stores more depleted, the ship more worn-out, the general morale weaker, the lugubrious Dutchman more openly sceptical of our chances – perhaps I might yet be saved by our turning home. It was a coward's hope, as well I knew. Yet in the grip of the equal miseries of seasickness and dysentery, not to mention every other common hardship of sea-borne life, I should gladly have proclaimed my cowardice to all who would listen.

I had hidden the snuff box again by the time the injured Coronel was brought down to my room. In those minutes I had also prepared the main table, sweeping it free of books, journals and manuscript pages, and made sure my other instruments and remedies were to immediate hand. Coronel Ramos was in a state of considerable agitation as the midshipmen press-ganged him into the room, for even in his confused condition he was bigger and stronger than any of them. It took four to get him onto the table, and they had a struggle to make good his restraints as he thrashed and twisted like some muscular eel.

'He was unarmed while agitated?' I asked Mortlock, who was one of the four assistants, and the only midshipman I knew by name.

'That's the lucky part, doctor. He's always polishing that flintlock of his, and he had it in one hand and a cleaning pipe in the other when the block came down, and it made him drop the pistol. Mister Murgatroyd got hold of it before it got washed through the gunnels, but I think if he hadn't, and the Coronel had still had it in his hand, you'd be digging a bullet out of one of us.'

'Let us be thankful for small mercies, then.'

Since the wound was on the back of his head, I had dictated that they secure him to the table face down. He had bled profusely, so I swabbed the affected area as gently and thoroughly as I could, being careful not to depress the bone until I had determined to my satisfaction that there was no serious fracture. My examination was helped by the fact that Ramos was quite bald, not just about the crown but around his whole blocky, boulder-shaped head. Some hair still grew, but he shaved it away each morning, sparing only his beard and moustache, which he maintained with the same devotion shown to his armaments.

'It doesn't look too bad,' Mortlock offered.

'There is no penetration of the skull, nor any fracture that I can detect. He is made of stern stuff, our Coronel. But the impact has knocked his brain about, causing his present distress. There is likely a build-up of pressure – blood or cerebral fluid – which must be relieved by means of trephination.'

Mortlock's eyes drifted to the exquisite French brace, poised in its now-open box.

'You're going to drill into 'im with that Froggy thing?'

'It is the only thing that will save him.' I looked to the four men who had come in with the Coronel. 'It will likely cause him some discomfort, and you must be ready for that. But I am confident that the procedure will work, if we proceed speedily.' I pushed my spectacles back up my nose, countering their habit of drifting to the tip. Rolling up my sleeves I took the brace, and settled myself into the most comfortable and stable position for the procedure.

Master Topolsky and Milady Cossile burst into the room without warning. The former was a cloud of black, the latter an apparition in yellow. I glanced up from my preparations, squinting through a loose lock of hair.

'What is this?' asked Topolsky, heavily clothed, wet and windswept from being out on deck.

'A medical emergency, Master Topolsky.'

'The doctor's going to drill into 'im,' Mortlock explained, with as much eagerness as if he had just graduated to the position of Assistant Surgeon. 'His brain can't breathe in and out, see, so it's squeezing his thoughts.'

'A most commendable summary,' said Milady Cossile, her fingers steepled. 'I expect Mister Mortlock will soon be composing the standard monograph on the subject?'

Mortlock looked at me doubtfully.

'Is the young gentlewoman being sarcastic again, doctor?'

I nodded sympathetically at the midshipman, who was straining every muscle to hold Ramos still. 'Pay her no heed, Mortlock. You are doing very well.'

'Is there need for this?' asked Topolsky, looming over the table. 'The Coronel is a hale man with the common vigour of his kind. He just needs a little rest, not to be drilled into like a brandy cask.' His tone sharpened. 'We still have need of him, Coade!'

'And my purpose is to ensure that he remains at our disposal, Master.'

Ramos muttered something from the table. It sounded like *trece* to me, the Spanish for thirteen.

He was not a true-born Spaniard but a citizen of New Spain. He had been a soldier – hence his title – but he now owed his allegiance to no army or king, and offered his services for hire to men such as Topolsky. I knew very little about him, for Ramos was a taciturn man, quite the opposite of his boisterous employer. But we had spoken now and then, usually in the quiet moments between watches, when one of us might encounter the other on deck, pensively watching the sea.

Some political or religious difficulty – more than likely the same thing – had forced him to leave the Americas: I understood a little of it, piecing together such crumbs of biography as Ramos chanced to offer during our nearly silent communions. Turning against his father, Ramos had developed sympathies for the independence movement led by the Jesuit Hidalgo.

'Better men than I have found themselves before the Court of Inquisition,' Ramos had confided to me. 'But I had the means to leave, and they did not. It does not make me brave, merely astute.'

Now this softly spoken giant – Ramos said that he owed his size and strength to his mother, who was of *criollo* descent – lay on my table, whimpering and foaming at the mouth. I was glad that his face was averted, facing the floor, because I could not have stood to look into his eyes as I began to work the brace.

'*Trece*,' Ramos murmured. Then, after a pause: '*Cinco*.'

I applied firm but steady pressure on the brace, while turning the handle at a slow, constant rate. The three-tipped bit was already biting into bone, etching a coin-sized groove. Mortlock kept glancing at my work then tearing his gaze away, while the three other midshipmen seemed incapable of mustering even a glance. I did not blame them for that: trephination was hardly something to be encountered in the normal life of the sailor.

'A question of terminology, if I may?'

Sweat was already in my eyes. It was the first time I had found my cabin anything other than intolerably cold since leaving Bergen. I paused in my work and pushed my hair and spectacles back again.

'By all means, Milady Cossile.'

'*La vigilia* . . .' Ramos said, on a note of rising concern. '*La vigilia! La vigilia . . . de . . .*'

'Concerning the procedure you are employing.' Milady Cossile still had her fingers steepled, tapping their tips against her lips between utterances. She had perfect lips, I thought. Not even the brush of Gainsborough could have captured their fullness. 'I have encountered the term trepanation as well as trephination. Would you presume that the two forms are etymologically related?'

I resumed my drilling. 'I cannot say that I have given the matter much consideration.'

'But still – would you presume?'

'I suppose I might.'

Even with my eyes focused on the drilling site, I still detected Milady Cossile's gleeful response to my answer. She skipped forward, clapping delightedly, her feathers bouncing jauntily, before re-steepling her fingers.

'Then you would presume incorrectly, Doctor Coade! The two forms are etymologically quite distinct! I am surprised you were not aware of this.'

I continued with my work.

'Do enlighten us, milady.'

Ramos said: '*Trece . . . cinco. Trece . . . cinco! La vigilia de piedra! La vigilia!!*'

'Trepanation derives from *trepanon*, which in turn derives from the Greek *trupanon*, meaning an instrument for boring. Trephination – or *trephine* – derives instead from the Latin, in particular *tre fines*, or three ends. Whether the latter term was first coined by Fabricius ab Aquapedente, or John Woodall, a century later, is a question yet to be settled.'

I looked up from my work and nodded. 'Thank you, milady. I am sure we are all most enlightened.'

'Never mind enlightenment,' Topolsky said, leaning very close in to the drill site. The Russian was a stout, pot-bellied man of about forty, with a wide, cherubic face, densely circumscribed by a curly mass of beard, sideburns and fringe. He had the sort of twinkling, searching, jocular eyes that suggested an agreeableness of temperament lamentably absent in the man himself. 'Will he live? We need this brute, Coade! Our expedition cannot proceed without him! He may not be learned, and his manners distinctly those of the New World rather than the Old, but who among us understands the placement of gunpowder like the Coronel?'

'I agree entirely,' I said. 'And if you value him as much as you say, you might refrain from projecting spittle into the wound site.'

Topolsky swore at me in Russian, his lips largely hidden behind the prodigious eruption of his beard, which was as voluminous and roomy as Ramos's was neat and manicured. His hair glistened and smelled faintly of perfumed oils. Regaining something of his usual composure he continued: 'Your reputation is satisfactory, Coade. I only wish that this were not the time to put it to the gravest test.'

'In my experience, Master, serious accidents rarely happen on a convenient schedule.' Suddenly I felt the opposition to the brace lessen as I bored through the last, sliver-like layer of bone. I had an image in my mind's eye: the tip of a drill bursting through the underside of a layer of ice, into the dark water beneath. Ice as bone, water as dura and brain. 'We are through. Master, if you might assist: that small implement like a sugar-spoon? I must lever away the bone fragment. Had there been more time I might have attempted to form an osteoplastic flap, but . . .' Abandoning my commentary I put away the brace and closed my fist around the tool Topolsky had passed me. To my immense relief the coin-sized section of bone levered away willingly, and with it came an immediate expulsion of thick, sticky blood from a severe epidural haematoma.

'It's like raspberry jam, doctor!' Mortlock declared excitedly.

I smiled at him. 'But perhaps a tad less palatable, even with your mother's best bread and butter.' I watched Ramos for a minute, until I had convinced myself that there was a definite easing in his distress. 'That must work,' I declared. 'It is, in any case, all I can do. To go beneath the dura would kill him. Medicine has done what it can, gentlemen – the rest of his fate is between Ramos and his god.'

'His god,' Topolsky muttered contemptuously. 'Can you imagine such a debased deity? Half Papist nightmare, half whatever Inca savagery came down to him from his mother.' Laughter lines creased the skin around his eyes and mouth, as they did when he was pleased with an observation he had either uttered or was about to utter. 'Better no god at all, I might venture!'

The expulsion of blood was easing. I did not think there was continued bleeding under the skull, although it would likely be many hours or days until we could be assured of his survival. Longer still before we knew that Ramos would recover entirely. I was not so sanguine, for I had seen and read about the lingering influence of concussion and other maladies of the brain on otherwise healthy men. If he carried only the physical scars of this day, he would be fortunate.

'Will you pop that bit of bone back into his head, doctor?'

'No, Mortlock – it would only become infected. But the hole is as small as I could make it. When I am sure that the pressure has been relieved, I shall close up the wound with stitches.' The unwelcome imagery of my recurring dream sprang to mind unbidden: the stone passage, the hood about me, my own face reduced to a hollow skull. I winced it away as one winces away a sour aftertaste. 'I think the Coronel will consider himself fortunate to have come through this day, even if he must live with a weak spot on the back on his head.'

'A commendable effort,' Milady Cossile said. She was dressed all in yellow, with a short-brimmed hat that seemed mostly made of yellow feathers. 'Perhaps there is something to be said for our provincial schools of medicine after all.'

'I shall be sure to convey your estimation to my tutors in

Plymouth. Thank you also for the lesson in etymology, which could not have been more timely. Do I have that right? I sometimes forget which one is to do with words, and which is to do with insects.'

She smiled patronisingly. 'You have the right of it, for once.'

'I still say he'd have been ship-shape with a bit of rest,' Topolsky complained, eyeing the now much less agitated form on my table. Ramos was still murmuring, but now his words slipped out of him drowsily and without any conveyance of inner turmoil. '*Trece . . . cinco. La vigilia de piedra.*'

'Without this intervention he would have been dead within the hour, Master. Now he has a fighting chance.'

'Good. Then if you're done with your infernal sawing, I suppose I can ask the captain to resume our northerly progression?'

'Far be it from me to interfere in the priorities of the expedition, Master. Dare I enquire: exactly how far into the ice floes will we sail, before giving up on your quarry?'

'Concern yourself with potions, doctor: leave the work of discovery to those of us who have the imagination for it.'

'That I shall gladly do.'

Topolsky and Milady Cossile departed. I told the midshipmen that they had been of great assistance, but were now free to go about their duties. Since *Demeter* would surely be about to resume turning and turning-about, zig-zagging her way north, I presumed that they would be needed on deck, assisting in the great coordinated dance of rope and canvas which made us sail.

Mortlock lingered after the other three had gone.

'I'm off duty now, doctor, so if you'd like someone to sit with the Coronel and keep an eye on 'im, I'd be more than willing.'

'That is very kind of you, Mortlock.'

His gaze fell upon the restful giant, still bound to the table. 'He's a quiet, brooding sort of cove, isn't he. The men said he was aloof, to start with, like he was better'n the rest of us. P'raps he is. But out of all of 'em that came with Master Topolsky, I think I like 'im the best.'

'I venture our opinions are not entirely unalike.'

Mortlock put on a half-smile. 'Is that your way of saying you agree with me, doctor, but you can't quite come out and say it?'

I reflected on my answer as I set about cleaning and packing away the parts of the trephination brace.

'You have the right of it, as Milady Cossile might have said. Now will you help me turn the Coronel? I fancy he will be more comfortable on his back.'

After he had assisted me Mortlock slid one of my chairs across the timbers and sat down in it wearily, without waiting on invitation. He was about my age and height. There all essential similarities ended: Mortlock was a burly, red-headed Yorkshire-man; I was from whippet-thin Cornish mining stock. Mortlock had been at sea since he was a boy and survived action, mutiny, flogging, shipwrecking and two bouts of scurvy. Since coming aboard, I had merely been afflicted by racking seasickness and a near constant dread of imminent catastrophe. In my mind, every creak and groan of the ship presaged the splitting of her fabric from bow to stern. I was not made for the sea and all the men knew it to one degree or another. But, of all of them, only Mortlock seemed not to judge me for my failing.

'Concerning her ladyship, doctor – and I don't mean to speak out of turn here – but she's a bit of an arse, isn't she?'

'An arse, Mortlock?'

'Pardon my French, I mean.'

'It is quite all right. And in point of fact I see no reason to find fault with your assessment.'

Mortlock relaxed into the chair. 'Why's she got it in for you all the time?'

'I think that is merely her manner, Mortlock. I imagine she was raised to consider herself among inferiors at all times.

Doubtless life has reinforced this admirable opinion of herself at every turn, from cradle to college. She has never had the slightest cause to be disabused of it. There may even be a grain of truth in it. I do not doubt that she is intelligent and well-schooled.'

'I didn't go to a school at all.'

'Then my point is proved. With no schooling, save for the humble education you have received at sea, you have proved yourself a far more agreeable companion than Milady Cossile will ever be. Granted, you are not so fair to the eye, nor so free of blemishes, nor do you deport yourself with such maddening—' I curtailed my train of thought before I blushed at him. 'But we must make allowances. Master Topolsky picked his expedition partners himself and we must strive to see the value in each of them.'

Mortlock leaned back in the chair, reached for a shelf and began leafing through the papers I had shoved from the table.

'Did you know of her before you came aboard?'

'As she is at pains to remind me, I am a provincial surgeon from the West Country while Milady Cossile moves in well-connected intellectual and academic circles in London. I am informed that she is on as equally agreeable terms with the likes of Byron as she is with men such as Davy. Our spheres, dare I say it, do not greatly intersect.'

'First it's circles, then it's spheres. Make your mind up, doctor!' He scratched at the rough red skin on the back of his neck. 'I just don't understand why she needles you all the time. It's like you offended her in a past life!'

'I am equally at a loss, Mortlock,' I said wearily. 'I can only suppose that Milady Cossile sees it as her gainful mission to occasionally improve another soul. Regrettably, for the duration of this expedition, I am the target of that undoubted altruism. But enough of our redoubtable etymologist.' I glared at him as he continued rummaging through my papers. 'Can I help, or are you quite content to dig into my writings on your own?'

'No, you're all right, Doctor. I was just hoping to get ahead of the others, you see.'

It was my fault. When Mortlock had come to me with his abscess, I had allowed him to quiz me on my progress with the manuscript, and at length had even allowed him to glance through the next couple of chapters, going so far as to gauge his opinion on one or two troublesome points of narrative. It had been my way of taking his mind off the treatment. But Mortlock, being an open, trusting sort of soul, had taken this as immediate licence to treat my papers as his own.

'I think perhaps we must draw a line under the narrative.'

Mortlock looked up, as stricken as if he had just read his own death warrant. 'You can't do that, Doctor Coade! There'll be . . . well, I shan't say mutiny, because that's a black word on any ship, even a privateer like *Demeter*, but there'll be 'ruptions if the midshippers don't get to hear the next part!'

'Ructions is the word you seek. But surely the midshippers haven't heard any part of it. You are the only man of that station who has come to the captain's table.'

Mortlock scratched around the diminishing swelling of his abscess. 'That isn't quite true. I hope you don't mind, but I've been memorising bits of it, as much as I can, leastways, and then going over it again when I'm down below.' He fidgeted in the chair, as restless as any boy summoned to their headmaster. 'I didn't mean anything wrong by it, but a lot of the men down there can't read or write, and a story takes 'em out of things. I tried them on *Gulliver's Travels* but they said they liked your story more, so I kept on with it.'

'I see.' I held my silence for a few seconds, not entirely out of some mean enjoyment of Mortlock's discomfort. 'You say they find some interest in it?'

'Oh, yes.' Mortlock leaned in eagerly. 'Especially that part about the ship with steam in its belly!'

'A steam-driven ship is no more than a logical progression of current developments.'

'And the thing the men are sailing towards – you can't leave 'em not knowing what it is, doctor!'

'Would that the question were entirely settled in my own mind, Mortlock. I am afraid that is not quite the case. When I read a passage to the captain's gathering, I am seldom more than a chapter or two ahead of it in my own process of composition.' I gestured at the papers he held. 'That is the difficulty. Between you and me, I am torn about the direction of the narrative.'

Mortlock turned to the start of the manuscript. His finger moved along the line at the top of the page.

'The Stone . . .' He paused. 'Viggil?'

'Vigil,' I corrected him. '*The Stone Vigil*. That is the title I have finally settled upon.'

Mortlock read on. '*The Stone Vigil*, or *The Edifice in Ice*. A romance by Doctor Silas Coade.' He nodded his appreciation. 'That's got a nice ring to it, it has.'

Next to us, Ramos murmured: '*La vigilia de piedra*.'

'He approves!' Mortlock said, laughing. 'I wondered what he was coming out with when you were drilling 'im. That's just the Spanish for your book, isn't it?'

I nodded through a faint uneasiness.

'You have a keen ear for languages.'

'Comes with seafaring, I suppose. I've heard every tongue under the sun. I can eff and blind in half of 'em, too.' He gathered the manuscript pages back together and returned them to the shelf. 'Well, I said I'd keep an eye on 'im if you like, and I meant it. And I promise I won't go peeping into the chapters you haven't read out to us.' Earnestly he added: 'But you've got to keep going with it. For the men's sake, if not the rest of us. They'll have my guts for gibbets if I make 'em go back to *Gulliver's* bloody *Travels*, and we don't even speak about *Robinson Crusoe*.'

'I shall . . . endeavour to.' I smiled inwardly, not entirely unflattered by the thought that the men below – rough-formed as their tastes undoubtedly were – preferred my scribblings to the efforts of Swift and Defoe. 'Although it must be understood that my surgical duties take priority at all times.'

Mortlock looked fondly upon Ramos, quiet again now. 'We're a lucky ship, Captain Vannie says. I'm sorry for the Coronel that he was the one, but that'll be our one bit of bad luck out of the way now, mark my words.'

'For an intelligent man, Mortlock, you harbour a deplorable streak of superstition.'

'I'm afraid that's another thing that comes with being at sea,' he replied unapologetically. 'As you'll find out, if you stick with it long enough.'

'I doubt very much that my career at sea will be of any great duration,' I replied.

Chapter Two

Content that Mortlock would keep watch over my patient, I gathered my deck clothes, putting on as many layers as was feasible before facing the savagery of the wind and waves. I was buttoning my coat when lightning flickered against my cabin windows. I waited for the roll of thunder to arrive, but the sounds of the ship must have muffled it.

'There is always lightning,' I murmured to myself, as if some deep truth lay buried in those words.

Exactly how far north we had come was neither my professional concern nor my private interest. The last accurate point of reference I committed to memory was when we stopped in Bergen to augment our supplies, but we had been sailing up the Norwegian coast for a further ten days since then, making between forty and sixty miles of northerly progress in each twenty-four hours. Our course was seldom direct, though, since the wind was coming at us from the Arctic Circle and Captain Van Vught was obliged to plot a laborious, zig-zagging route.

I noted the changes in the heading and tilt of the ship the first twenty or so times they happened: there was always a commotion of shouts and footfalls above my cabin as sails were reorganised. Eventually – like all the rhythms and routines of maritime life – these disturbances dropped beneath the threshold of conscious observation, except when they caused me to lose my footing or tip a candle across my desk.

That we were indeed far to the north of Bergen – perhaps four or five hundred miles – was abundantly obvious as soon as I ascended the ladder (the companion-ladder, I should call it) that brought me onto the top or quarterdeck. The wind knifed against me with an escalating, impersonal malice as I went up rung by rung, until the full, fierce force of it was striking my whole body.

The planking was icy. The wheel was nearer to the stern than the ladder so I had to resist the wind's efforts to send me skidding bodily along the quarterdeck. By this point, though, I had learned to emulate the stable, splay-footed stance of the older hands, not just because this habitual posture aided progress on a rocking, slippery deck, but because it helped against seasickness, to which I had already proven abundantly susceptible. The men had found it amusing that of all the maladies which could befall their surgeon, I was afflicted with the one for which there was no ready remedy except time.

I made my way along the wind-whipped quarterdeck. I spied three men standing close together by the wheel. The captain was one of them, Topolsky another (no other man had quite his build), but the third was not readily identifiable. I did not think it was Milady Cossile, nor one of the senior officers, so – with Ramos excluded – that left one of the two other men brought aboard by Topolsky: Monsieur Dupin or Herr Brucker, both of whom were suitably alike in stature. I continued my cautious advance, allowing my gaze to lift to the sails and rigging and the celestial depths beyond. It was ten at night and the skies were clear, still and transparent. Polaris sat high above us and a full moon transformed the ship into a gleaming spectral blue vision, ghostly except where there was a smudge of orange from a brazier, a lantern or a wavering pipe, cupped close to the mouth.

Off the port side stood an immensity of dark, foam-crested water, continuing all the way to a black horizon. On the starboard side, to our east, loomed a continuous wall of sea-cliffs, craggy and barren, underscored by a drool of surf. We were about a mile off these cliffs, and had been sailing alongside them – allowing for the zig-zagging course of the ship – ever since we had departed Bergen.

Occasionally there had been an inlet or an island to interrupt the tedium, but the overall impression was of some dreary iteration of the same pattern, like a roll of wallpaper fashioned into a continuous, nauseating strip. I wondered how even the keenest navigator could be confident of our position now. Van Vught had shown me his charts in the days after Bergen. They started off quite accurately, with each tiny feature of the coast mapped and named, but then became progressively less detailed with increasing latitude. He had stopped identifying islands and inlets some days ago, relying instead on measurements of stars and his consultation of chronometers and tables. That was easier said than done on a ship in rough waters, often under clouded skies.

I came within easy speaking range of the three men, and identified Dupin as the third member of the party. Van Vught had his hands on the wheel, Topolsky next to him; the captain's weatherworn features illuminated by the meagre glow from his pipe. Had Rembrandt painted him, he could easily have been some stoic Biblical patriarch of immense and improbable age. The captain was about fifty, but looked older, as men who had lived at sea often did. He had a beard and a prominent, ledge-like moustache, stiffened like the bristles of an old and dependable broom.

'How fares Coronel Ramos, Doctor Coade? Master Topolsky tells me you drilled into his head.'

The captain's English was beyond reproach, but he still

softened his esses, 'fares' becoming 'farezh', 'his' becoming 'hizh', and so on.

'A simple trephination, which I hope will have the desired outcome.'

'He went at it like a man who wants very much to justify an expenditure,' Topolsky complained to the captain.

'I am sure we can rely on the doctor's good judgement.'

'I shall be glad to – provided he does not insist on drilling into the rest of us.'

Topolsky was much shorter and broader than the captain. 'I have the constitution of a Cossack wrestler,' he had assured me early in our acquaintance, when I had noted how easily he became out of breath climbing up and down companion-ladders. Yes, I thought: but only if that hypothetical wrestler had spent a year indulging in enormous feasts and heroic bouts of idleness. Perhaps his blood was indeed Cossack, but there was so much about Topolsky that was bluster and misdirection I took none of his assertions as proven fact. He spoke English and French very well, and had clearly spent time in London and Paris. He only ever spoke Russian to curse, though he often alluded to his familiarity with the Imperial Court. 'Ah, yes, as Catherine herself once confided to me . . .' or 'It reminds me of an exquisite *objet d'art* shown to me by Peter himself, in the private annexe of the Hermitage . . .' and that sort of thing. Attempt to pin him down on any of it, though – such as when he was last in Russia, and what had caused him to seek his fame elsewhere – and the topic was quickly and skilfully dodged.

This much I could be sure of: he was wealthy enough to fund this expedition, but not so wealthy or generous with his money as to fund it lavishly. The ship was fifth-rate, by definition, and in mutual arrangement between Van Vught and Topolsky she ran with a very small crew, so that the men were at constant risk of being overworked. Costs had been cut in a hundred miserly ways, from the provision of the cheapest sort of salted beef to second-hand sailcloth to my surgical supplies. I was also one of those expense-saving measures: a surgeon, but not one of great repute, nor one who could afford to dictate his terms of employment. I, in other words, was as meagrely provisioned as the beef.

'We have resumed our course north?' I asked.

Van Vught smiled enough to lift the stiff, horizontal extremities of his moustache. 'We will make a navigator of you yet, Doctor Coade.'

'I would take credit for my observation, but it takes very little learning to notice that Norway is off to our right – to starboard, I should say.' I nodded at one of the other men standing near the wheel. 'Has Monsieur Dupin spied your objective, Master?'

'I have not,' Dupin answered.

He did not look at me, nor otherwise shift his gaze, for Dupin had his eye to a small, dainty spyglass. He had the spyglass aimed ahead of us and a little to the right, fixed on the line of cliffs about a mile north of *Demeter*.

Raymond Dupin was a very young man, perhaps the youngest of any of us save the greenest midshippers. I believed him to be about twenty but in his appearance there was nothing to suggest that he was anything other than an earnest, slightly sullen schoolboy. Prodigious tufts of yellow hair erupted from beneath the woollen cap he wore against the weather. His face was long and sharp-edged, with a chin that could split flint and cheekbones like razors. He was all shadow and light, like a sketch of a man rather than the finished work. Not a hint of beard hair showed anywhere around his mouth or in the line of his jaw. His deep, close-set eyes were as cold and grey-green as the waters in which we now sailed.

In service to Topolsky, he had come aboard as the expedition's private cartographer and authority on all matters of navigation. Naturally, Van Vught had experience of his own to call on, as well as such charts and instruments that were already aboard *Demeter*. These resources had clearly been deemed insufficient for the expedition's needs, and so Dupin had his own spyglasses, sextants, clocks and so on, all of impeccable quality (there at least, no expense had been spared) as well as trunks of maps, charts and almanacs. These items he guarded like crown jewels, clutching them jealously to his chest if another man (especially one of the regular crew) should show the slightest inclination to touch them, or even look too closely. The fine instruments – some of which had undoubtedly been furnished by the other member of the party, Herr Brucker – came and went from his plush-lined cases like infants being raised and lowered from cribs.

In that respect, I could find no fault in him: I was no less protective of my braces, knives and bone-saws. Both of us were born to a trade, and both of us knew the value of our implements. Mine were for dividing and suturing flesh; his sliced and ligatured distance and time.

'What exactly . . .' I began. 'What exactly . . . is it that we are looking for?'

'The fissure!' Topolsky said. Then, with unmasked irritation: 'Coade, have you been completely oblivious to our conversations, across all the evenings when we have gathered?'

'I was merely minding my own business, Master.'

'The doctor has enough concerns of his own, without us adding to them,' Van Vught remarked.

'Yes, I suppose it must be a very taxing business, thinking up a fairy story.'

Van Vught glanced at the other man with a surprising asperity. 'I did not mean that. The doctor writes only in his spare time, such little as he has. And I know that the men find it a pleasant distraction from the immediate concerns of our voyage. Even Milady Cossile takes some pleasure in it.'

'Yes,' I said, since the objectionable etymologist was not about.

25

'The same sort of pleasure as the hound takes in the fox.'

'Criticism too much for you?' Topolsky asked. 'Perhaps writing is not your vocation after all.'

'A man may have two vocations,' Van Vught mused.

Topolsky did not like my narrative, but his objection to it was of a much more transparent nature than that of Milady Cossile. When we first set out, Topolsky had been lord of the dinner table. He had many stories he wished to declaim, and for a little while he had been gifted with an attentive, if sceptical, audience. I posed no challenge to his oratory, and so he liked me. His eyes twinkled, the sherry flowed, the cigars were consumed, the tall tales encouraged. But as the wind put more leagues behind us the shine had gradually rubbed off his boasting and name-dropping. There was a sameness to it, a certain predictability, as if we had all heard the stories many times over. They were the sort of account which tended to conclude with Master Topolsky leaning back and declaiming "Of course I was proved right in the end" or "naturally, if they had listened to me, none of that would have happened" and various permutations thereof. When, during a lull, I was persuaded to read aloud from my romance-in-progress (which Murgatroyd and one or two of the other men were aware of) I had displaced Topolsky in the general affections of those evening gatherings. That had not been my intention, but now I suffered the daily consequence of that reckless impertinence. How dare I be the more popular dinner speaker!

'You may be relieved, Master, to hear that I am minded to discontinue the narrative. Mortlock would have me continue it—'

'That bumpkin thinks a brain is the same as a lung.' He tapped a finger against his nose as he prepared to offer me some shrewd advice. 'I would value his opinion a little less highly if I were you, Coade. He is a man of little learning and even less discernment. Choose your confidants more carefully.'

'I shall keep that in mind, Master.'

'Besides, your fancies already strain our credulity overmuch. Ships that sail by steam, cannons that fire volleys without being reloaded, and paintings that compose themselves by light alone!' He turned to the cartographer. 'What do you think's next, Dupin? Men bestriding the air? A picnic on the Moon?'

Dupin grunted his uninterest. He was still sweeping the cliff, angling his spyglass at a slowly moving point about two miles ahead of us.

'Let us speak of our position,' Captain Van Vught said. With one hand still on the wheel, he used the other to jab his pipe down at the angled chart table positioned at the wheel's side.

It was an improvised affair, somewhat like a lectern, with a sheet of glass that could be clamped across any open map or set of tables to protect them from the elements. Suspended above the lectern was a lantern, bucking and swaying with the wind and the motion of the ship.

'Where do we think we are?' I asked.

Van Vught tapped the pipe-stem against the glass, and by implication against the portion of the chart immediately beneath it.

'My conviction is we have just shortly passed the sixty-eighth degree of latitude, putting our position approximately here. Monsieur Dupin, on the other hand, contends that we are still some way south of the aforementioned line of latitude: no more than sixty-seven and one half degrees north.'

'Sixty-seven degrees and twenty-two minutes of latitude,' Dupin said mechanically.

'I wish I could offer an opinion either way,' I said. 'All I know is that it is cold, and the sun seems to reach a little less high in the sky from day to day. But I suppose it does that every winter.'

'The difficulty,' Topolsky went on, 'is this: it is agreed – quite agreed – that in all matters where a decision must be taken our excellent captain has the commanding authority. That is quite, quite beyond disputation! But the difficulty—'

'Then there is no difficulty,' I interrupted. 'If the captain considers the sixty-eighth degree to be the absolute limit of our northerly progress, then that is his decision.'

'But the difficulty,' Topolsky persisted, 'the very grave difficulty, is that since we cannot agree upon our position, we do not have the luxury of deferring to the captain's unquestioned authority. Since it is not yet a settled matter that we are indeed north of the sixty-eighth degree, the conditions for the captain's decision – however that should fall – have not been activated!'

'With no disrespect to Monsieur Dupin, ought not the observations taken by Captain Van Vught and his ablest men take precedence? The captain knows his ship and his instruments. He knows these waters well.'

'I have sailed close to these shores,' said Van Vught, who was too modest not to offer a clarification. 'But never as close to these cliffs as we are now.'

'Monsieur Dupin is quite confident in his observations,' Topolsky said. 'Aren't you, Dupin?'

Dupin lowered his spyglass momentarily. Despite the cold, a sheen of sweat showed on his brow and along the sharp ridges of his cheekbones.

'I have sufficient confidence.'

'In these matters,' I ventured, 'it may be wise to cleave to the precautionary principle. We have two sets of measurements, and neither can be said to be more trustworthy than the other. The captain knows his instruments and his methods, and we must presume no inferior capability on Monsieur Dupin's behalf.'

Van Vught jammed his pipe into his mouth and used both hands to make an adjustment to the wheel. From somewhere beneath the decking I felt the groan of rope and timber as his intentions were communicated to the rudder. A few clipped commands had men scurrying about the sails and rigging, fearless of the wind, ice or the tumultuous waters below.

Van Vught spoke out of the corner of his mouth, the pipe waggling with his words.

'Would you suggest that we split the difference between the positions?'

'No, I would suggest that we treat your reading as the one to act upon, not because it is more inherently believable, but because it is the one that places us furthest north and therefore in the greatest theoretical peril. Have you any incentive to exaggerate our northerly progress?'

'I have not,' Van Vught said. 'In fact I shall be denying myself a bonus if we do not locate the objective Master Topolsky seeks. If I did not believe my reading, I should be very content for us to sail on.' He crunched his jaw down tighter on his pipe, a habit which made me wince. 'But I do believe it, unfortunately. And even if I did not have the evidence of my measurements . . . there is *that*.'

He was staring ahead in a sudden and deliberate fashion, like a dog that has just spied a rabbit: something new and cold sparking in his eyes, as if a few wayward chips of the moon had lodged themselves within his pupils.

'Ice,' he said.

'We have seen ice before,' Topolsky said.

'Small pieces of it, no threat to us. But that ice is a mile off and there is a lot of it.'

'Is it serious enough for us to turn around?'

'Not just yet, Doctor Coade. We can sail between the icebergs. They are only about the size of a house. But there will be bigger ones. There are always bigger ones.'

I shivered. It was one thing to confront my own fears of destruction at sea. I had no doubt that many of them were irrational, or wildly amplified. But it was another to stand next to a man such as Van Vught and feel a breath of his own fear, and know that it was well deserved.

Dupin spoke.

'I see it.'

'The ice?' Topolsky asked.

'No, not the ice.' His hand shook on the spyglass. 'The fissure!'

Topolsky took the spyglass, lifting it to his eye with similarly trembling hands. He aimed it at the cliff, sliding the smallest tube in and out to adjust focus. 'Where, Dupin, where?'

Dupin reached over and steadied the spyglass. 'A little nearer. About there.'

'I don't see anything.'

'It is not obvious.'

'Then help me, for pity's sake!'

'Look for an irregularity in the line of surf.'

'An irregularity?'

Van Vught unclamped the sheet of glass on the table and drew out one of the drawings that had come aboard with Topolsky. He held it aloft under the lantern, comparing the sketched profile of the cliffs with the faint, moonlit apparition before us. As the lantern moved, so the drawing seemed to breathe in and out, as if etched onto the skin of some living organism.

'I think you have your fissure, Master Topolsky.'

I fancied I could see something where they were focusing their attention – a break in the surf, as if a pen had stuttered while scratching out a line of white ink – and perhaps a suggestion of a declivity above it, a recess in the cliff. But my night vision was nothing to boast about: generations of mining forebears had not gifted me any sort of exceptional faculty in that regard. I was all too aware that the brain was apt to deceive itself into seeing almost anything, if the desire was sufficient.

Did I desire it, or did I not desire it? That was a different question.

'It could just be a deep notch,' I offered.

'It's nothing of the sort,' Topolsky said. 'Use your eyes, doctor.'

'I am attempting to.'

'There is a clear break in the line of the cliff, all the way to the summit. It's the fissure, the inlet, the defile, exactly as described. Each second improves the correlation! Good grief, there's that skull-shaped outcropping, on the near-side – just as in the drawing! It is the very thing, and practically in our grasp! By the morning we shall be through to the other side!'

Some dim inkling of their intentions reached me. 'You mean we're to sail through that gap? It looks rather on the narrow side.'

'We're a narrow ship, Coade. Why else would I hire this fifth-rate sloop? No offence intended, Captain Van Vught.'

'None taken, Master. It is true we are narrow across the beam. Our draught is shallow also, and we are copper-bottomed. That will serve us well.'

'We've passed many indentations in the coastline,' I said. 'Fjords. Too many to name. What makes this one significant? They must all have been sailed into at some point. Norwegians and Danemen must have been sailing these waters for a thousand years. There can't be much left to be explored.'

'This is not the same, Coade. Tell him, captain.'

Van Vught sucked on his pipe for a few moments. 'The fissure was not here when my charts were compiled. There was just a continuous cliff. That is how it must have been, about a hundred years ago.'

I nodded. 'And now?'

'The cliff must have become worn away, until there was just a thin wall separating the sea from the inland water. A dyke of rock. It could have been like that for a long time. Even as long ago as when these charts were made. No one would have known that there was a body of water on the other side.'

'Until the cliff collapsed, creating your fissure.'

31

'And exactly when that happened, no one can say, not even Master Topolsky, except that it must have been before his drawings and charts were compiled.' Van Vught sucked some more on his pipe. He was calm at all times, but never more so than he was on deck, at the wheel. The vagaries of weather and sea seemed to have no bearing on his degree of inward repose. I could not have believed any man could be more at home, and more fully at peace with himself, in their favourite chair, in the warmest, snuggest parlour, than this man at the wheel of his beloved ship. 'They are quite recent, are they not, Master Topolsky?'

'No more than ten years old,' Topolsky said. 'The collapse of the sea-cliff must have happened between a century and ten years ago, but beyond that we can only speculate. Perhaps more will become clearer as we traverse the passage.'

'There is a hazard in that, I imagine?'

'Most certainly,' Van Vught answered.

'Then I trust that whatever is beyond that fissure is worth the risk to us?'

'We did not sail all this way just to look at cliffs, Coade.'

'Then what is it?'

'We seek a construction – a stone-built edifice at the eastern limit of the inland body of water.' Topolsky scrutinised my expression. 'Do not look so gloomy, man! It will make your fortune just as surely as it makes mine. Surely you are not afraid of a little adventure?'

'You speak as if this construction were already known to us.'

'Its existence is known to a select number of individuals, including society men and women of considerable fortune and even greater discretion. My sponsors, in other words. But they only know it because *I* brought word.'

'But you haven't been here before. If you had, you'd have known exactly where to find the fissure.'

'*Intelligence* came my way, Coade.' Some calculation worked behind his eyes. 'A crew sailed these waters. Being of an exploratory disposition, they ventured into the fissure. The unworthiness of their ship prevented them going any further, but it was sufficient for them to glimpse and chart the object of our interest.'

'And the name of this ship?'

'*Europa*. Though the name will mean as little to you as some minor bone or ligament does to me.'

'But if the men of *Europa* saw this . . . edifice, of which you speak . . . why have they not made their fortunes in place of you? Surely priority trumps all other concerns, in matters of discovery?'

'A glimpse is not a discovery. They did not see enough to capitalise on their exploit. Better that the intelligence be . . . traded, to a man such as myself, with the means and connections to make the most of it.'

'Is this settled, captain?' I asked. 'We are really going through that fissure?'

'The matter will be decided when we have light,' Van Vught answered. 'And if the passage is navigable – if I judge it so – then navigate it we shall.'

I could not explain why an unaccountable dread had begun to fill me at the idea of threading that passage. But fill me it had.

Chapter Three

Mortlock looked up from a book as I came back into my cabin. His eyes blinked a little readily, for it was clear that he had been asleep, or nearly so, until the moment of my return. The volume in question – Woodville's *Medical Botany* – sat precariously in Mortlock's fingers, nearly upside down and only a twitch away from falling to the hard varnished floor.

'The pictures are very pretty, doctor. I've never seen a book so nice.'

'Nor so expensively procured, Mortlock, so kindly return it to the shelf before it succumbs to catastrophe.' I softened my words with a smile. 'You are welcome to come here and read whenever it suits you, but I think it would help to be awake while doing so. Furthermore, most scholars agree that Woodville is best appreciated the right way up.'

'Oh.' Mortlock fumbled the book around in his lap, then closed it delicately. 'I didn't shut my eyes for more than a moment, I promise. I said I'd keep a watch on the Coronel, and I meant it.'

'Your diligence is not remotely in question. How has he been?'

'Quiet as a mouse, for the most part. Mumbles something now and then, but we all do that when we're sleeping, don't we?'

'Unconsciousness manifests itself in varying degrees. A word here and there is no cause for concern. He seemed . . . comfortable in himself? No convulsing?'

'Not a twitch. Sleeping like a babe, I'd say. You put him right with that Froggy drill.'

'It was not without risk, but I daresay it was the only action that would have saved him.' I made a gesture of gentle encouragement in the direction of the door. 'You may leave, with my thanks. I will mention to Van Vught that you have been of particular assistance. Though you are off duty, you may wish to go on deck. They have found the elusive break in the line of cliffs. The fissure, Master Topolsky calls it.'

'The fisher? Fishing for what?'

'*Fissure*, not fisher. A narrow passage, which may allow us to reach an inland sea, a sort of lagoon, I suppose, although that word does not sit well with these freezing latitudes.'

'All this way for more sea?'

'I gather there is something of interest in the lagoon itself, although Master Topolsky would not say too much. Perhaps, if we are lucky, we will soon see it with our own eyes. There is talk of fortunes to be made, so I gather it must be something out of the ordinary.'

'Pardon me for saying so, doctor, but you don't strike me as the sort out to make a fortune.'

'I am not, Mortlock. I shall consider myself amply rewarded if I have served this ship and crew satisfactorily, and we make it back with the minimum of casualties.'

'That'd do me as well, if I'm honest.' He paused a moment. 'Well, if you don't mind, I'll take my leave and see what's going on with this fission . . .'

'*Fissure*, Mortlock. Fission is a . . . very different process.'

When I was certain that the midshipman was in no danger of returning, I allowed myself a pinch of opium to restore the clarity of my thoughts, then scraped my chair around so that

I could sit comfortably at the side of Coronel Ramos. I lifted the bandage away from the area where I had cut into his scalp, satisfying myself that the expulsion of blood had ceased and that there was no suppuration of concern.

I had not meant to disturb Ramos from his sleep, but he must have been closer to awareness than I guessed, for his eyelids fluttered and a word emerged from his lips.

'Doctor.'

I answered softly: 'Yes, Coronel. Please be still. You are in my cabin. There was an accident.'

'An accident?'

'Yes. A few hours ago. You were on deck, and . . .'

He did not open his eyes. 'Am I . . . maimed?'

'No, you are quite intact in body and limb. But you did suffer severe concussion. I had to open your skull to relieve the pressure. Please do not be alarmed . . .'

'I have seen worse things done to men. And I have seen men survive worse things.' With the mild interest of someone enquiring after next week's weather, he added: 'Will I live?'

'I think it very likely. But you must rest, for now.'

For a man of such stature, and whose hairless, heavy-jawed head was so imposing, the Coronel had remarkably gentle eyes. They opened now, degree by degree.

'You drilled into me?'

'I did.'

He chuckled once. 'I have been sliced, stabbed and penetrated by shot. Sometimes by the enemies of Hidalgo, and sometimes by his friends. Twice by the husbands of his friends. But never drilled, until now.'

'I had no choice.'

'You need not explain yourself. If you did it to me, then I know that it was necessary.' He reached against his restraints, striving to touch my hand. I closed my fingers around his. 'I thank you, Silas. Not only for saving my life, which I am sure that you did, but for giving me another story to tell.'

'I would think a man who had lived your life would have stories enough.'

'There are many, it is true. But I have never found it easy to speak in the company of other men. I have nothing to say to men who speak only of whoring and drinking. But if I have a story to tell, I am sometimes able to fill the silence. There have been many silences, and many stories. Another is always welcome.'

'Then I am . . . glad to have been of service. But I will insist that you rest.'

'I will rest. But first, what happened to me?'

'A block of wood – do not ask me its function – came down from the rigging.'

'Better that we sail on steam, as in your book.'

I was pleased that he remembered, for it indicated little or no loss of recent memory.

'For now, we must confine ourselves to reality. Coronel – may I ask something?'

'I could deny you nothing, Silas.'

'You were talking in your sleep. You said *trece*, which I think is thirteen, and another word was *cinco*, which I believe is five. Thirteen, and five – several times. Do these numbers have some significance?'

He shook that massive head. 'I do not think so. Perhaps, in my sleep, I was wagering. My father tried to beat it out of me, but if there was a way to gamble I have always found it, even in my dreams. I have won and lost a thousand fortunes while abed.'

'There is one other thing.'

'Please.'

'You said *La vigilia de piedra*. The vigil of stone, or the stone vigil.'

He tried to lift his head. 'I did?'

37

'It is an odd thing to say. It is the title of my narrative, or at least the title I have presently assigned it. But I have mentioned that title to no one. Mortlock saw it just now, when he was nosing through my belongings . . .'

Ramos made to stir as if duty called him. 'He has betrayed your trust?'

'No – no! Not at all.' I placed a calming hand on his chest. 'Mortlock is kind and well-intentioned, and he insisted on watching over you when I was on deck. Mortlock is not the mystery! The mystery is the similarity between my title and the words you uttered.'

'I have not looked upon your narrative.'

'No, and not for one instant did I imagine you had. But if the words are familiar to you, in your native tongue, then it must betoken something. The originality I thought was mine . . . cannot be so. Where do those words come from, Coronel?'

He looked at me, his eyes open and truthful.

'I do not know, Silas.'

'You have no recollection?'

'I do not. Not of the numbers, not of the words. I do not think it is a story, or a song, or a poem. I have never remembered such things before, so why . . .' He paused. 'There is someone you could ask, Silas. Someone among us who knows everything about words.'

'Milady Cossile?' I nearly laughed. 'Dear Coronel, if it came to that, I should sooner drill into my own skull, and keep going.'

*

It was late, much later than was usually the custom, but in view of the discovery now upon us, Captain Van Vught had called *Demeter*'s senior figures to his stateroom. No meal was to be served at this exceptional hour, but sherry and cigars had been set before each place, and Master Topolsky was already making very commendable inroads into both his glass and his cigar, his eyes red, his cheeks inflamed, and his mood ebullient to the point of boisterousness.

'Savour this evening, gentlemen,' he was declaiming loudly as I came into the room. 'It will be the last before your lives are changed utterly! Tomorrow we cross the Rubicon.' He paused to fan away his own gauze of cigar smoke. 'We stand on the threshold of eternity. Our names will be uttered in the company of Polo, Magellan and Columbus! Mere cartographers like Cook, Mason and Dixon will be swept into the annals of deserved obscurity!'

'Perhaps,' Van Vught said mildly, attempting to temper his client while remaining within the bounds of civility, 'perhaps a *little* caution is in order, Master Topolsky, until we have completed a thorough survey of the passage by daylight.'

'Captain,' Topolsky said amiably. 'I know you far too well, dear fellow. You are a man of passions. A man of boldness. You will not be daunted by a modest constriction of rock and water. Yes, by all means conduct your survey – I'm sure these things must be seen to be done. But let us not pretend that by this time tomorrow *Demeter* will be anywhere but the other side of the fissure!'

'Silas,' Van Vught said in a companionable manner, inviting me to take the seat that he had kept vacant by his side. 'Is the news all that we might hope for, concerning our dear friend from the Americas?'

'Yes, doctor?' enquired Herr Brucker, the owlish instrument-maker. He was completely bald, save for a narrow stripe of black hair running from crown to nape, just as if it had been applied by a single stroke from a tar-brush. 'The news is good, *ja*?'

'Coronel Ramos is awake and lucid,' I reported.

'Excellent!' said Lieutenant Henry Murgatroyd, the second

most senior man on the ship. He thumped the table and encouraged a general round of thumping, clapping and toasting.

'I have urged him to rest,' I said, smiling at the party. 'It is my fervid hope that he will make a full recovery, but there is still peril in the coming days. However, Coronel Ramos is as strong a man as I have known, and it is my expectation that he will rally.'

'Did you mean fervent hope?' asked Milady Cossile. 'It is true that the two words are commonly taken to be interchangeable by those of modest learning, but they are not exact synonyms.'

'Are they not?' I asked, feigning sincere interest.

'Fervid may be said to imply a degree of unreasoning feeling beyond mere intensity of desire. A man of scientific inclination would adhere to the use of fervent, unless he wished his fellows to think him possessed by irrationality.'

'I would not want that,' I said, with the quiet satisfaction of one who has set a trap and seen it sprung.

'Please, milady,' said Murgatroyd, leaning over to pour a little more sherry into her glass. 'The doctor has had a trying evening. Perhaps his education could be adjourned, temporarily?'

'If we will not educate ourselves, Lieutenant, then we must depend on the kindness of others.' She took a delicate nip of the sherry. 'But you are right. It must be a very tedious business, to see a man helped towards the light, when he is not willing to be led.'

'Perhaps the man wishes only to find the light for himself,' I answered. 'But your kind efforts are noted, milady.' Before she could get in a rejoinder I said immediately: 'Captain Van Vught: is it indeed the case that we have found the inlet?'

'All the drawings agree, Silas, although there is only so much we can see by moonlight. It should be navigable, I think. Master Topolsky tells me that *Europa* was broader of beam than *Demeter*, and heavier of draught, although I do not know the ship for myself. We will observe the tidal flow in the morning, and judge for ourselves when it is best to thread the needle. I think we will go with the tide, if we have the wind at our backs. Before we do that, though, perhaps we may speak more openly of what the expedition expects to find, besides a lagoon. There was a need for secrecy, when we were putting in and out of port, but that time has now surely passed.'

Dupin glanced at Topolsky and received a nod of assent. The young cartographer had cleared a space before him on the table and unrolled a chart that I did not think I had seen before. He weighted its curling edges down with cutlery.

'Explain, please, for the benefit of our hosts,' Topolsky said, puffing vigorously on his cigar with one hand, scratching at the oiled, perfumed mass of his beard with the other.

'It's the lagoon,' Dupin said, his voice breaking on the words. He was sweating profusely, his complexion clammy. The sharp angles of his face stood out as if chiselled.

'That we may charitably have deduced for ourselves,' said Murgatroyd. He was a well-bred Irishman whose handsome countenance had not been greatly diminished by the loss of an eye to the Americans. He now wore a patch, and seemed to compensate for the absent eye by injecting a surfeit of expression into the other. No man on *Demeter* was better able to communicate his feelings through so limited a vessel, even if it were achieved with the merest narrowing of his lids or the slightest telling aversion of gaze. He was loyal to Van Vught, and still more loyal to the ship, which I think he fancied was due to become his in turn. Of our expeditionary guests, he regarded them as one might regard some troublesome but profitable cargo: an annoyance which must be tolerated, even pampered, in the interests of later reward. He did not like any of the guests except the absent Ramos, and his seniority allowed him the privilege of not masking his sentiments. In his defence, his animadversion owed nothing to nationality or creed. We were not presently at war with anyone, and so our motley assortment of Russians, English, French and Spaniards (if Ramos was still to be considered subject to Spain) were accorded excellent indifference.

Master Topolsky jabbed his half-consumed cigar in the general direction of Dupin's chart, allowing hot sparks to rain down on the drawing.

'Observe, please, the general shape of the feature, as that will have an important bearing on what we may expect to see by daylight. Note the shape of the lagoon: firstly how it extends inland and to the east by about six miles, never more than a mile across, but also how it bends gradually to the south, describing an arc or sickle. Note also the prominence jutting out from the southern shore, which will hinder any direct sighting of the lagoon's easterly limit.'

'Which is where you expect to find this . . . fortress?' I asked, noting a small, black, spiderlike impression which lay on the chart at the rightmost extent of the lagoon.

'Edifice, we are calling it, *ja*,' replied Brucker, and the emphasis in his reply caused me to capitalise the word in my imagination, as if it had unique significance and stature. Not merely an edifice, but the Edifice.

'Edifice, then,' I replied. 'And what are these curious lines?'

I gestured at a net of curving marks, enclosing the lagoon like wood grain around a knot.

'Contours of elevation,' Dupin said, using a trembling hand to flick the cigar sparks aside. 'An innovation of Hutton's, from his work on Schiehallion.' He dabbed perspiration from his brow. 'Along each line, the height above the sea remains constant.' He coughed, spit dappling the table like the first drops of a rainstorm. 'Where the lines are closest—'

'Are you feeling quite well, Monsieur Dupin?' I interjected.

'The boy is simply a little overworked,' Topolsky said. 'Instead of loafing around in his cabin, he has been on that deck, with his spyglass, for three continuous watches.'

'Then he needs to rest.' I regarded the young man sternly. 'You will rest, Raymond?'

He sniffed. His grey-green eyes regarded me. 'I was telling you about the contour lines.'

'Yes, and I appreciated your explanation.' I smiled, wanting the boy to know that I only had his best interests at heart. 'And I see it now. The lines get very close at the near end of the lagoon, where the cliffs must be nearly vertical. Then the slope becomes less severe, on the opposing shores, but it becomes very steep again near this mark. This is your fortress, I am sorry, Edifice?'

'It is.'

'It looks like a fat, furry-legged spider, or a little black octopus. These arms are . . . defensive fortifications? Walls, trenches, or suchlike?' Frowning, I reached across to tap a nail against the chart. 'The lagoon is drawn to scale?'

'Naturally,' Dupin said.

'Then if the lagoon is – as you say – a full six miles from end to end, six miles from the fissure to the eastern limit, then this black mark must be . . . a quarter of a mile across!'

'I shall astonish you further. The men of *Europa* reported that the fortress was as tall as it was broad!' Topolsky pressed his face nearer mine, so that I got a full, heady waft of his perfumed oils. 'Imagine it, Coade: a pile of stone sufficient to render the pyramids mere pimples on the pustulent face of Egypt! Does that not stir the soul, even your soul?'

'I suppose it does. I might also wonder who made this thing, and whether they are at all inclined to be visited.'

Topolsky dismissed my qualms with a flick of his wrist. 'No hint of life moves in those walls. In all probability our quarry has lain empty and desolate for hundreds of years, forgotten to time, its purpose – even the hand that commanded it to be built

– lost to fathomless antiquity. We may disturb dust and ghosts, but little else.' His twinkling, sherry-tinted eyes roved over my face, searching for the fundamental flaw of character that he surely knew to be present. 'Dear God, man, are you not in the least part moved by such a prospect?'

'I am neither moved nor unmoved,' I admitted. 'If you had resolved the riddle of heredity of physiognomy, or devised a lens for discerning bone through living tissue, or shown me how to render a patient insensible to the agony of surgery, I might be moved in the manner you expect.'

'Your indifference will crumble at the first glimpse of those soaring fortifications,' Topolsky assured me. 'But in the meantime, let me appeal to somewhat baser instincts.'

I smiled. 'By all means.'

'What we find here will make all of us very famous, and very wealthy.'

'I desire neither.'

Herr Brucker looked doubtful. A judicious smile creased Milady Cossile's lips. She had extracted a yellow feather from her hat and was tickling the side of her mouth as she examined me.

'Then I assume you will be publishing your manuscript pseudonymously, and with all royalties redirected to the destitute?' she asked.

'I will not be publishing it, milady. It is abundantly plain that the work is beyond salvation.'

'That would be a very great disappointment, doctor.'

'I am surprised that you feel that way, milady. At every turn you seem to have found more fault than good.'

Milady Cossile looked about the other guests, her face a mask of wild surprise. 'But I thought my criticisms perfectly timid. Generous, even.' She consulted the instrument-maker. 'Would you not concur, Herr Brucker?'

Brucker blinked and answered in the manner of one very much inclined not to cause trouble.

'Always generous, *ja, ja!*'

'Perhaps *you* thought your observations generous,' I said.

The others put on tense smiles and feigned an awkward interest in their sherry glasses and half-spent cigars. Herr Brucker rubbed at the improbable stripe of his hair. Murgatroyd scratched an itch under his eye-patch. The ship creaked and the waves slapped against her sides.

Milady Cossile would not be deflected.

'Have they not helped you improve the narrative, in certain regards?'

I had to fight hard to contain my anger. I had tried to draw milady's venom with the deliberate usage of 'fervid', knowing she would pounce. That achieved, I had hoped to be spared any more of her criticism, at least for that evening.

'Improve things? They have compelled me to go back and redraft passages, if that is what you mean. You did not agree with the type of ship my adventurers employed, so perforce I had to amend it. You said that there were deficiencies in my depiction of the customs of shipboard life – a misunderstanding of elementary matters of navigation and rank, and so I tried to improve those areas. You said that I had the weather quite wrong for the specified time of year, and that the winds I described were absurdly unrealistic for the given circumstances.'

Milady Cossile nodded encouragement. 'But all of these alterations have been to the betterment of your tale, Doctor Coade!'

'It is a fact, nonetheless, that each change had consequence. My story has become clotted . . . overburdened with detail, and forced to explain that which needed no clarification. Thanks to your interventions, I am spending as much time redrafting as pushing forward.'

Judging by her pretty frown, she found my answer perfectly bewildering. 'But if the story were constructed on dubious foundations . . . was it not better to shore them up now, rather than continuing to build an ever less stable structure?'

'You may see it in that light, milady. All I know is that I cannot now proceed.' I looked around the table. 'Please, dear friends. Let us speak no more of my vanity. There is, besides, another reason why I must discontinue.' My cheeks tingled. 'It is an awkward thing to discuss, but in light of this evening I would have no choice but to abandon the narrative completely.'

'What has happened, Silas?' asked Van Vught.

I stirred in my seat, uneasy under the inquisition of my peers. My clothes felt sticky, my eyes itchy with the after-effects of opium and sherry. 'I had a certain direction in mind,' I said. 'An objective towards which the story was racing. That objective was a structure of forbidding proportions. What you might almost term . . . an Edifice.'

'What good tale doesn't have a big old castle in it?' asked Murgatroyd cheerfully.

'It is not just that, Henry. We have followed my characters over water, to the brink of their first glimpse of the castle . . . Edifice.' Unconsciously, I was capitalising the word just as surely as Herr Brucker had done. 'They were about to be stirred and daunted, torn between a terror of the sublime unknown and their craving for notoriety. The latter impulse compelled them to enter this Edifice, whereupon . . .' I shook my head, thoroughly dispirited, not even willing to continue my own thought.

'Whereupon what, Coade?' Topolsky probed.

'Events of a disturbing nature were to befall them.'

'You can't give up on the story, doctor,' pleaded Mortlock. 'For the men downstairs, if not for us! It were just getting good, sir. I mean, not that the earlier bits weren't good as well, they were, but now it was getting *proper* interesting. For King and

Country, sir, don't have me reading to the men from Swift and Defoe again!'

I lifted my sherry glass to him, tipped it deferentially.

'You are kind, Mortlock.' A sudden gripping anxiety had me desperate to leave the room at any cost. 'Dear friends . . . I must attend to the Coronel. I have left him alone for far too long.' I turned to the clammy-faced boy. 'Raymond? May I count on you to take some rest? You are in urgent need of it.'

'See to the brute,' Topolsky said, as if we were speaking of a useful dog or pack mule. 'I'll see that Dupin rests. But before you depart, Coade, you must satisfy our curiosity in one respect.'

'By all means,' I said guardedly, beginning to rise from my chair.

'What were the events of a disturbing nature?'

I did not answer him. I could not have done so had I wished. Although I knew that the events set to befall my characters were in all respects abhorrent, and that in some sense I had already devised these horrors in my mind, with dramatic foreshadowing, I could not at that moment bring a single facet of those vile consequences to mind.

It was as if I did not wish to remember what had already happened to those poor souls.

Chapter Four

Ramos stirred as I loosened his restraints, satisfied that he was
not likely to do himself harm before morning.

'Where have you been, Silas? Surely you should be sleeping?'

'I will sleep now, Coronel.' I rubbed at my stinging eyes. 'I
have been up to the captain's stateroom. You know of the inlet
your employer has been searching for?'

'I knew of his folly.'

'You didn't believe in it?' I poured him some water and offered
it to his lips. 'I would have thought it a prerequisite for being in
Master Topolsky's service.'

'Not so, dear Silas. Master Topolsky demanded of me only
that I swear to serve him in matters of security, contract law and
such military expertise as may be called upon. This you know
very well. Your captain is an honourable man, and I think fair
in his relations, but we do have a contract with him and I am to
remind him of the terms should our opinions vary.'

'And enforce those terms, if needed?'

'I think a persuasive word would be sufficient. Hidalgo
achieved far more with words than gunpowder and I try to walk
in that man's shadow.' He looked ruefully down the length of his
body, still lying on the table where we had operated. 'Besides, I
am but one, on a ship of hundreds, and now I have a hole in my

head. The men below are not soldiers, but I would not wish to make enemies of one of them.'

'Nor they you, Coronel.' I began to undress, while I still had the energy to do so. 'But for what it is worth, the folly is real. Dupin has found the fissure – that is what they keep calling it – and if our Dutchman is satisfied then tomorrow we will sail through it, into the body of water now screened from us by cliffs. I suppose you know of the fortification Topolsky expects to find at the eastern end of the lagoon? Brucker called it the Edifice.'

'I know only that I may be called to find a way into it.'

'Do you believe it will exist?'

'I did not believe that we would find this inlet. Now that we have, I am ready to accept the rest of it.' He paused. 'But my involvement remains practical. As we near the Edifice I will advise on safe lines of approach. If he wishes that we should blast our way in, I will advise in the setting of powder. When we are within, I shall guard against traps. The nature of the thing is a problem for other men.'

'He thinks it could make your fortune.'

'If he is right, then money will be of help to my friends in New Spain. And one day, perhaps, if their enterprise succeeds, I shall be able to return to Valladolid without looking over my shoulder. Money can help with that, as well.' I sensed the pain it caused to him to speak of his own concerns, his eagerness to deflect onto another subject. 'What of you, Silas?'

'What of me?' I smiled, having to think for a moment. Even as I did, a sort of picture began to form before my eyes, un-folding itself as colourfully and tantalisingly as a child's paper theatre, made of clever folds and hinges. 'I should like to return to Plymouth and become a doctor on dry land.'

A great sceptical crease split the boulder of his forehead. 'Not in London? I thought all you Englishmen were drawn to London like flies to *guano*.'

'No, Plymouth would suit me well enough,' I said, grinning at his understandable misperception. 'The air is fresher, for one. A view of the sea would suit me, but not too *near* a view.' The picture unfolded itself still further. 'A modest white-painted cottage, a little orchard, perhaps even a wife, if she tolerates my day-dreaming. I should call it Hilltop Cottage. There would be vines and honeysuckle, and perhaps some fine oaks about. I should like enough patients to balance my books, and sufficient that I may be of some service to the townsfolk, but not so many that they interfere with my writing. Does that seem unreasonable?'

'I think you are better suited to the sea than you realise.'

'And I am content that this will be my first and last voyage. I have not been truly happy at any time since we set sail. If I am not seasick, I am cold. If I am not cold, I am exhausted. When I am none of those things, I am frightened. Yet if there is one part of it that I shall not regret, it is our acquaintance.'

'It is not every friend that drills into another friend's head.'

'Human affairs would be curious indeed, if that were the custom.' I appraised him again, still as a friend but through the discerning filter of my surgeon's eyes. 'Is there anything you feel you need, before I retire?'

'Only that I might satisfy your curiosity concerning that title. *La vigilia de piedra.*'

'You have traced the source of it?' I asked with rising interest.

'No, Silas.' He looked at me as fondly and regretfully as a father having to tell his favoured son that he could not keep a puppy. 'I have searched my memory and I am as confident as I can be that it means nothing. *Nada.* It is not a poem or song from my home country, nor a painting nor anything that I can remember. I must have overheard the words, and dreamed them into Spanish.'

'But not from me!'

'Men speak things in their sleep, as you have learned. On a ship, it is easy for such things to reach the ears of other men, even if they are themselves asleep. A ship is a dream of whispers.'

'You mean well,' I said kindly. 'But I am afraid my curiosity is anything but satisfied.'

'Sleep well, Silas, and in the morning you will be troubled by other things.'

I smiled at the austere truth evident in this. Life was indeed a continuous lesson in finding ways to be less troubled by certain things, so that we might make room for new concerns, which arrived with the promptness and regularity of mail coaches.

Ramos closed his eyes and became still. For twenty minutes I watched him for signs of agitation, until satisfied that his sleep was agreeable. I ought to have gone straight to my own bed then, but some masochistic compulsion pulled me back to my desk. I opened my manuscript at the last completed page, glared at it in resentment, feeling an equal enmity for the book as I did for the architect of its destruction, the damnable Milady Cossile. I tore out that last page, crumpling it into a ball, and was about to attack the previous one when some wiser instinct stilled my hand. As much as I hated the work, as much as I detested the sin of pride that had seen me embarking on the enterprise, I could not dismiss the good opinion of Mortlock and the midshippers. Perhaps their tastes were not so well formed as that of Milady Cossile and her ilk, but if my words had given those men one moment of respite from the tedium of their lives, what right had I to deprive them of another?

I took a pinch from my snuff box, and was soon lost to oblivion.

*

I must have fumbled my way to bed, because that was where I woke, with a watery light trembling through the cabin windows, where I had neglected to draw the curtains. A dream was dissipating, like a smoke sculpture being drawn apart by breezes. I had been wandering that lightless stone tunnel again. The pattern of it was always the same: a stumbling progression through darkness, a hood about my head, until at last I emerged into a chamber where a glimmer of light from above struck against a plane of polished rock, serving as a crude mirror. In the mirror I glimpsed my hooded reflection, and with a terrible inevitability I pushed back the hood until the light found the contours of a skull, empty of socket and grinning of jaw, and without fail I moaned or screamed myself to merciful consciousness.

I rose, shivering fit to rattle the dream loose from my head. Why did it plague me so? There was ample fuel for nightmares on a ship, so why did I dream of lightless tunnels and hooded skulls, instead of drowning or the horrors of battle?

I glanced at Ramos, observing the slow, massive rise of his chest, like the Earth itself straining, and the peacefulness of his face, as unburdened by worldly concerns as any sleeping saint. My scream must have been the silent kind, for it had not disturbed him.

Steadying myself against the rocking of the ship, I washed and dressed, and then chanced to see the crumpled sheet still resting on my desk. Crumpled, but not balled, as if it had been patiently unrolled and flattened while I slept. With a gathering unease I sat in my chair and took the crumpled sheet between my fingers, flattening it further.

My words were as I remembered them, right up to the point where the flow deserted me and my pen dabbed a line of expectant dots: the roots from which words might flower, when once again inspiration had me in its thrall. But those words were not the entirety of the torn sheet. In larger, bolder strokes, cutting mercilessly across the prior text, three words had been blotted down:

Inversion!
Inversion!
Eversion!

I stared at the rude adornment, noting how the ink skipped and snagged its way across the ruts and creases in the paper, indicating that it had been made after I balled up the page. I glanced again at Ramos, entertaining for an instant the notion that he might have risen from his recuperation and scrawled this palimpsest across my work.

But in truth I already knew well the author of the crime. The hand was mine and mine alone. At some point between my last clear recollection and waking, I had unrolled the ball and set my pen to it again. Some delirium of the small hours, fired by the last pinch of opium, had driven me to this vandalism. But in the literal light of a new day, I could see no sense in the words I had left myself.

'Eversion,' I said aloud, as if, like a spell, the meaning of the word might disclose itself through being spoken. But the significance was lost to my conscious mind. I felt that I ought to know what my own unconscious will had wrought, but there was nothing. Nothing except the assumption that, since *Inversion* had been set down first, and then angrily amended (the pressure of that crossing-out had nearly been enough to gash the paper through to its other side) then the two forms must have been similar enough to be confused in my mind.

An image flashed before me: my drill penetrating Ramos, as in the trephination procedures, yet instead of wielding the brace I was *under* the vault of his skull, a watcher from within, looking up to the ceiling of bone. Then the bone became paper, and the drill became a slicing nib, breaking through from outside.

A call sounded from above, a scuffle of footsteps signalled some urgent but doubtless routine business. The ship heaved about, timbers groaning, as if, like some indolent mouser, it had become exceedingly comfortable lying just-so and did not wish to be disturbed. The commotion, perfectly ordinary as it was, roused the Coronel. I was glad of that, because it gave me something to think about besides myself.

He yawned and forced open an eye.

'Are you refreshed, Silas?'

I re-crumpled the paper ball, and made a point of consigning it to the feeble little stove which was all that served to warm my cabin. It was not lit now, but it soon would be.

'I am very tolerably refreshed, Coronel,' I lied to him. 'And looking forward to what the day brings.'

*

I arrived on deck. The wind had eased, and although we remained anchored, the swell was not as nauseating as it could have been. The sea was more grey than blue or green, and the sun a paltry yellow smudge that had only deigned to lift itself a little above the line of cliffs. Small icebergs – if they could indeed be called icebergs – drifted past us and to the south in an amiable procession, like white cattle seeking fresh pasture. The cliffs were mostly in shadow, with only the uppermost part of them catching any of the sun's direct radiance. It was enough, though, to afford a much improved view of the inlet, and the water beyond it.

The inlet was wider than I had feared by night, and the idea of going through it no longer seemed entirely preposterous. The cliffs – at least, where they had been broken through at this point – formed a sheer-sided but narrow wall, about four hundred feet high. The gap was about two hundred feet across, five or six times wider than *Demeter*, and the narrowest part of the channel extended about three or four hundred feet in from the sea, before widening out into the lagoon. It was, I realised, only the severe aspect of the cliffs which made the idea of going through the inlet troubling to the imagination. Had the cliffs been harbour walls, I would never have doubted that the passage was navigable.

Van Vught, Topolsky and Dupin were by the wheel again. The captain and Master Topolsky were in easy, animated conversation about some aspect of the operation ahead of us. Van Vught was gesturing into the rigging with the sucking end of his pipe, pointing out sails and lines, Topolsky nodding like an eager student. Dupin had his angular head bowed, studying something in his hands: a little construction of paper, smudged with ink, which in turn made his fingers blue.

'Good morning, gentlemen,' I called out.

'Good morning, doctor,' Van Vught answered. 'The Coronel is satisfactory, we trust?'

'Yes, very well rested. Which I think is more than we can say for Monsieur Dupin, who I did not think to see on deck.'

'I am well enough,' Dupin said, not lifting his attention from the paper object. It was a sort of ball or lantern made of folds, expanding and contracting like a bellows as he worked his fingers against the hinge-points.

'Be sure Ramos is secure,' Van Vught said. '*Demeter* may move around a little as we thread the fissure, and we would not want him to fall.'

'I shall do so. I sense that a decision has been reached?'

'Indeed it has.'

'The captain has satisfied himself that the passage is safe,' Topolsky said.

'Those were not my *exact* words,' the captain corrected. 'I have decided – after consulting with my officers – that the risks are no worse than sitting out here in this ice flow, which as you will have noticed is greater in concentration than it was yesterday. In

55

the lagoon, I expect that we will not be so troubled by icebergs. By ice, perhaps. But that is a different problem, and I do not think the lagoon will freeze over until later in the season.'

'You are satisfied that we can sail through that gap?' I asked.

'Sailing will be only a small part of it, Silas. I was just explaining to Master Topolsky that we will rely on the tidal flow more than the wind, which is likely to be unpredictable in the confines of that passage. But the tide comes and goes with regularity, and provided we have sufficient depth in the channel . . .'

I tried to stop my voice rising with alarm.

'There's a *doubt* about that?'

'The rocks that once made up that cliff – the part that is missing – must have gone somewhere. We must trust that they have spread far from the breach, rather than lying just beneath the waters.'

'I would hope we rely on something more substantial than trust,' I said.

Dupin looked up from his paper toy. His cap was jammed down over tufts of sweat-matted yellow hair. 'This has been discussed in your absence.'

'Has it?'

'Our charts show deep enough waters. We have no reason to disbelieve them. As a precaution, soundings will be taken as we approach the channel.'

'By which time we will be in the tide's grip!'

'We will anchor if the need arises,' Dupin said unconcernedly.

'Lieutenant Murgatroyd has sent spotters to the mast tops,' Van Vught said. 'They observed the tidal rush as it came and went and the water showed no sign of disturbance by anything below.'

'I am . . . reassured,' I said uncertainly.

'Don't concern yourself with these matters of seamanship, Coade,' Topolsky said, as if I were sticking my nose into someone else's private business. 'All your unreasoning fears will dissipate once we are inside the lagoon and have rounded that headland.'

I turned to Van Vught. 'Dare I ask when the tide is next in our favour?'

'We will have raised anchor within the hour. We shall sail nearer to the cliff until the flow has us, then strike sail quickly. You are welcome to be on deck, of course, but I must warn you that there will be a great deal of commotion as we approach the inlet – much activity, shouting, and a considerable mass of men moving around.'

I smiled at his tact. 'You are worried that I will get in the way, although you are far too kind to say it.'

'No. But it is as well to mention that the work will require delicate coordination from the men, and there is a reasonable prospect of injury.'

'Nothing serious, I hope.'

'The men are well trained and careful. But if ever your services were likely to be required, this would be the occasion.'

I nodded, half filled with trepidation, half with the tingling anticipation of honest work. 'Let us pray for nothing more than a dislocation, or a simple fracture, easily set. I will make sure the table is prepared for any eventuality. I think Coronel Ramos may be persuaded to take a chair, if I can stop him running up ladders.'

'We will be all right, Silas,' Van Vught told me. '*Demeter* has always been a lucky ship.'

'Let us hope it remains so,' I answered.

Chapter Five

He meant well by that reassurance, but it had very much the opposite effect on me. I nodded my leave, returned to my cabin, and explained to Ramos that it would help if he were to take a chair. The Coronel needed no encouragement or assistance from me to swing his legs off the table. I watched him for signs of giddiness, but he seemed sure on his feet.

'Sit down, and I shall bandage your head anew. The wound has suppurated a little, but to no great concern.'

'I have no need of further rest, Silas.'

'The patient is always the least reliable witness in these matters. You are as bad as Dupin!'

He lifted his eyes to mine. 'Our mapmaker?'

'I've insisted that the boy rest, but he will not. Is it Topolsky that drives him so?'

'In this instance, no. Dupin has only one master.'

'Himself?'

'Mathematics. His mistress and his tyrant. Gambling, whoredom and violence are the things that kill some men. For him it will be numbers, I am sure of it. Numbers and symbols, as deadly to his spirit as any addiction or vendetta. That said, I am in no position to judge another man's vocation.'

'So long as he doesn't die on us before he has exhausted his usefulness,' I said, before blinking at the unanticipated callousness of my own words. 'If you can find a way to persuade him to rest, perhaps he will listen to you.'

'I fear I may be just as bad a patient, Silas.'

'But somewhat more agreeable company. Please heed my advice, and if it irks you to be confined here without occupation, then I shall gladly deputise you as my assistant surgeon.'

'I know nothing of surgery.'

'But I imagine you do know a thing or two about holding men down against their will.'

'That I do,' he said ruefully.

'It will likely not come to that. But let us hope for the best, and prepare for the worst.'

He nodded his approval. 'A sound dictum, in peace as in war.'

When Ramos was seated I re-dressed his scalp, nodding quietly at my own work, not out of any sense of vanity but rather taking reassurance in seeing that I had risen to the demands of my calling.

As always the dichotomies of my profession loomed large in my thoughts. I had no desire to hurt or mutilate any of *Demeter*'s men, but if their injuries called for my intervention I would act with urgency and something not entirely divorced from enthusiasm. I would be depending on skills that were not only mine alone aboard the ship (so far as I knew), but which had been acquired through diligence and toil. Even though my training had been in the provincial schools of Plymouth, rather than the hallowed institutes of London or Edinburgh, I considered myself the equal of any man when it came to the blade and the suture.

'You look contented, Silas,' Ramos observed, as I thrust a clean sheet across the table.

'I am in my element. This is the work I was created to do. All else is distraction.'

'You exist only to save men.' He gave me a slow approving nod. 'It is a nobler calling than my own.'

A commotion on deck, a coordination of calls and shouts, signalled the weighing of *Demeter*'s anchor. I felt a gradual alteration in the ship's motion as the wind gathered in whatever portion of the sails remained spread, and we sliced through the ice-pocked swell rather than rising and falling on it. Slowly, the angle of the sun's light – low and pale as it was – moved about my cabin as the ship pointed its bow at the inlet. Since my cabin was near the stern on the port side I could see nothing of our intended destination, but only the more distant northern extremities of the cliff. Seated at my bureau, and making a preliminary entry into the medical log – reporting our intentions and my state of readiness – I noticed very little alteration in the cliff's aspect over the next several minutes. But then quite suddenly it was palpably nearer, and a smoother aspect to the ship's motion suggested to me that we were already in the irrevocable grip of the inflowing tide.

I set down my pen, listening intently. The ship creaked and groaned constantly, but I had become accustomed to these mindless complaints and had trained my ears to listen for the sounds beyond them: the footfalls, the calls – the individual accents and voices – and the complicated symphony of snapping, rushing and rustling noises that attended some significant alteration in the disposition of canvas and rope.

I could offer no useful description of any part of the process, but I could say that the noises fitted into a familiar pattern that I had begun to recognise, a reassurance that the work being done, while demanding, was proceeding in an orderly fashion. I heard Murgatroyd and the other senior officers quite distinctly, and while there was a seriousness to their commands and enquiries, I heard nothing of panic or concern in their utterances. Now and then Van Vught interjected a remark, but the captain's manner was that of a man who had the utmost confidence in his inferiors, and was quite content to observe rather than direct. Presently, too, I heard the periodic calling out of soundings, as one of the men measured the depth of water beneath us.

The cliff was near enough now that I had a much readier appreciation of its height, and how greatly it loomed over the highest mast of *Demeter*. All at once I was struck by an overwhelming impression of the cliff's size and mass, and how utterly inconsequential our little prison of wood and sail was. It seemed, in a sickening reversal of perspective, that our ship was a fixed thing, almost the centre of the universe, and the cliff an implacable moving surface, an advancing shield of ageless rock against which we were about to be shattered, reduced to a few wet, ragged and bloody human splinters.

'It will do you no good waiting here, Silas,' Ramos said. 'You are turning green before my eyes. Go above, and be assured I will be here when you return.'

'If there are injuries,' I rationalised, grateful, 'it is perhaps better that I be nearer to the origin of them, so that I may offer the most expeditious assistance.'

'That seems very wise,' Ramos answered.

*

By the time I made it to the quarterdeck the tide had borne us to within two hundred feet of the inlet. A hurried shedding of sail was now in progress, requiring many hands both on deck and in the wind-whipped heights. *Demeter* had needed some portion of sail to guide its entry into the tidal flow, but now the race was on to reduce the ship to a skeleton of masts and crossbeams. Murgatroyd and his men were calling out with increased urgency now, and even the captain's interjections came more frequently. But still there was no sense that any sort of crisis was afoot. The crew had been trained to strike sail quickly when the weather turned, and all that was now being asked of them was to do it under somewhat milder circumstances.

Van Vught was at the wheel, and now his interventions were becoming sharper and more rapid, as he sought to thread *Demeter* into the deepest part of the channel between the two opposing jaws of cliff. The soundings continued, and although I did not catch all of them, the general impression was that the depth of water was decreasing, but not so severely as to cause alarm.

No more than one hundred feet now separated us from the opening of the inlet. Although the sun was still up, no part of its light reached us directly. The ship had entered the cliff's shade, and the inlet itself was at the wrong angle to admit any sunlight. The shadow brought an inauspicious chill to my bones, and with the nearing of the cliff-sides the air became heavy and damp, as if it lay draped across the deck like a funeral shroud. All at once the voices grew muted, the calls less frequent.

The distance to the cliff was now much less than the length of the ship. The soundings had ceased: there was no purpose to them now, given the speed of our passage. The walls soared to the north and south: black and glistening on their lower flanks, paler and mossy near their overhanging tops. Horizontal striations of rock called to mind books jumbled on books, a library tipped on its side, so that the tomes pressed closest to the earth had begun to rot and mulch under the pressure of those above. I did not feel oppressed, though. Rather, I was giddy with the realisation that this traversal would be over nearly as quickly as it had begun. Our speed was tremendous, and that was daunting, but the flow would be done with us very swiftly. I glanced at Van Vught and saw concentration but not terror.

'A wreck!' shouted Murgatroyd, pointing off to port.

I followed his cyclops gaze and saw nothing except water, cliff and shadow. But my two eyes were not so well trained or acute as the one remaining eye of the lieutenant. He had seen what did not belong, and after lengthier moments I saw it as well, pressed into the gloom of the cliff like a mashed insect, and nearly indistinguishable from the hue and darkness of the rocks. It was a ship, indeed. There was not much left of it: merely the broken carcass of its hull, impaled so firmly against the cliffs that it was fixed there, insensible to any motion of water or wind. The stumps of its masts projected above the hull, attenuated to a quarter or a fifth of their proper extent, and over these wooden bones draped a mossy shroud of collapsed sail and rigging. I stared and stared, willing the ship to melt back into the shadows and become a mere phantom of perception. But it would not oblige.

Murgatroyd lifted a spyglass to his eye and sighted on the hulk. He studied it wordlessly, then lowered the instrument.

Steady on his feet despite the angle of the deck, he walked back to Captain Van Vught.

'You should see the name of her, captain.'

'She does not look as strong as *Demeter*.'

'I doubt that she was. But you should still see the name.' Murgatroyd, testing the limits of rank, nearly forced the spyglass to the captain's eye.

Van Vught studied the apparition as silently as his lieutenant. I could only guess the object of their attention. To my eyes, the wreck was the colour of an old boot, and uniform in its drabness. Something near her front was drawing the captain's interest, though: some darker blemish against the rotten, weather-tormented wood of her bow.

The captain lowered the spyglass. He turned to the man who had sponsored our voyage.

'Master Topolsky, would you care to comment?'

'I did not say that they succeeded!'

'Nor did you say that *Europa* was wrecked.' The captain's voice was low, and seemingly without rancour, and that was the worst part of it. 'You led us to believe that these men did not come to grief.'

'I never claimed to know the fate of *Europa*!'

'Are you saying that you did not know she had been wrecked? That she met her end in the same inlet to which we are now committed?'

'How can you not have known, Master?' Murgatroyd asked rhetorically. Something broke in him: some reserve that had been under strain for weeks. A wild fury showed in his unpatched eye, rendered all the more vivid by its asymmetry. 'By not disclosing this, he has violated the letter and spirit of our agreement, captain. All is now void! While Ramos is indisposed, I strongly recommend that Master Topolsky be confined to his cabin and treated as a prisoner! As for the rest of his men, they must all be culpable! They each kept this lie to themselves! Lock them all up and let the courts fight over our contract!'

'What of survivors?' the captain asked.

'I . . . cannot speculate,' Topolsky blustered. 'I did not think we would sight this wreck. I thought it would be long beneath the waves, instead of scrawled across that cliff like the writing on the wall! If it would not be visible, I was not required to mention it!'

'How many survivors?' Van Vught persisted. Then, to me: 'Now we understand why the men of *Europa* have not already made their fortunes with this discovery, Silas. They were too busy being drowned.'

'I don't know that there were survivors,' Topolsky admitted, lowering his head. 'There may have been!'

'How did you come by your intelligence?' I asked.

'Exactly as I said! I came into possession of charts and documents—'

Murgatroyd grabbed Topolsky by the lapels of his coat, as

roughly as any thief. 'Damn your evasion, man! What was it? Did you plunder this wreck? Did you feign ignorance as to its location, so that we might fall for your game?'

Topolsky wriggled in Murgatroyd's grasp. Dupin looked on with a distant interest, as if observing a street brawl in which he had no personal stake. He still had that smudged ball of paper between his fingers, squeezing and caressing it like a charm.

'Lieutenant Murgatroyd,' Van Vught said. 'Your zeal is noted, but perhaps you would unhand our guest temporarily.'

'Temporarily!' Murgatroyd snarled, releasing the Master so suddenly and violently that Topolsky toppled back on his heels and had to flail to regain his balance.

'Thank you,' the captain breathed.

'The intelligence,' I repeated.

'A trunk must have escaped the wreck.' Topolsky was more red about the cheeks than usual, and nearly out of breath. 'I do not know the specifics. It floated on the outgoing flow and reached open water. Later, it was found by another ship . . . the men from whom I brokered its purchase, along with the contents.' His breath came hard and fast, like an exhausted racehorse. 'They were simple fellows, with just enough wit to realise that they might make a coin or two from selling the trunk to me.'

'Why to you?' I probed.

He dismissed my question with a flap of his hand. 'It is common knowledge among such crews that I will pay for nautical exotica. Charts, drawings, artefacts of mysterious provenance. Bring them to me or one of my aides and you will be offered a fair price. I have people in every port of any significance: a great cobweb of influence, with me at its throbbing heart.'

A heavy, unsteady step sounded on the deck planks. I turned to face it with a desperate foreboding, certain that I knew its source.

'Coronel Ramos – you should not be about!'

He had seemed strong on the table, and no weaker in the chair. But forced to walk, forced to move through the ship, his frailty showed. His face was pale, his eyes narrowed to a frowning squint, as if even the pale light of these latitudes was an affront to him. His bandaged head sat on his vast shoulders at an angle, as if it had been dropped carelessly into place.

'I heard shouting. I could not remain below.' Approaching us, his eyes flashed from one protagonist to another, appraising our altered relations.

'Thank goodness, Ramos! You have not forgotten your obligations after all.'

'Coronel,' said Murgatroyd, giving the other man a respectful nod. 'You and I have no fight.'

Ramos answered mildly: 'That is true, for now.'

'He rough-handled me, Ramos! The man is no more than a common thug! Strike him down, and teach the bog-trotting dog some modicum of civility!'

I took Ramos's arm, feeling that the giant might vomit or topple at any moment. 'There has been a . . . misunderstanding,' I said. I pointed to the wreck, already slipping away behind us. 'That is the wreck of *Europa*! He lied to us, Coronel. I am as certain of that as I am that you had no part in this deception.'

'I did not.' Then, to Topolsky: 'Did you lie, Master Topolsky?'

'Concern yourself with knives and powder, Ramos, not the machinations necessary for greatness! Lying is the grease that lubricates progress! If the world were entrusted to truthful dullards, men would still be wearing animal skins!'

'That is how he thinks of you,' Murgatroyd confided in the Coronel. 'A truthful dullard. Throw your lot in with us, man. At least you will have the respect of your fellows. Is that not so, captain?'

'A moment, Henry.'

I had not heard Van Vught address Murgatroyd by his

66

Christian name, not even in the most avuncular of moments around his table, and the slip spoke to a moment of distraction on the part of the captain. Something had commandeered the greater portion of his concentration – something beyond even the wreck of *Europa*.

We jerked.

I nearly lost my footing. Ramos did lose his, for his sense of balance must have been precarious. Murgatroyd tried to soften the larger man's crashing descent to the deck and knelt by the fallen giant as Ramos vomited a frothy, pink-stained phlegm onto the planks. Then his eyes began to roll and flutter, and a quivering palsy took authority over his body.

The captain wrestled with the wheel. We had hit something, surely: perhaps the same submerged rocks that had done for *Europa*. I waited for the awful crunching as our lower timbers were ripped asunder. But nothing of that nature came. The ship was still moving like a thing afloat, with the relative motion of the rock faces to confirm it.

'What is it?' I asked, torn between attending the shaking Ramos and the nearer terror of wrecking and drowning.

'The rudder is not answering,' Van Vught told me.

Rather than making corrections, a touch clockwise, a touch to the contrary, he was spinning the wheel continuously, counterclockwise, as if he wished to make a sharp turn to port. But the ship's bow was veering in the opposite direction. The ship had become a dark compass dial, intent on pointing to the southerly pole. Some current, or wind eddy, or combination of such factors, now toyed with us, and we could no longer keep a straight course through the fissure. The walls continued to constrict ahead of our motion. What had been easily traversable when the ship was moving bow-first was no longer wide enough to permit passage.

In an instant, the little contretemps that had played out

between parties became an insignificant element of the larger drama now befalling *Demeter*. Ramos's fate was a mere detail now. Men were rushing about, obeying bellowed instructions and their own hard-won instinct for preservation. Some hands were scrambling back aloft, with the seeming intention of restoring a portion of sail: I could only imagine that, with the incapacity of the rudder, the wind had become a potential ally rather than foe. Other men were unshipping long poles, several of them at each, and moving to the sides of the ship so that they could fend off the rock walls. But it was all happening too slowly, and the tidal flow offered no quarter.

I caught the captain's eye for an instant. He looked at me, and between commands seemed to invite a question.

'Are we in trouble?'

He nodded.

'We are indeed in trouble, Silas. Will you help Coronel Ramos, nonetheless?'

I had been stupefied into inaction, but now I remedied it. I threw myself down beside the shaking form of my friend. Murgatroyd had his head cupped between his hands, trying to prevent it knocking against the deck as the Coronel thrashed. Blood spilled out between Murgatroyd's fingers, the bandage already as red as a banner. Ramos vomited again, and then the violence of his motions intensified, as if he were some immense shuddering machine which had lost its governing restraints, and would now dismantle itself piece by piece.

'He is choking, Murgatroyd!'

Murgatroyd looked into my eyes, his own eye wide. It was not quite terror I saw in it, for I do not think men like Henry Murgatroyd permitted themselves the capacity for such an emotion, but terror's desperate near-cousin, wild, destabilising uncertainty.

'You healed him!'

'I did my best. He was still weak, and should have remained below.' I had my fingers in Ramos's mouth, trying to clear the obstruction in his throat. It was like trying to extract a morsel from a snarling, rabid dog.

'Save him,' Master Topolsky decreed, looking down on me. 'Save the brute, Coade, or I swear I'll have you ruined!'

Murgatroyd stood up with an easy, unhurried manner, and punched Topolsky into a condition of instant unconsciousness. The swiftness of that transition was a thing of medical beauty, fit for the textbooks. The Master fell, heavy and silent as a sack of grain.

'Now I will have a broken jaw to attend to,' I said, as Ramos bit into my flesh and our blood mingled in his mouth.

'That may be the least of your concerns,' Murgatroyd said, rubbing at his knuckles.

I followed his gaze along the busy deck, to where a curtain of rock slid past the bow, nearer by the second. The men with poles were rushing forward. I watched them as if in a dream. wondering why they bothered. It was obvious that none of their efforts stood the least chance of success. The ship was too heavy, too ponderous, and the cliff moving too fast. One pair of men managed to project a pole out beyond the length of the bowsprit, but as soon as it contacted that moving surface of the rock the pole was wrenched violently aside, injuring both men by the violence of the action. One man lay instantly limp and still on the deck, and the other attempted to scramble to his feet but could not, for some part of his leg was hurt. The other men with poles were less keen now, seeing how unequal they were to the task before them.

Ramos gave a last violent shudder and then became quite still. I extricated my pulped and bloodied fingers and searched for a pulse.

'He is gone, Murgatroyd. I could not save the poor man.'

'Then save another, if you can!'

Nursing my damaged fingers – if they were not broken or dislocated, it was a miracle – I left the Coronel and staggered forward across the deck, leaning against the sickening, veering angle of the ship. Was the ship as a whole in peril? I did not know. *Trouble* could mean several things, from the likelihood of imminent destruction, to an inconvenience of delays and repair, costly to the accounts. But even if we were all about to drown, I could not have set aside my professional obligation to those men.

I do not think I had covered more than half of the distance to them when the bowsprit met the rock, and jammed itself into that irregular surface like a knife between ribs. I might have expected it to snap away cleanly, but I had underestimated the extent to which it was an integral extension of the ship's primary fabric. The main part of the bowsprit held, and the ship underwent the most violent deflection, accompanied by an appalling protestation of wood: a groan of agony issuing from the belly of the vessel itself. The deck tilted like the steepest street in Devon. *Demeter* had become a cruelly handled plaything, caught between the cliff and the tidal eddies. The deflection loosened men from the masts, now tilted at a considerable angle from the vertical, and they came down screaming and flailing. Depending on the height from which they fell, they met either the deck, the gunnels, or fell into the raging waters, where rocks could not have been far beneath. Those who entered the water were beyond all salvation, but I still felt an overwhelming compulsion to tend to the broken men on deck. Yet as I surveyed the spectacle of injury and pain laid out on *Demeter* like some awful carnival, a paralysis of action overcame me. I knew my presence to be futile: I could tend to one or two of the men, perhaps, but my ministrations would amount to nothing but a prolongation of their agonies. And which among the fallen should I favour with a surgeon's touch, when all was nearly lost? Surely we were all done for.

The ship writhed between rock and tide and at last something gave way at the bow. Wood sundered and the bowsprit broke apart, with one end still embedded in the cliff. Hope rallied with me: damaged as we were, at least the ship had freed itself. If the tide could now bear the ship into the lagoon, even rudderless and with damage to her bow, repairs could likely be effected once we were sheltered from the wind and ice.

Yet with the severing of the bowsprit, the tensioned forces of the rigging were now fatally unbalanced. A sequence of failures attended, beginning with the foremost mast. Two thirds of the way up, where two sections of mast were spliced together, the upper part broke away and came crashing down.

Onto me.

The mast smashed me to the deck. It lay across my waist, shattering bone and crushing vital organs. I knew this instantly, and without the least shred of doubt. I could visualise the damage as plainly and dispassionately as if I gazed on an anatomical drawing of my own catastrophe.

Rather than pain, I felt the lower part of my body turn numb. It was as sudden and shocking as the slamming of a door, silencing a quiet domestic conversation that had been going on, without ceremony, for the entirety of my life. I had become a house divided.

I tried to breathe and realised that I could not.

Through a reddening fog Van Vught and Topolsky came into view, leaning over me, exchanging words of consternation. I strained to hear their words, though, over the growing roar in my brain.

A yellow form joined them. She leaned in as well, and even as the rest of my world dissolved, her face and voice were the last things to remain clear.

'Oh, Doctor Coade,' said Milady Cossile, plucking a feather from her hat and chewing on the end of it. 'This dying really won't help us, you know.'

Chapter Six

A ship is a dream of whispers, the dead man said.

Whispers and dreams.

So I dreamed.

I found myself in the stone-walled tunnel again, without preamble or explanation, stumbling and groping my way towards a distant, feeble suggestion of greyish light. I was not cloaked this time, but encumbered by a suit of metal, the jointed armour of a knight. I shuffled against the tremendous resistance from each creaking, rusted articulation. I had felt that paralysing weakness in many other dreams, and with that realisation arrived a momentary chink of lucidity. This was also a dream, and since I was in it, I was also the architect of its narrative. I could submit to it, shape it – or break it.

I had not the will.

The lucid moment glimmered out like a star eclipsed by a darker body – or perhaps the distant Sun, obscured by some little moon of Jupiter, Saturn or cold Uranus. I shuffled on, striking for the light. It was not a phantom after all, but an opening in the tunnel, a wider part where paths branched off into deeper darkness and illumination fought its way down from above, through a maze of cracks and shafts. An opening from which I might yet find a point of escape.

The lustre of the walls threw back my countenance. I stared at my own dusky reflection: the gleam of old metal, the beaked visor, the plume on the helmet's crown. I creaked up my arm and squeezed my stiff gauntleted fingers against the visor. It lifted, but as grudgingly and grindingly as an old drawbridge.

I stared into the void inside the helmet. The void stared back. There was blackness there, and for an instant I thought it a complete absence of form, as if the helmet were entirely empty. But I needed only wait for the light to worm its way inside. By degrees, a face emerged.

It was not really a face at all.

It was a skull, garbed in only the thinnest mantle of withered flesh.

To the dream of whispers, I added a scream.

*

Mortlock knocked before entering, and that was a mercy. I gathered myself at my desk, scraping sleep from my eyes, jamming on spectacles and in all respects attempting to make it seem as if I had not been asleep a moment earlier. I took up my fountain pen, and went over the last line I had written, so that the ink still shimmered.

'Mortlock, come in,' I said, raising my voice in glad fashion.

He poked his head into my cabin. 'I heard a cry, doctor, as I was getting near. Is all right?'

'An exclamation of delight, dear Mortlock, and no more than that. In a flash I saw my way through my current narrative impasse. I'm afraid I rather allowed my exuberance to get the better of me.' I twisted in my bureau chair, wondering how likely any man would find my explanation. 'I heard your footsteps and knew you were about to knock. What ails you now? The abscess is still giving trouble?'

'Not that, sir.' Mortlock lowered his scarf and dabbed at his jaw, which – although raw from the abrasion of the wind and the scarf – bore no trace of its former swelling. 'You got at it very well, sir, doctor, I mean. I hope I won't be making more work for you either, but I've been telling the other men how you knocked me out cold, and how I didn't feel so much as a tickle.'

'I am pleased. If knowledge of the ether's efficacy encourages other men to come to me with their complaints, rather than suffering in silence, I shall be glad of it.'

'Wouldn't that be a distraction from your scribbling, sir?' Mortlock asked eagerly, nodding at my manuscript.

'Quite honestly, I should welcome the work. The captain calls *Demeter* a lucky ship. He may well be right: other than your abscess, Coronel Ramos's mishap – thankfully remedied – and a few exceedingly minor injuries, the butcher's bill has been very small indeed. Long may that continue, of course, but if the crew or our guests continue to abstain from accident and infirmity as they have done, I almost fear that I will forget the rudiments of my profession.' Seeing his immediate concern, I smiled over my half-moon glasses. 'I do not mean that seriously, Mortlock – but it is good to be employed, is it not? On some other voyages, the surgeon of the ship has also been a naturalist or botanist: a very useful way of making the most of these months at sea. But the pursuit of knowledge is scarcely an option in these dismal, damp latitudes. The further we venture, the more my spirits seem to fade. The seas grow greyer, the skies paler, the procession of land more monotonous, when we are in sight of it. Have you seen so much as another living thing since we rounded Cape Horn?'

His eyes went to the ceiling as he racked his memory. 'A bird or two sir, and I reckon a seal, although it was a long way off.'

'Slim pickings for a monograph, I think we can both agree.' I put away my pen, stoppered my inkwell, blotted the manuscript and closed it carefully. 'What is it, Mortlock? We seemed to run quite close to those cliffs just now. Has something happened?'

'It were a little touch and go, I think, sir, but we squeezed through quite handsomely in the end.'

I frowned. 'Squeezed through?'

'Master Topolsky's fissure, sir. Doctor. That gap in the cliffs the Russian's been looking for. They found it last night, the captain took a look at the tides and winds, Mister Fitzpatrick put some more anthracite in the boiler, and through we went, easy as a greased rat.' He squinted at me as if one or both of us were suffering some temporary derangement. 'Didn't anyone tell you what was afoot?'

'They may have done,' I confessed, remembering how my mind had wandered at the last captain's table as soon as the talk turned to matters of navigation. 'Something about venturing into sheltered waters, pursuant to something of interest to Master Topolsky?'

'You have it, sir, and no mistake. But I reckon you'd best hear the rest of it from the captain himself. That's why he sent me below: to bring you up.'

'A matter of medical concern?' I asked with some faint rising interest.

'No, not that, sir, doctor. But you being a man of learning, and all, and this curious *eddy-face* that keeps being mentioned . . .'

'I think that would be the Edifice, Mortlock,' I corrected gently, something of last night's conversation at last penetrating to the forefront of my memory. 'The spiderlike blot on Dupin's map.'

'Dupin's map, sir? I'm not sure I've clapped eyes on any of old yellow-mop's maps. Very possessive of them he is. Won't let 'em out of his trunk if there's another soul around.'

'Well, perhaps you were not there when the map was explained to us, but I remember the feature quite well, along with its apparent size. If it exists – even if it is a pile of rubble – it will indeed be the marvel of the age.'

76

'You don't sound all that bothered, though.'

'Oh, I shall be perfectly content if it is real, because then Captain Van Vught will see some of that bonus he has been promised, and that will be good for *Demeter* and her crew. And I suppose I would not reject my share of that bonus, either. But there my interest ends. There is no law that says every man must be driven by the same compulsions as his fellows.' I looked at him astutely. 'What drives you, Mortlock?'

'Pie, mainly,' he reflected, a hand drifting to the shrunken belly he undoubtedly wished to fill. 'And a little grog. And a tale, if it's told well. Like yours is, I mean.'

'You are too kind.'

'I'll let the captain know you're on your way, shall I?'

'No need – I shall be there quicker than you could possibly convey the word.'

Mortlock looked past me to the manuscript. 'I mean it, by the way – it is good, and you ought to keep on with it. I'm sorry if I distracted from your writing, by my knocking?'

'You did not, Mortlock.' I patted the now sealed manuscript. 'Have no fear of that. The wind is in my sails again. I believe I may even have settled on a title. What do you make of *The Stone Vigil, or The Edifice in Ice. A romance by Doctor Silas Coade*?'

'I think it should fly off the shelves, doctor, when you've decided on which one it is.'

*

When Mortlock was gone I opened my desk drawer, tied off my forearm, and injected myself with surgical morphine. Hypothetical Edifice aside, The hypodermic syringe was a marvel of our age, as adept at administering curatives to the men as it was at furnishing my own steepening addiction.

Thus fortified – however temporarily – I emerged into the

cold low light of a sun that had only just had energy to haul itself above the cliffs, inlets and glaciers of Patagonia. We were creeping up the Pacific coast of South America, having rounded the Cape after sailing south from Montevideo. We had been there for the winter, and the city had been unseasonably damp and overcast. Yet after weeks of perpetual stormy seas, lacerating winds and insidious cold, Montevideo had become in my memory a vision of balminess, a bounteous oasis of comfort, plenty and life upon whose quaint and colourful streets I would have gladly prostrated myself to kiss.

My forearm still tingling beneath my sleeve, I surveyed our situation. Walls of ice-dappled cliff were peeling back on either side of *Demeter*. In the ruffled waters astern, they narrowed until nearly the point of closure. The dismal southern sky bit down into the cliff where a part of it had collapsed away, forming a neck of water between the sea and the saltwater lagoon into which we were now forging.

The lagoon grew wider ahead of us, and the cliffs toppled back into gentler – if still forbidding – slopes of rock, ice and snow. The inlet we had traversed was about two hundred feet across, but the lagoon widened until there was a mile or so between its northern and southern shores. I could not see how far it extended inland, but that observation triggered another belated recollection from the night before: the lagoon was curved, and we had anticipated that a headland would block our sight of its inland, eastern extremity.

So it proved. I could see the headland quite plainly, about two miles ahead of us on the starboard side. It was a skull-shaped mass of rock which projected from the lessening slope of the cliff. The skull seemed to be balanced precariously, as if it would not take much more than a gust to send it toppling into the lagoon.

Van Vught and Topolsky stood by the wheel. Dupin, the

cartographer, was next to them, and next to Dupin was Coronel Ramos, bandaged about the scalp (he wore nothing else on his hairless head) and showing commendable recuperation after his accident.

'Silas,' Ramos said, nodding once.

'Good morning, doctor!' Van Vught called out. 'Forgive me for summoning you. I know that this is not exactly medicine, but we did not think you would thank us for allowing you to miss it. Is that not so, Master?'

'Whatever suits Coade,' Topolsky answered indifferently, and I knew then that it was the captain who had thought of me – and perhaps Ramos – but not Topolsky, to whom I was but a complicating nuisance of his contract with Van Vught.

I watched my footing on the deck as I neared the gathering. 'It's a charming lagoon, gentlemen.'

'Not just any lagoon,' Topolsky said, mirthful eyes twinkling in the narrow margin between woollen hat and scarf, the latter drawn over his nose. 'This body of water is on no chart in the possession of any maritime power. Past or present! Save for our own maps, it is totally unknown. And yet here we are, beholding it with our own eyes! Consider yourself fortunate indeed.'

'There is water,' I admitted. 'And rocks. And some ice. And quite a lot of sky above us. 'And that headland is, I suppose, of some distinctiveness.'

Topolsky shook his head in disgust. 'Exploration is wasted on you, Coade. Your imagination has turned in on itself, through repeated misapplication. Mere fiction has no place in this bold new world of ours.'

'I shall bear that in mind.'

Topolsky turned to the young cartographer. 'Dupin: any hint of our quarry, as yet?'

The sharp-featured young man averted his eyes from the curious optical instrument he wore on a strap around his neck. It consisted of two squashed telescopes joined side by side, spaced the same modest distance apart as his own close-set grey-green eyes.

'No,' he reported, and went back to his observations.

'What is that thing you look through?' I asked.

'A pair of binocular telescopes,' the young man answered without looking at me. 'Porro's recent patent, but with improvements in prism collimation by Herr Brucker.'

'Only the latest fruits of science for our expedition,' proclaimed Topolsky, as if he were still trying to drum up sponsorship.

'While we skimp on everything else,' Ramos murmured.

'I trust the passage through the inlet did not disturb you too badly?' Van Vught asked, fingering the stiff projection of his moustache. 'I would not have wanted to chance those waters without the assistance from our marine boiler, but in the end we came through with very little difficulty.'

'I am very glad to hear it. I did see something of the cliff getting nearer, but I presumed that if it were of concern, I would have been informed.'

'There was no real prospect of accident,' Van Vught said. 'Which is not to say that we did not take all precautions, nor that we should be any less alert as we proceed into the lagoon.'

'Will we sail all the way to the Edifice? Monsieur Dupin's chart looked very detailed to me, but only you will know whether we can sail all the way east, or must make part of our journey along the shore.'

Topolsky complained to Dupin: 'I thought we agreed not to disclose the confidential charts until we were safely within the lagoon?'

Dupin levered his binocular telescopes away from his eyes. His cheeks were sunken, the colour of ruined milk. His cheekbones stood out like a pair of treacherous mountain ridges. 'The topographic chart remains in my care. To have seen it, he would have needed to go through my sealed possessions.'

Coming from any other man, such a suggestion would have been grounds for an immediate and unconditional apology, followed by a demand for satisfaction if that apology were not forthcoming. I knew better than to hold Dupin to such standards. He could not help himself. He could no more control his tongue than other men could control the beating of their hearts. There was no intended provocation in his words, merely an assertion of the facts as he saw them.

'I did not, Monsieur Dupin,' I said levelly. 'I have a clear recollection of seeing the chart on the captain's table, over sherry and cigars. I believe it was the same evening that I advised you to take more rest, for the sake of your health.'

'A similar chart, perhaps one of our own,' interjected Van Vught diplomatically, offering me a way to save face, and trying to keep the peace between his guests and *Demeter*'s newly hired physician. 'Murgatroyd and I marked up several of them by way of speculation as to our objective. Doubtless it was one of those that you saw.'

I nodded keenly. 'Of course, it must have been.'

Dupin went back to his scouting. Topolsky gave me a cautious look, while Ramos only frowned, making no judgement except to signal his unwillingness to take a side.

'In answer to your very reasonable question,' Van Vught said, 'we will likely not risk *Demeter* anywhere near the shore. But in the calm waters of the lagoon, far from the tidal rush near the inlet, it will be perfectly practicable to go out in the boats. If the topography of the shore permits, Murgatroyd can arrange for the setting up of a camp, so that the boats do not have to come and go unnecessarily.'

'Would Silas join us?' asked Ramos.

Van Vught must have already considered the question, for his answer was immediate.

'If the doctor is not overburdened with work on *Demeter*, then it would seem the most sensible arrangement, in case of sickness or injury among those who go ashore.'

'There is no *if* about it,' Topolsky said. 'It is there in the contract. Where there is a conflict of work, Coade is to give priority of treatment to the expeditionary party.'

'My priority,' I said, 'would be to the man most in need of my care.'

'Then you will place your captain in forfeit of his obligations!'

Gently Van Vught said: 'I am sure there need be no disagreement, and no need for us to put contractual matters above Doctor Coade's commendable scruples.' He leaned in confidingly. 'Besides, it may be to your advantage, Silas. A few days on dry land, away from seasickness and the confines of *Demeter*, would do wonders for your constitution.'

I smiled. 'Has my retching been that obvious?'

Topolsky scoffed. 'Had we known our surgeon would be prone to seasickness, as well as flights of fancy, we might have cast the net a little wider than the barbarous hovels of Plymouth. I allowed myself to think you were related to the Exeter Coades, Coade! I thought that with the money that has flowed to that renowned and respectable family, we could be sure of the calibre of your education. It was a mirage!'

'I am not responsible for any assumptions made about my name,' I replied. 'Besides, I am related to Lady Coade. I believe I may be a fifth cousin or something similar.'

'A fifth-rate cousin on a fifth-rate sloop! How apt!'

'I would not be standing here if Silas was anything less than capable in his arts,' Ramos said.

'You, Ramos?' Topolsky asked scornfully. 'I would not be so quick to use you as a benchmark for Coade's capabilities! You have been soft in the head since he drilled into you. Why do you not defend me when our contract is reduced to a legal mockery?'

'I see it,' Dupin said.

'See what?' I asked.

'The Edifice.'

'You *see* it?' Topolsky asked disbelievingly. 'Preposterous, Dupin! We haven't even begun to round the headland!'

'Nonetheless, I see it.' Dupin's voice was as barren of excitement as if he were dictating last year's news. 'There is a projection above the headland.'

Topolsky snatched the binocular telescopes out of Dupin's fingers and jammed them into the slot between his hat and scarf. He swept them around the massive obstruction of the headland, until at last something caught his eye.

'Good grief, Dupin!'

'Now you see it,' the cartographer stated.

'I see what I *think* you also saw. A fingerlike grey projection, like the top of a tower?' But it cannot be what it appears! That skull-shaped mass of rock must loom eight or nine hundred feet above the lagoon! If there is something beyond the headland which rises up enough to be seen over it, then it must be taller still! There is no possible ambiguity!'

'May I view it?' I asked.

Dupin still had the binocular telescopes looped around his neck, but his faintly trembling hands lifted them off for my benefit and he watched with some visible concern as I peered into the eyepieces. A wheel lay between them, for adjusting focus, similar to the arrangement on a microscope. The headland was sharp through the excellent optics. I tracked along its barren, moss-less upper edge – the gleaming grey crown of the skull, so to speak – until I detected the protrusion the other men had already observed. It was very small, hardly more than a vertical grey sliver, like a solitary fence post standing sentinel atop a hill.

'I confess, gentlemen, that I cannot easily discern the nature of the object. Were I to have stumbled on it for myself, I might easily have dismissed it as being nothing more than a vertical stone resting atop the headland.'

Dupin patted a prickly line of sweat from his brow, dislodging a curl of yellow hair that had fixed itself there.

'It moves.'

'It what?' I asked.

'Our relative motion, is what he means,' Topolsky said. 'We are yet under steam, albeit progressing at only a very low rate of knots – the captain's wise caution prevailing – and yet our movement is enough to differentiate the projection from the headland! It is a little like the effect of parallax, whereby our astronomers determine that one star is not in fact at the same distance as another! The stars do not move, but the Earth does, as it wheels around the Sun. We are the Earth!'

I nodded slowly. 'I see now.' The little finger was inching along the skull from right to left, but one needed to watch it for several seconds to be confident of the motion. 'And yes, I see by implication that it must lie at some higher point than the top of the headland. Higher and more distant. But it could still just as easily be a natural pinnacle of some kind.' I passed the binocular telescopes to Van Vught. 'Captain?'

He did not seem to have been permitted to handle or examine them before because his fingers lingered over them for a moment before lifting them to his eyes. I wondered if he thought them a fancy, inconsequential toy, but was too polite to say so, or whether he coveted them over his own old but rugged spyglass.

He looked through them for a moment, then passed them back to Dupin. Ramos said nothing, and it was obviously agreed among the Topolsky party that this distant glimpse was of no interest or concern to the soldier.

'I do not know what it is, to be sure,' Van Vught said. 'If it is a tower, then it must be at least eleven or twelve hundred feet above the lagoon. If that is an indication of the size of your Edifice . . .' But he permitted this wild conjecture to go no further. 'We shall see soon enough, when we no longer have the headland in our way. I think about two hours will be sufficient.'

'We shall commemorate the moment,' Topolsky said. 'The light is fair, the deck not moving around too much.'

'You mean to make a photograph,' Captain Van Vught said, with the air of one who has just realised his worst fears.

Topolsky's eyes glittered with sudden enthusiasm, the lines around them deepening to ravines. 'We must move with the times, gentlemen! Or rather – since I shall require quite a long exposure – we must ardently *not* move!'

Chapter Seven

Topolsky's photographic equipment had not seen the light of day at any prior point on the voyage. It came out onto the deck in straw-packed crates, which Topolsky set about opening and rummaging through. There were contraptions that needed to be unfolded, others than needed to be screwed together or disassembled and reassembled in some different fashion than they had been put into the crates. Topolsky approached the task with confidence, but before very long he stood frowning and squinting at the centre of a small explosion of pieces, none of which seemed to belong to each other. That was when Dupin intervened and wordlessly and efficiently imposed order on the chaos, with Topolsky standing in a sort of squatting, muttering dejection with his hands on his hips. 'Yes, Monsieur Dupin, that piece there, indeed,' he would declare at intervals, when it was plain to all observers that Dupin already knew exactly what to do and needed no guidance or encouragement in the matter.

But by turns the equipment took shape, and Topolsky entertained himself by exposing some plates of the surrounding rock slopes and the deck of *Demeter*. The ship's continued cautious progress was bringing us around the headland, affording an ever-extending view down the length of the lagoon. Part of me remained fully sceptical about the stony projection, but as we caught sight of more and more of the surrounding terrain, so it began to seem still more improbable that there could be any mass of rock large enough to have loomed over the headland from our then vantage point. The average height of the terrain was falling, rather than rising, with the eastern end of the lagoon being flanked by much lower and gentler slopes than the rock walls which fringed the western inlet.

Topolsky sent Ramos away to make sure that the relevant parties were gathered on deck in anticipation of our first direct sighting of the Edifice.

'Dear Doctor Coade,' Countess Cossile greeted me as she arrived, wearing a yellow coat, yellow gloves and an extravagantly feathered yellow bonnet. 'You have partaken, I suppose?'

'Partaken?'

Her eyes seemed to drift to my forearm. 'Breakfasted, I mean. You were not with us at the main table. Or did you think I was referring to something else?' Beneath the brim of her hat, her expression turned reproving. 'It is not a habit one should cultivate.'

'What isn't?'

'Breakfasting alone. Whatever did you think I meant?' She lifted her gaze from my arm, turning her beam-like attention instead to my face. 'Or were you taking the opportunity to forge ahead with your narrative? One must admire such doggedness in the face of insurmountable odds.'

'You are convinced that my narrative will be a failure?'

'No, I am convinced that it has already met that condition.'

I shrugged good-naturedly. 'The men seem to like it.'

She looked to the deck, and the layers of ship beneath. 'Ah yes, the illiterate and unschooled. Perhaps you have indeed found your natural audience.'

'If it really isn't to your taste, Countess, then perhaps the kindest thing would be to direct your energies elsewhere.'

'That I would gladly do, doctor. But in the absence of ancient writings, half-forgotten alphabets, cryptic codes and symbols, there is a distinct lack of occupation for a mind such as mine. These long days at sea tax the spirit dreadfully. I have read every book that came with me, and every other book that I can find aboard. I have even listened to your efforts in the direction of a novel.'

'How kind. Was it perhaps a mistake to join the expedition in the first place, if your intellectual gifts are so rarefied?'

'Time will tell,' she answered, treating my question as if it had been sincere. 'Perhaps, in the Edifice, Master Topolsky will find the lexical puzzles I have been put aboard to unravel. In the meantime I must confess that I have been retained at quite a generous rate, so at least I shall not return destitute, whatever the consequences of our endeavour. You have been retained under similarly favourable terms?'

'I wouldn't know. I was hired at the standard pay for an Assistant Surgeon, and since I expected to learn from the experience I saw no reason to question my salary.'

'An Assistant Surgeon? Then there is another, to whom you answer?'

'No, a ship of this rating would normally muster only an Assistant Surgeon – usually no better than a butcher or carpenter, and with about as much concern for hygiene.'

'Then we must be very glad of your employment, since you are clearly a cut above those occupations. The neurosurgery you performed on Ramos was not without merit.'

'Thank you.' I frowned at the unfamiliar term. '"Neurosurgery" – is that how they speak of such interventions, in London?'

'It is how they may come to do so.'

'You are an exceedingly odd travelling companion, Countess.' I smiled stiffly. 'Quite the oddest I have ever met, I feel sure. But

I suppose it is better to be in the company of interesting souls, however challenging their manner.'

'You find me interesting?'

'I find you fascinating.' The word nearly stuck on the tip of my tongue, but it had slipped loose before I could reconsider it. 'By which I mean as infuriating as any puzzle. And yet, I have never met another individual who seemed to have taken so automatic a dislike to my entire being.'

'I find your book disagreeable, doctor. I have no fixed convictions about you.'

'Yet you seem to find endless disappointment in my every action, my every utterance.'

'I see what you can be, but have not yet become. What you might be, with the right direction. The right instruction. The right training.' She nodded peremptorily between these statements. 'Perhaps, instead of seeing me as your adversary, you should see me as one who wishes to shape and encourage your development.'

'I have asked for no such shaping.'

'You have need of it, nonetheless.' She plucked a feather from her hat and tickled her cheek with the end of it. An absurd vision flashed into mind: Countess Cossile leaning over me, chewing on the end of her feather, while I lay pressed to the deck of *Demeter* by some immense, crushing mass of wood, my innards destroyed.

She studied me with sudden concern. 'Are you all right, doctor? You have quite lost your colour.'

'It's nothing. This seasickness dogs me, even in these calmer waters.'

Some ghost of sympathy haunted her features. 'This is hard for both of us. But if you insist on thinking of *Demeter* as a ship of the sea, seasickness will be a part of it. Can you not make the adjustment, at last? It will be so much easier when you do.'

'What adjustment?'

'That which you resist. That which will bring you to a full understanding of our predicament.'

'I do not know what remains to be understood. Our predicament seems plain enough: we are aboard a ship navigating the islands and inlets of Patagonia, under hire to a private expedition.'

'There is vastly more, doctor. But the difficulty is this: as soon as you catch a glimpse of the larger truth, you are apt to push it away – as you will doubtless push me away any instant now, on some pretext conjured up by your—'

'Coade!' barked Topolsky. 'The sighting is upon us, man! Not a second more of your dilly-dallying! I want our entire party captured in the moment of my . . . our . . . triumph! You too, Ada.'

'I am sorry, Countess,' I said hurriedly, realising – with a sting of envy – that it was the first time I had heard her forename, and that it distressed me that Topolsky could utter it so carelessly, while I would have given the world to hear it tumble from her lips. 'Let us continue our discussion . . . our very curious discussion . . . at some other opportunity?'

She shook her head: disappointment, exasperation, some yet deeper flavour of despair I could not yet categorise?

We assembled into a formal group on deck.

Captain Van Vught and Master Topolsky to the fore (the latter would insist on nothing less) and then the members of the expeditionary party on the second row: Dupin, Herr Brucker, Countess Cossile and Coronel Ramos. I had been hired on at the same time as the rest of the party, but I was not to be considered part of it and so I joined Murgatroyd and the other senior officers in the third rank, and then Mortlock and an assortment of respected midshipmen lined up to form the fourth, merely to make up the numbers.

I wondered who Topolsky was going to delegate to work the camera, but that consideration was already taken care of. Brucker had equipped the camera with an ingenius clockwork mechanism which opened and closed the shutter automatically.

'We are clever in Stuttgart, *ja*?' asked Brucker, leaning in so that I felt his breath upon my neck. 'You men in England scurry about like mice, but we have clockwork to do our bidding!'

I twisted around to address the odd, owlish man, his curious brush of black hair fully exposed now that he had his hat in his hands.

'I am sure the men of Stuttgart are to be congratulated on their industriousness,' I replied. 'But do we really want a world run by clockwork?'

Distractions of foreign innovations aside, the business was fully as tedious as expected. I had been photographed before – such advancements had even reached the West Country – but it was one thing to remain quite still and expressionless on land. On a deck, even a deck moving as gently as ours did, the body resisted such stillness. It was difficult to keep our balance while remaining motionless, and soon the movement of the shore began to make me feel reliably nauseous, over and above such lingering seasickness as never quite left me. Topolsky insisted on exposing six plates, to add to the ordeal. The strain of remaining perfectly still proved too much for Dupin, who fainted suddenly, collapsing down onto the shoulders of Captain Van Vught, who caught the boy before he came to any further harm. Dupin, in a daze, made his stumbling way to a crate where he sat down in a funk of pale dizziness.

'You must take better care of yourself,' I told him, pinching back his eyelids while he remained seated. 'You have worked yourself to the brink of exhaustion, Raymond. You also have a fever.'

'That chart was always in my room.'

'I don't doubt it. As the captain kindly explained, I saw a different chart. Does that satisfy you?'

'I think I'm nearly there,' he said, in a low, somnambulant sort of voice.

'Nearly where?'

Dupin rummaged in his coat pocket and produced a soggy-looking mass of crumpled paper, blue with ink. 'I'm nearly there. I can nearly see it.' He pressed his fingertips against the mass of paper, making it spring open along certain folds and hinge tighter on others. 'It's just a folded piece of paper. I haven't cut it or anything.'

'You need to rest.'

'You can't see it, but it's possible. It's a sphere, you see?' He pinched the paper between two extremities, making it balloon out like a soggy attempt at a paper lantern. 'It's a sphere. I think it was always a sphere, and then something went wrong. That's the topology.'

I looked to the land speeding by us on either side of *Demeter*. 'Topography?'

'No. Topology. Surfaces and volumes. Transformations. Homotopic transformations. Can you see it, doctor?'

'See what?' I asked gently.

'How to make it inside-out. There's a way. I can nearly see it.'

I could see that he was profoundly troubled, consumed by a fever of speculation: as real, perhaps, as the fever of the blood which warmed his brow. 'I don't think you need to waste your time on that. You can't turn a sphere inside-out.'

He looked at me with a sudden, brittle shock, as if I had just told him that his favourite puppy had been shot. 'No!'

Topolsky ambled over with something glassy in his hand. I had no time to react before he spirited it into position beneath Dupin's nose. Dupin sneezed violently and nearly crashed onto his back off the crate. I grabbed the boy by the scruff of his neck with one hand, and seized Topolsky's little vial with another. Rage nearly made me crush it. I only had to waft it within a foot of my nose to detect its awful pungency, smothering even the oils Topolsky worked into his beard and hair.

'He's my patient, you Cossack bastard,' I said.

'And he's my employee,' Topolsky said. 'As are you, Coade.' He glared at me, retrieved his vial, then glanced down at something on the deck. It was Dupin's paper construction, fallen from his fingers as the sneezing fit hit him. Some trick of the impact had caused its paper hinges to react in a quite specific way, making the object snap from one soggy state to another. Now it had become quite an odd shape, less like a sphere or lantern and more like a cross between a marine screw (like the one that propelled *Demeter*) and a twisted, stubby-limbed octopus.

Or, perhaps, a fat-limbed spider.

Topolsky jammed his foot onto the object, reducing it to a pulp of blue-stained papier-mâché.

'Cossack bastard or not,' he said quietly, 'I still own this expedition.'

Dupin was still pinching his nose and sneezing, his reddened eyes streaming tears.

*

Demeter continued around the headland.

Minutes passed, with barely any human voices to disturb the muffled chug of the marine engine beneath the decks. All eyes were on that extending shoreline. There was no beach as such, merely a drab margin of broken, ice-speckled stone between the water and the start of the hillside. Surely we were already far enough around the headland that we ought to have seen something?

93

And then quite suddenly it was there. There had been no warning: no hint of outlying works or ground disturbance. Emerging into view around the lowest part of the headland was an abrupt, soaring grey wall of such perfect smoothness and regularity that I immediately banished any thoughts that I might be seeing a natural feature.

Another wall interposed itself, set at an angle to the first, and then a third. Slowly I realised that we were seeing a series of projecting ramparts of varying heights and widths, laid out on curling paths, like the coiled arms of a thick, muscular octopus. From our low vantage it was all but impossible to construct a coherent impression of how these features were arranged and connected. There were many of them, some ending in turrets, some seeming to curve back in to the main mass of stone. I was, however, struck by a singular impression: that if an ordered, rectilinear, geometrically sensible fortification were graven onto some medium such as thick, foamy coffee and the liquid then stirred, stretching and distorting along axes of rotation, the resultant form might begin to resemble the spectacle we saw before us.

More of it came into view as we progressed, extending both vertically and horizontally. The walls lifted higher and higher the further back they were, resembling terraces cut into a sheer hillside. I had no reliable sense of distance, and nothing else in the scene that offered anything by which I might gauge the wall's height. Not a man, tree or house, however imperfect such yardsticks might have been. But my skin-prickling intuition was certain enough of one thing.

The innermost walls were *too* tall.

'An estimate of height, please, Dupin,' Topolsky said.

Dupin, his eyes still watering, and still (it seemed to me) only a flutter away from fainting once more, had resumed his role as cartographer and surveyor. Instead of binocular telescopes he

94

now made use of an even more intricate device assembled from engraved quadrants, fine balances and jewel-like lenses.

'Seven hundred and fifty,' he reported.

But this was not a verdict on the height of the innermost walls, merely an interim report.

'Eight hundred,' he called again.

Then:

'Eight hundred and fifty.'

'We have the upper limit!' Topolsky said excitedly.

The succession of walls had finally stopped climbing. Now we were viewing horizontal battlements laid out on the top of the walls. They rose and fell in sickly, sinuous waves, like saw-backed reptiles stretched out on undulating ground.

'Eight hundred and eighty feet,' Dupin reported.

My mind reeled at the notion of the masons who had laboured to throw those immense walls up into the air. I could, at the limit of my vision, begin to discern wavering lines of regular blocks, hundreds upon hundreds of them. They ought to have reminded me of brickwork, but instead they brought scales to mind. Perhaps it was the movement of the intervening air over the cold water of the lagoon, but the walls seemed to breathe in and out as my eye swept across them.

Nor were the walls the end of it.

Projecting above the sinuous battlements was a stone-built citadel: the prize, surely, that these monstrous defences sought to enclose. Like the walls, it thrust back in a succession of layers, each higher than the last. There were gatehouses, keeps, linking walls – many such walls, rising in dizzying stepped tiers – and more towers than I could easily count, jostling together like the sky-blackening chimneys of some dream of industry. Up and up the great towers soared, lessening in number with progressive height until a dozen or fewer, the mightiest peaks of the range, stood sentinel. The topmost part of one of these towers, surmounted by a stone finial, must have been the object we discerned above the headland.

Our slow progress disclosed the full extent of the structure. It ended as it had begun: without any sign of surrounding formations or encampments. The quarter-mile succession of walls terminated abruptly, with just a rocky margin of shore and mud-coloured slopes beyond it. The Edifice stood alone, without context, without explanation.

Topolsky was in a sort of stupor. Dupin, with more presence of mind, was executing a quick, methodical sketch, his fingers still blue-stained from his paper construction. We had the photographic equipment, of course, but from the moving deck the image could never be entirely sharp, and I think Dupin wished to commit *something* to paper, while there was a chance.

'Well,' Van Vught asked. 'Is it all that you hoped for, Master?'

Topolsky tried speaking and came out hoarse with excitement. He had to thump his own windpipe before he could proceed. 'What I hoped for, dear captain? I stand before you struck mute with wonder and astonishment. There was a part of me that doubted, even until that first glimpse, that it could be real. Yet here I stand: silent, upon a peak in Darien!'

'Not entirely silent,' Van Vught answered.

'There is something wrong with it,' I said.

'Of course there is something wrong with it, you imbecile,' Topolsky said, nearly laughing at my evident stupidity. 'Its very manifestation is a wrongness! The Edifice should not be here! Its presence is an affront to order and sense!'

'I mean that it does not look quite right. There is something...' I faltered, searching for the words that would not condemn me as a fool. 'Something askew. Do you not see it? It is like a thing seen in a mirage, twisting and rippling in the air, yet frozen in one particular aspect of its changing. Those curving, coiling battlements make me seasick.'

'You are never not seasick, Coade.'

'It is more than that. Those towers lean in or away from each other to a small but troubling degree, like skittles about to topple.'

'Your eyes may serve you for the humble examining rooms of Plymouth, but I am afraid they deceive you where distance is concerned.' Under his breath, but audibly, he added: 'These bastard's eyes are not so afflicted.'

'I see the wrongness just as clearly,' Van Vught said.

'Then it is a trick of the eye, brought about by the motion of *Demeter*,' Topolsky said.

'It is not the first time I have sighted something on land,' Van Vught replied. 'Would you care to comment, Monsieur Dupin?'

Dupin continued his sketching without interruption. I had always quite liked watching another man make marks on paper, but Dupin's strokes were more like impressions laid down by an engraving machine: faultless and precise, but in their very exactitude deadening to the eye. I noticed, in amongst his drawings of the scenery about us, and the object itself, sketches which seemed to convey steps in the deformation of his paper construction, now ruined. It was as if, despite the thing before him, his mind could not resist returning to its prior occupation.

'There is a deviation from the expected regularity along a number of axes,' he said. 'When we have closed in I shall be able to quantify the degrees of this deviation, and its probable causes.'

I nodded slowly, glad that my observation had been confirmed.

'I suppose there may have been subsidence in the walls, or whatever foundation those towers emerge from. But it can't have been very serious, or we'd see rubble all around the base, where other towers have already collapsed.'

'Let us not venture into supposition, when the facts alone will guide us,' Topolsky declared. 'The new science of *photo-graphy*

97

will resolve all ambiguity. Set aside your obsolete sketching, Dupin! Such rude handiwork belongs on cave walls, not in our learned institutions! Thanks to the good offices of Monsieur Daguerre we have no further need of such daubings!'

The photographic equipment was made ready again, the clockwork timer wound, and we were encouraged to take up formal poses behind the captain and the master, while that monstrous mass of stone rose behind us like an architect's fever dream.

Dupin's fingers kept jerking. There was nothing between them now, not even a pencil, but I fancied he still imagined himself holding that ball of folded paper. What had he seen in his mind's eye, I wondered? What had troubled him so? What was still troubling him?

Chapter Eight

In the evening, with the ship's mood caught uneasily between cheer that we had weathered the inlet, and faint foreboding that we might yet sail closer to those staggering, mirage-buckled walls, the captain convened his usual companions for dining and sherry.

There was, to begin with, really only one conceivable topic of conversation, and I was perfectly content to lean back and observe it as a nearly mute witness, except when I was prodded for an opinion. The plates had come back, with Monsieur Dupin's drawings (which were as fastidious and neat as architectural prints) spread between them, and I watched as Murgatroyd, Topolsky, Dupin and Brucker ran rulers and protractors across them, comparing dimensions and angles and trading supposition and inference concerning the relative sizes of features in the Edifice.

Ramos, who said as little as anyone, watched this discourse with an unlit cigar pinched between his lips.

'Logic dictates that there will be a point of entry, presumably concealed within the complexities of those walls,' Topolsky said, riffling excitedly between the papers and plates. 'Doubtless, since those walls are clearly defensive in function, any opening must be enclosed within them, invisible from our present vantage. If there is not a gatehouse, there will be a concealed door, tunnel, or perhaps a set of stairs cut into the wall, or even a bridge feeding in from the uplands beyond.'

'You count on a way in?' Van Vught asked.

'There must be one.'

'Not if it's a tomb, sealed up after construction,' pointed out Countess Cossile. 'Or a prison, of the sort where inmates were tossed over the walls and left to rot within.' She eyed me coquettishly, as if we shared a private joke – or perhaps the same private nightmare. 'Perhaps, when you breach those walls, you will be overwhelmed by a tidal wave of skeletons.'

'There are window-slits in the walls and crenellations along the tops of them,' Murgatroyd said, tapping a finger against a fuzzy detail in one of the plates. 'To me they speak of defence. Whichever forgotten Norse warlord made this thing, they meant to keep it for themselves.' He nodded at Topolsky. 'I think we will find a way in. No matter how well-built a fortress, even if it had its own water supply, and perhaps room enough inside those walls for sheep pastures and orchards, there would still have been a need for supplies.'

'If there isn't a door,' Ramos said, 'one can be arranged, provided the blasting powder is of sufficient potency.'

Cossile reached over and tapped Ramos on the wrist, not without some chilly affection. 'Dear Coronel: you really will not rest until you have blown something up, will you?'

'One way or another, there will be a way in,' Topolsky said. 'And if we must depend on Mister Ramos's munitions, Ada, then we shall. In a little while the fog of distance will lift and we shall gaze on our adversary with sharpened eyes and sharpened wits!'

I could not resist an interjection: 'Our adversary? Other than standing there a little ominously, it hasn't done us any harm, has it?'

'I speak figuratively, Coade: it is our adversary in that it represents ignorance and the unknown. And as men – and woman – of science may we agree that such deficiencies in our understanding will likely be rectified with no small measure of struggle and set-back? Be it the work of nature or the work of man, secrets and mysteries are never willingly divulged!' He finished one cigar and lit another. 'If they were, wherein would lie the glory, the nobility, of scientific conquest?' He leaned in confidingly, looking up and down the table. 'The Edifice will exact a toll from us, friends – of that I am certain! But we shall best it, and such scars as it inflicts on us – scars of body and soul – shall be all the more proudly worn, for we alone shall know the cost of them! Gentlemen in England, now abed, shall think themselves accursed they were not here!'

'Or extremely glad to have had a lie-in,' Cossile murmured.

I smiled. She caught my eye and smiled back.

Murgatroyd picked up one of the plates and held it closer to his own singular eye, examining something near the base of the Edifice: a little dark smudge pressed between the shoreline and the first flank of stone. 'What is that, gentlemen? I don't recall seeing it when we were on deck.'

'A flaw in the plate,' Topolsky dismissed.

'It is not a flaw,' Brucker said. 'It is real. The same thing is shown on this plate.'

'It is distinct from the Edifice,' Dupin commented. 'Eighty feet long, I would estimate, and perhaps fifty or sixty in height.'

'May I?' asked the captain politely.

He took the first plate from Murgatroyd and studied it carefully. Then he set it down slowly. 'I think it is a wreck, gentlemen. The masts are discernible, and perhaps a funnel. The main part is the hull. It is a steamship, like *Demeter*. I do not think any other sort of ship could have navigated the fissure.'

'How old could it be?' I asked, willing to expose my ignorance of maritime propulsion.

'We will know when we are a little closer. Certainly not more than thirty years. I think she may be a paddle-steamer, rather than screw-driven.' He turned his face to Topolsky. 'Did the men of *Europa* know of this wreck, Master? If so, it is curious that you have made no mention of it until now.'

'Their intelligence mentioned no wreck,' Topolsky said dismissively. 'And it need be of no concern to us. Ill-equipped ships come to grief all the while. We are anything but ill-equipped.'

'Still; we will approach that shore with caution.' Van Vught ruminated between sips of sherry. 'We shall anchor just off the headland, and then send out the boats the rest of the way. They will have a little further to row, but the men will not mind the exercise if there is a promise of dry land and extra grog at the end of it.' He nodded at Murgatroyd. 'Perhaps you will even find a patch of ground level enough for cricket, Lieutenant: I know you miss your strange English game. In the meantime, if there are useful stores in that wreck, we shall make them ours.'

'And bodies?' I asked tentatively.

Van Vught nodded sombrely. 'I hope there are none, Silas, but if there are we shall treat them with the respect due to all brothers of the sea.'

I picked up one of the plates that had been taken of the formal group, with the Edifice behind us. The plate had been chemically fixed, so it could be exposed to light, but it had not yet been duplicated as a photographic negative. As a consequence, all that was light was dark, and all that was dark was light. *Demeter* was a spectre of itself, its gunnels pale as bone, floating on a milky sea beneath an ashen sky. I turned the plate upside down, so that the ship seemed suspended from a ceiling of ice, with an immensity of sucking darkness clawing at it from below.

'Do you notice, doctor, that the crew haven't registered at all?' Countess Cossile enquired. 'They were scurrying around like rats, while the rest of us stood still enough to be captured. Other than the occasional phantom, where some man lingered long enough to leave a trace of himself, it as if we haunt a ghost ship – as if we ourselves are already dead.'

'You have a morbid streak, Countess,' said Murgatroyd, smiling awkwardly.

'It is a failing,' she agreed.

'The image is inverted,' I said, turning the frame the right way around. 'Everted . . . no, inverted. May I ask, Countess, what is meant by "eversion"?'

She frowned in my direction. 'Is there such a word, doctor?'

'There is,' Dupin interjected excitedly, a fusillade of spit bursting between his teeth. 'But its usage is rather specialised. Among mathematicians, it refers to the act of being turned inside-out . . .'

Brucker scraped a hand along the ribbon of black hair which divided his cranium. 'As the starfish everts its stomach, *ja?*'

'In mathematical framing, the definition is rather more rigorous,' Dupin said. 'But you have the crude sense of it. As a matter of fact, the problem is of interest to me. Consider the question of sphere eversion in a three-dimensional space—'

'Enough, boy,' Topolsky said. 'Some of us will be everting our own stomachs, rather than listen to you babble on about spheres and spaces.' His tone turned patrician. 'Concentrate on the here and now, as you are paid to do, rather than this airy-fairy nonsense.'

'I do not think it is nonsense to Dupin,' I said, struck by a protective urge towards the boy, for all his peculiar single-mindedness. 'In fact, I should like to hear more about it. I'm afraid my own mathematical education progressed no further than Napier's bones.'

'How many bones did he have, sir?' asked Mortlock.

'Two hundred and six, just like everyone else,' Countess Cossile said. Then, to me: 'Do you really mean to rectify your ignorance of matters mathematical, doctor? If so I imagine it will only be a matter of time before the shadow of Pythagoras falls across your literary imagination!' She clapped delightedly. 'Spare us the torment, doctor: what is next, for our gratification?'

'I am spent,' I said, pressing back into my seat. 'You have all been kind, but I fear the time for fiction is at an end.' I held up one of the photographic plates. 'Nothing that I might imagine can begin to compare with that. Besides, I sense I may already have strained the patience of my friends.'

'Oh dear,' the Countess said, pursing her lips in a mock pout. 'Have my little observations really been so wounding?'

'It has nothing to do with your observations, Countess, wounding or otherwise.'

'Why then I must implore you to continue.' She looked around the table for support. 'The doctor is entirely too self-effacing about his efforts. I am sure I am not alone in finding that his narrative gave me much to think about.'

'Much to pick holes in, you mean,' said Mortlock spiritedly.

'Midshipman . . .' Van Vught rumbled, warning him not to overstep his welcome in such elevated company.

'I still do not understand what is meant by a submarine,' Brucker lamented.

'A ship that moves beneath the waves,' I said.

'A ship of metal, no doubt,' Countess Cossile said.

Beyond our lagoon, somewhere in the warren of channels and inlets to the west, a distant storm discharged its fury. There was no thunder, but a single pulse of lightning limned the cabin windows, etching them in a tracery of blue light.

'There is always lightning,' I mouthed to myself.

Ramos sat quietly in my cabin. Often, when the dinner guests had dispersed from the captain's table, the Coronel and I shared a small cigar or a little snifter of brandy between us, each of us content not to speak for the sake of speaking, but to enjoy our silences as deeply as our conversations. Sometimes Ramos brought a little guitar – it was made of an almost impossibly delicate and translucent wood, so that one could nearly see through it – and played Spanish and Mexican folk tunes he had been taught in his childhood. His fingers were clumsy on the frets and strings to start with, but after a few tries he invariably settled into the task, gaining in confidence and fluency as he went. We spoke now and then of poetry and music, sometimes of our childhoods (though I more readily than he) and then occasionally of our intentions for the future, beyond our days on *Demeter*.

'I have fallen foul of Topolsky,' I said, pouring a little more brandy into the other man's snifter.

'Easily done.'

'But perhaps not so enthusiastically as was witnessed today. First I called him a Cossack bastard.'

A mild shrug. 'He is both of those things.'

'But it is not gentlemanly to make such an observation.'

'What was the provocation?'

'I was tending to Dupin after that fainting spell. I was concerned for the boy. He needed rest. Topolsky sauntered over and . . .' I waved aside my own recollection. 'No matter. No provocation excused my words. Dupin was my patient, but . . .'

'You said "first". And the second thing?'

'Perhaps the more serious insult. I spoiled his moment of triumph, when the object came into view. It was his to enjoy, by any measure, yet I had the reckless temerity to point out that there was something imperfect in his Edifice.'

He rolled the snifter in his fingers, dipping his nose to the rim.

'Again, you only spoke the truth. He is a bastard, and that object is crooked.'

'But it might not have been so unwise of me to hold my tongue. It is a failing of mine, as it is a failing of Dupin's, and indeed the Countess.' I sighed. 'Although we do it for different reasons. I am moved to rage when a man gets between me and my duty of care. Dupin is an innocent who has no choice but to say what is in his mind. There is no malice in him, just that awkward compulsion.'

"Mm,' Ramos said, nodding faintly. 'I agree. And Countess Cossile?'

'Of the three of us, I think she is the only one who enjoys wounding. She is infuriating. And yet . . .'

'And yet . . . ?' he beckoned, smiling at my candour.

'She beguiles me.' I grunted, irritated at myself for speaking so freely. 'She is also not the problem! I offend her by existing. With Master Topolsky, although I ranked low in his estimation, I did at least hope that there might be scope for improving my standing.'

'Perhaps it is not his estimation that matters.'

I looked at him guardedly. 'You think not?'

'I knew such men when I served under Santa Anna. At first, they command your attention because of their noise and grandiosity. They are always the loudest men in any room, and it is understandable that we should want their favour, as the flower seeks the favour of the sun.' He shifted, equally uncomfortable with such freedom of expression. 'But during our assault on the Alamo I learned that the worth of a man is not to be found in the strength of his voice, or even his convictions. Convictions are . . . what is your saying? Two a penny?' He made a dismissive swatting gesture. 'They die like flies. No, Silas: I saw the best and the worst of men at that battle, men on both sides of our little dispute, and I saw the humblest of them become lions and the proudest of them reduced to braying lambs.'

'Must you respect a man to be in his service?'

'No,' he answered carefully. 'But since it helps to be paid, you must respect the fullness of his pockets. In that regard, our boastful friend may be relied upon. I have already sent funds back to Mexico, and more will follow when we finish our expedition.'

'Is your family safe now?'

'As safe as ever.' My question seemed to cause him some amiable puzzlement. 'It is kind of you to ask. But did I mention a concern?'

'I thought that there was some difficulty – a religious or political matter.'

'In Mexico we are inclined to make little distinction.' The huge man shrugged, lantern-light burnishing the dented gleam of his skull. 'No, my grandfathers made the right choice in siding with Miguel Hidalgo over the King of Spain. The enemies they made are safely in the ground now, their ghosts grow weaker each year, and our country is unshackled.'

'I am glad of it, and I am sorry if it seemed as if was prying into your private affairs.'

'When one man has looked into the head of another, Silas, there need be no secrets between them.' He took another sip and it seemed to loosen something in him. 'I shall tell you something more of Master Topolsky, although it must remain between us. I think it will help you understand him better, and – perhaps – forgive him some of his failings.' He gathered himself. 'When I was first in his service – before I met you – he spoke to me of an episode of illness in his childhood.'

I smiled wryly. 'The Master seems too indomitable to succumb to any known malady.'

'He puffs himself up, runs around a lot, and makes an impressive noise, but that is also true of the plump, stupid birds that you English like to shoot for sport. Beneath the feathers there is often less than meets the eye.' His own observations seeming to trouble him, Ramos gave a shake of head, one part negation and another shame. 'Still, I would not work for a man I considered completely without honour. He is a bastard, but then so am I. He is brave, has never lied to me, and I do not believe he will lead us astray. We each of us have our armour.'

'And what of this illness?'

'A fever. Confined to bed, adrift from all sense of time and place with nothing to occupy his senses but the fluttering of bedroom curtains. This was in the long white summer nights of his homeland, already a strain on anyone's soundness of mind. Once, in the endless warm evening, he fancied that the curtains flew apart by an impossible degree, such that the view between them was the entirety of his universe.' A note of awe entered Ramos's retelling. 'And he saw it, Silas: as the curtains parted, so for him did the thin veil of reality. Beyond it stood a glittering clockwork of such complexity and perfection as to make our friend Brucker weep. That sight of it did not last long, but by the way he spoke of this episode, I believe it has cast a shadow of desperate longing across his entire life.'

I thought of the times I had been abed with illness in Plymouth, an unwilling prisoner of my own reeling imagination.

'Surely the wiser part of him knew it to be a consequence of fever?'

'Indeed. But our wiser parts are not our masters.'

'Would that they were,' I reflected. 'But you are right, of course. And I see now that he must have been hoping to see a facet of that perfection in the Edifice. Perhaps, for a second, he did. But then I undid the spell by pointing out the wrongness of what we saw before us.'

'You broke the spell, but if you had not done it Raymond Dupin would have said something, and if not Dupin then Henry Murgatroyd or even our captain.'

'When one is being stabbed, I am not sure it matters that there might be other daggers waiting in the wings.' I bowed my head in regret. 'Still, if there is one salvation: his opinion of me was low enough to begin with. There is scarcely room for it to go any lower.'

'As I said, you are not to be blamed. A doctor ran off with his mother: ever since then, he has held your entire profession accountable and contemptible.'

'Regardless of their opinions, most men eventually have use of us.'

'Indeed: and he is not so foolish as to think we could weather these seas without a physician – and that was before this.' He rapped a knuckle near the spot where I had opened him. 'And I mention his illness – which he only confessed to me in a blaze of drunkenness – only that you should better understand the man we follow. He speaks of fame and fortune, but what he truly seeks is one instant back in that fever-bed, with the curtains flung wide, and all heaven spread before him like a banquet.'

'He will never have it.'

'No,' Ramos agreed. 'But be sure of this, Silas: he will not be denied in his search. And a man like that is to be feared as much as he is admired. That bastard will lead us to one of two things: glory or ruin.'

I topped up his glass, and mine as well. 'It is a strange thing, Coronel, that your misfortune has been the cause of a friendship. I ought to regret any injury that befalls a man, especially one as serious as yours. But I fear I am not as sorry as I should be.'

Ramos touched my glass with his. 'Nor I, that it happened, dear Silas.'

Chapter Nine

Demeter anchored in the middle of the lagoon, about a mile further east than the headland, and lowered two boats into the water. With the captain's encouragement – and since none of the men needed my attention come morning – I clambered awkwardly down the ropes (my equipment lowered in advance) to board the pinnace, the larger of the expeditionary vessels. Both the pinnace and the smaller jolly boat were sturdy, white-painted craft. The pinnace took ten men, the jolly boat six, together with ample supplies to outfit a camp for several days. The pinnace was the only one with a mast, but it was not used today. Each boat carried rowers, made up of midshipmen: six in the heavier pinnace, two in the jolly boat. Mortlock was the only one I knew by name, and he was already in the pinnace, fussing with a bandage around his palm. Ramos came aboard as well, since this boat carried the bulk of the powder barrels and fuses that were his responsibility. The remainder of our non-rowing party was made up of Murgatroyd and Dupin, at least to begin with. But then there was some discussion among *Demeter*'s hands about the relative weights of various belongings, and it was deemed that Dupin's surveying materials had to be put into the other boat for the sake of balance. Since Dupin would not travel without them, even if they remained in plain sight for the entire crossing (and no man was likely to be so idiotic as to tamper with them) it was arranged for Dupin to climb over into the other boat, and Countess Cossile to take his place in the pinnace.

'Well, doctor,' the Countess said, facing me as she positioned herself on one of the cross-planks. 'It seems that Monsieur Dupin cannot bear the thought of us being separated.'

'I doubt that Dupin had a thought in his head save for the jealous protection of his instruments. He is like a schoolboy guarding his homework from the other boys.'

'It is true that he has found his one vocation, and will not countenance another trespassing into his expertise.'

'I doubt that any of us has the slightest interest in doing so.'

'Ah, but you were the only one of us who asked about that word, clearly cutting to the heart of his interests. What is a cartographer but a very specialised kind of mathematician?'

'I had inversion in mind, and eversion slipped out,' I said testily. 'No more needs to be made of it.'

'Oh dear.'

'Oh dear, what?'

'I shall have to break it to Monsieur Dupin that the doctor is in a *very* disagreeable mood.'

I said nothing. If my eyes lingered on the line of her jaw for a second longer than prudence dictated, then I hoped that the error was beneath the threshold of her observation.

And yet she beguiles me . . .

Murgatroyd nodded to the men to begin rowing, and with strong, regular strokes the pinnace and the jolly boat began to slip away from *Demeter*. Across the cold water, the grunts and murmurs of the men in the other boat reached us as if we travelled hull-to-hull. Topolsky was quiet, I noticed: not his usual rambunctious self. He sat small and slope-shouldered, like a dark, slumping sack of coal, his back to the direction of travel. Something in the imperfection of the Edifice had roused troubling ideas within him. He brooded rather than boasted, and when he spoke – to Dupin, Brucker, or across the water to one of our number – he made a noticeable effort to avert his eyes from the very thing that drew us.

'How is your wound, Coronel Ramos?' the Countess asked brightly, looking over my shoulder.

'I do not think it will be the thing that kills me this time.'

'This time?'

'I'm sorry?'

'You do not think it will be the thing that kills you this time? What a peculiar formulation. Is that a thing that men say to each other in Mexico? Perhaps, when the old religions still grip the imagination, it is not so unusual to speak of cycles of death and rebirth?'

'It was nothing, I assure you.'

She redirected her attention to me. 'Do you think it odd, Doctor Coade, to speak in such terms?'

'We are not all linguists, Countess. The Coronel was merely making friendly conversation in a language that is not his mother tongue. Would it not be a kindness to let the occasional error go unnoticed, or is that entirely beneath your capabilities?'

'You really have roused yourself with the wrong head on.' She dipped her head to my boxes of medical equipment, tucked low in the boat and protected from damage by masses of rope and canvas. 'I hope you brought *everything* with you, or your mood will be even more intolerable by evening.'

We progressed. The lagoon's banks were far enough away that I perceived no impression of movement, but after several minutes a backward glance showed the distance we had attained from the ship. Against a rising backdrop of rock and ice, *Demeter* looked dainty, toylike and fragile. How could such a little thing swallow a hundred men like a whale, and still feel empty and haunted in the quiet watches?

Slowly our course altered the angle between boat and ship, such that *Demeter* seemed to slowly revolve as if on a potter's wheel.

'They have repaired that mast very well,' I commented to Murgatroyd, anxious to establish a line of conversation that did not involve the Countess.

'The mast, doctor?' Murgatroyd asked pleasantly.

I frowned at him. 'The one that broke, Henry, during our passage. I am quite sure I remember it crashing to the deck.'

Murgatroyd gained the wary, tactful look of someone who is going to have to set another man right without causing insult.

'Oh, there was a bit of damage here and there, you're quite right, but nothing as serious as a mast coming down. That's a very bad thing indeed. I'm sure there was a lot of noise and shouting, even so – and if you're below-decks, that can sound a lot worse than it is.'

I was about to answer that I remembered it vividly because I had been on deck at the time of the mishap. But some rare caution stilled my tongue.

'Thank you, Henry. Time and again, I realise I should never venture to have an opinion on anything to do with the fabric of the ship, because I am quite sure to make a fool of myself.'

'You stick to bones, doctor, and we'll stick to sails and coal,' Murgatroyd told me amiably. 'And it's not foolishness, is it, Mister Mortlock?'

'Not at all,' Mortlock said, agreeing hastily with his superior officer. 'A ship's like a whole new world. You could be born on a ship, and you'd still go to your grave learning something new. I'll tell you what I learned last night! There's two hundred and six bones in a body! Imagine being dead, and all those bones rattling around inside you! I don't think I fancy being dead!'

A tunnel, a stone passage, a suit of armour: my own reflection disclosing a skull.

Being dead is bad enough, I thought. But there is something worse.

Walking around with someone else's bones inside you.

'We're back to mortality again, are we, gentlemen?' asked the Countess, as if she were privy to my very thoughts.

Absently, she plucked a feather from her hat and tossed it overboard, where the weak currents of the lagoon soon bore it away, a lonely little yellow messenger off on its own.

*

The boats crunched against the loose scree that bordered the lagoon's shallows. We disembarked, wading through two feet of shivering cold water until finding ourselves on dry, if slippery and ankle-twisting, land. Ahead of us stood the flank of the nearest wall, a mere prelude to the rising, undulating defences beyond, and between us and the wall lay the wreck we had spied from *Demeter*. It was indeed another steamship, but (as the captain had ventured) a paddle-wheeled vessel. We were looking at its starboard side, with the port side pressed close to the wall. The wreck was well above the shoreline: fifty or sixty feet beyond the present limit of the water, and a good ten feet of elevation above it, resting on a bank of large round pebbles and still larger, irregular boulders, some of which had pierced the hull, such that her planks had been split, forced apart and in some places cleaved clean away. Through the gaps where planks had split, or were gone, we made out the dark, musty promise of her holds, and whatever useful goods might yet lie within them.

Half-way along the hull was the starboard paddle wheel, or rather its greatly mangled remains. The wheel's semi-circular housing was nearly intact, but the main part of the wheel was a ruin of broken spokes and shattered paddles. Perhaps the weather had caused it to rot and collapse in gradual fashion, but I wondered instead if the wheel had still been turning, still revolving under the full force of steam, when the ship found itself tossed onto the rocks, the wheel shattering itself in a whirling orgy of self-destruction.

Like *Demeter*, she had carried masts and sails, but little now remained of these save three grisly stumps surmounted by sagging, broken cross-beams, draped with the skinlike remains of canvas. They made me think of three crude crosses raised above some ghastly Calvary, whose storm-racked sky was the grey rampart beyond. Of her name no trace was to be seen, had it ever been inscribed on her hull.

We did not go near the wreck to begin with. Ramos, Murgatroyd and Mortlock selected an area of relatively level ground where the rocks were small enough to be trod underfoot, and this was where we erected our camp. Canvases were laid across the stones, tents and awnings set up, latrines dug, and tables and chairs arranged for our temporary convenience. By the standards of comfort on land, it was spartan, but for most of us it was an immeasurable improvement to life on *Demeter*. The men did not need to sleep cheek-by-jowl; ablutions could be performed with some measure of privacy, there was room to wander around freely, there was a breeze, games of cricket and football could be staged, the ground did not rise and fall or tilt with every breath, a cup of coffee could be set down on a table and trusted not to spill itself and above all else there was silence, except for the men's cheerful voices and the gentle slap of the lagoon's water against the shore, a movement too feeble to be called waves. The presence of the wreck might have been expected to dampen spirits slightly, and perhaps it did, but those spirits were elevated enough that the men were still in an agreeable, playful mood, like schoolboys on the first day of liberation from their lessons. They knew in their hearts that whatever folly had befallen this earlier ship, it could not apply to the sturdier *Demeter*, with her modern lines and superior means of propulsion.

I had a tent to myself, and that was welcome, but it was also obliged to serve as my office, examining room and even operating theatre, should anything befall the men. So far they had all made it ashore unscathed, healthy except for the minor maladies of which I was already aware. Ramos was growing in strength from day to day, but I observed him carefully all the same. Although he had responded well to the surgery, it would likely be many months before we could be completely sure that he was out of danger. Exhaustion still dogged Dupin, but there was little I could do about that. Proximity to the object only stoked his enthusiasm for work, and we had barely touched land before he was springing around with his surveying gear, like some mad naturalist with a butterfly-net.

The wall which loomed above the wreck was but the nearest of many, and lower than the tiered ramparts which rose beyond it. But it was still tall enough to inspire feelings of the sublime. A green margin hemmed its base to about the height of a man. It puzzled me to begin with, until I realised that it was an extension of the tidal staining which marked some of the rocks and pebbles around our tents. I glanced back with some foreboding to the lagoon, wondering if its tidal range could possibly be so high as to submerge our entire camp. Surely, though, men such as Murgatroyd, with their knowledge of almanacs and tables, would have performed the necessary estimation of risk before deciding on our temporary base.

An urge overcame me and I retreated to my tent before the visible manifestations of my addiction became too stark. Drawing the flap behind me, I busied myself arranging supplies for a minute or two, while listening for footfalls and voices outside. Once I was satisfied that no one was near, or in danger of coming near, I quickly injected myself with morphine then lay down on my bed, listening to the racing whirl of my heart. Appalled and fascinated in the same breath, I visualised it as a paddle-like engine, spinning nearly to the point of destruction, and I wondered if the doctors of the future might yet perfect such a machine, for men whose hearts were ailing.

Without warning, a huge, bearded, bald-crowned face jammed itself through the loosely secured flap.

'Silas,' Ramos said, affecting no surprise at my posture. 'I called, but you didn't answer. I would not have interrupted so rudely, if I had known you were resting.'

I pushed myself up on my elbows, glad that I had taken the trouble to pack away the syringe and morphine. 'Just a little light-headed. It's curious, isn't it? I have been afflicted by seasickness for almost the entirety of our voyage, and most especially since Montevideo, dreaming of nothing but the fixity of *terra firma*. Yet now that I am upon dry land at last, I feel myself struck by a dizziness that feels very much like a close cousin of seasickness itself!'

'It means only that you are at last adapting to *Demeter*.'

'A good thing, then,' I said doubtfully, hoping that my story of dizziness was a satisfactory cover for the effects of morphine addiction and the remedy thereof. 'Although it does not feel like much of a good thing while I am in the bitter throes of it.'

His faint smile conveyed either sympathy or the wise understanding that I lied, but that he would not be so unkind as to remark upon it.

'Perhaps a little stroll will help.'

'I doubt that, but what do you have in mind?'

'Murgatroyd and I are going to investigate the wreck, while the light is still with us. We will take a couple of lanterns but it will still be dark inside. You are of course welcome to join us.'

I thought of the man I had lately offended, the man I had called a bastard to his face. 'Will Master Topolsky be joining us?'

'No, and he was very dismissive of our intentions, considering it a waste of our energies. He is with Dupin now. They are planning to go all the way around the Edifice before dark, looking for a way in.'

'Then I think I will join you, Ramos.' I gestured vaguely at my belongings. 'But please allow me a minute, if you would.'

'Of course,' he said, his head backing out of my tent like the moon vanishing between veils of cloud.

I met them at the rent in the starboard side of the hull, where the planks had ripped apart to create an opening through which a man might stoop with only moderate indignity. Murgatroyd had two Davy lamps, and he offered me one to carry, which I did gladly since it allowed me some illusion of usefulness. Ramos had a scimitar on his belt (I will call it such although I am no authority on swords) and a musket in his hands, and he was the first through, splinters of rotten wood crumbling away as his mighty shoulders and back squeezed against the timbers. He crunched down onto something then called back from the darkness, his voice echoing hollowly from within the hold. 'Come through, Henry. Then you, Silas. It is safe enough for now.'

I climbed through after Murgatroyd. The space beyond was musty, but not so dark as I had anticipated. The light of day fanned through the gaps where the planks had loosened or rotted, casting ladder-like patterns over my companions' faces. We looked striped and fearsome, warriors daubed for battle. Beneath our boots was a jumble of sound timber, rotten wood and ankle-twisting voids which went all the way down the lowest part of the ship. In places, rocks had burst through completely. At our entrance, a faint scampering sounded beneath the boards. I thought it odd that rats had survived in such a barren place, but only until Ramos showed me the grain sacks which still slumped against the sides of the hold, intermingled with coal and other provisions. Barrels, which might plausibly have contained potable water, had been toppled and spilled by the violence of the wreck. That was a shame, but not a catastrophe. While it might have been reassuring to find a reserve of supplies, *Demeter* was still well provisioned in the essentials.

While Ramos was going around the hold, Murgatroyd found a ladder which led up to a hatch in the ceiling. He called the other man over, handed me his lamp (so that he had both hands free) and he and Ramos began to strain at the trapdoor. I stood forlornly, rats scampering underfoot, unable to do more than watch. The hatch was stubborn – rotted into position, perhaps – but after a minute of brute effort Ramos was able to batter it loose with the stock of his musket, already generously dented from the cracking of skulls under Santa Anna. Murgatroyd reclaimed his lamp and we climbed out of the bottom-most hold, into one of the intermediate decks. Again, no portholes or ceiling grilles offered illumination, but the planks had eased apart enough to admit a tracery of grey light, revealing a hold or storage compartment smaller than the one beneath, perhaps for lighter goods. Crates had been tossed against each other, some upended and broken, with their straw-lined innards spilled onto the floor. Here and there the contents of these crates gleamed in our lamp-light. The equipment was at once inscrutable to me and in the same breath instantly familiar. I did not need to know what it did, or what it was called, to recognise it as being comparable to the instruments and devices brought aboard *Demeter* by Dupin and Brucker.

'They came with similar intentions to us, gentlemen. To survey.'

Murgatroyd lifted to his eye an object somewhat like a pocket compass. 'This lot doesn't look as fancy as what we have.'

'You are right, Henry, but I think that only speaks to this expedition being somewhat older than our own.'

'Master Topolsky never mentioned another expedition, did he?'

I glanced at Ramos before speaking. 'Well, he did, Henry – just not in terms of that ship coming to grief.'

'This cannot be *Europa*,' Ramos said, as if by assertion alone he might make it so. 'This cannot be.'

'What was his account of *Europa* to you?' I asked him, treading delicately, for I did not wish to imply any act of concealment or deception on his part.

'As he told it to you, Silas, and you, Henry, and your captain. That the crew of *Europa* caught sight of the Edifice. but could get no closer. They returned home, and sold their intelligence.'

'It's too soon to say if this is the ship,' I said. 'But if we can find our way to her helm or bridge, I imagine we will have the answer.'

'If they were in this ship when it ran aground,' Murgatroyd said, 'there are going to be bodies.'

'Let the bodies be my business, Henry,' I reassured him.

We had been moving towards a door at one end of the compartment, heading in the direction of the prow. It was of stout construction, panelled and varnished wood with a small circular window set into the upper part. As our lamps swung in our hands, and faint grey light played through the timbers, I discerned a pattern of letters written on the door. Excited, hoping that these words might confirm or negate our suspicions, I pushed ahead of Ramos and Murgatroyd.

The letters floated before me, faint against the varnish. They said:

PROPULSION CORE

NO UNAUTHORISED ADMITTANCE

Chapter Ten

I pushed my finger against the letters, tracing the curious spartan typeface, frowning at the strangeness of the words themselves. The lamp-light wavered as Murgatroyd caught up with me.

'Will it open, doctor?'

'I haven't even tried opening it. Do these words make any sense to you, Henry? Coronel? It is English, but . . .'

Their grey-striped faces were solemn. 'Words?' asked Ramos.

'These words!' I exclaimed, jabbing the wood.

But even as I spoke, I saw that my finger was touching only a few mottled blotches where the varnish had worn through.

'It is easy to be mistaken, when we are so intent on finding something,' Ramos said.

My throat had gone quite dry. 'I apologise, gentlemen. I . . . allowed my enthusiasm to get the better of me. Will you forgive me?'

'There is nothing to forgive,' Ramos said, holding the musket in one hand while he turned the door handle with the other.

Beyond, as I should have realised from the layout of the ship, was the engine room, with its enormous wheels and shafts driving the paddles on either side of the hull. All was still and cold, with scuttles of coal still waiting to be fed into the iron belly of the boiler. The damage to the paddles had led to some of the parts of the engine being violently buckled or thrown out of their fastenings. Even a layman such as I could tell that the steamship was past any possible point of repair.

We searched around the narrow spaces between these monstrous riveted masses of iron and copper, but no body or part of a body was to be found. My unease was now a tightening band around my chest. I had seen something on that door, and in some oblique manner its meaning was not completely at odds with the function of this engine room. Was this not also the means by which this ship gained propulsion?

I flashed back to the morphine injection. I had measured the dosage precisely, had I not? Or, in my haste, had I put too much of the drug into myself, and was my brain now loosening itself from the shackles of reality?

Or was it quite the opposite?

We departed the engine room. Beyond was a corridor with wooden compartment doors on either side. We searched a few of them, finding storage rooms and small cabins, but no trace of life. At the end of this corridor was a choice between another wooden door and a flight of stairs which led to the next level. We took the stairs, feeling them creak and groan beneath our boots. The ship was on a starboard tilt, so the effect was as if we explored some abandoned mansion that had begun to subside into its foundations, with every angle calculated to instill unease and trepidation.

Once we were on the upper level we moved quickly through the recognisable components of a ship. There were portholes on this level, allowing thick shafts of daylight to penetrate the interior. There was a galley, a separate dining room and a succession of cabins. We searched them all. Loose items had been thrown around, so that everywhere we trod there was broken glass, shattered earthenware, and splintered wood, but still no trace of present habitation. The library was all the more shock-ing because it appeared intact and inviolate, with its books still in neat, scholarly order on the shelves. They had been secured by chains and wooden lips on the shelves, ready for the perusal of ghosts.

I eased one such book from the shelf, opening it at random.

'*A speculation into the interior properties of the Galilean satellites,*' I mouthed, before snapping the text shut.

'It's beginning to look as if they weren't here when she wrecked,' Murgatroyd said. 'They might have got off in jolly boats and pinnaces, if they knew their ship had had it.'

'It's possible, Henry,' I allowed. 'It's also possible that the bulk of the men were still aboard when she ran onto these rocks, but that the event was not nearly as violent as we might imagine. The ship looks terrible to us now, but we don't know how much of that was the work of time and weather.'

'Where are they now, then?'

'If it was evident to them that the ship was beyond salvation, they may have ventured ashore with the purpose of striking north, in the direction of Santiago. I imagine they took their dead with them, to bury decently, and all the boats and supplies they could travel with. What is certain – if that was their plan – is that they will have left a record of their intentions.'

'Silas is right,' Ramos said. 'They will have left something. Which will either vindicate my master, or condemn him.'

We moved forward. Beyond the library was a wider area – a sort of hallway – with larger windows, rendering our lamps superfluous. On the port side of this hallway – the side facing the Edifice – was a door which led out onto deck. The door was ajar. Another door sat opposite it on the starboard side, facing to the lagoon. Although its pane was shattered, this one was still bolted from the inside. Ahead of us stood a pair of open doors leading into a room that I judged to be of some importance, for even from the hallway I could see that it was luxuriously appointed, with a grand table in the middle.

'I think, gentlemen, that is where we will find our answers,' I said.

But Ramos was stooping down, leaning on his musket for support. He traced something in the planks of the floor: white grooves, gouged deeply into the wood.

'What is it?'

'I do not know, Silas,' he said in a low voice. 'But if you observe these marks, they continue all the way out through that door, onto the port-side deck.'

Murgatroyd bent over. 'They look like scratches to me,' he offered. 'Like nail scratches.' He splayed his own hand and offered his fingertips up to the grooves. They matched excellently.

'See how they dig in here,' Ramos said. 'Closer to that room. Then they are pulled back, growing shallower. Then they dig in again.' He picked at something: perhaps a fleck of nail jammed into the wood. 'It is as if a man tried over and over again to stop himself being dragged out of the ship, by his bare nails.'

'It could be an animal leaving those marks, I suppose,' Murgatroyd said. 'A bear, or something.'

'You would rather it be a bear, Henry, and so would I. But those are indubitably human marks.'

'I don't like it.'

I nodded. 'I doubt very much that you are alone in that opinion.'

We followed the scratches into the room beyond the hallway. Our nerves, tested already, were now at breaking point. Ramos had the musket in both hands, held nearly horizontally, and he jabbed it from shadow to shadow as if he might fire at any instant. The room was as empty of life as the rest of the ship, though. Charts and diagrams lay across the tilted surface of the table, and various almanacs were still spread open, some on the table itself and some fallen to the floor, where they resembled a flock of dead birds with stiff black wings. In cabinets around the room were many more books, as well as a multitude of compasses, clocks, quadrants and so on. A few of these specimens were on the table, and a few more lay ruined on the floor.

'I am no judge,' I said. 'But it seems to me that these men, though they came earlier than us, were not ill-equipped.'

Murgatroyd leafed through the charts. 'These are as good as anything on *Demeter*. And I don't think these instruments would've disgraced us, either. They aren't as fancy as the ones Herr Brucker came aboard with, but they're better than the average ship carries.'

'Then we must put aside any thoughts that these men were lackadaisical in their preparations,' I said. 'They may not have had such a swift ship, or the benefit of Master Topolsky's connections, but they were not fools.'

'And yet,' Ramos said, swivelling around to take in the whole of the cabin, and by implication the ruined ship beyond it. 'They came to this.'

Murgatroyd stopped in his examining. He had become statue-like, a tableau of a man poised with his finger on the open page of a journal.

'Henry?' I asked.

He murmured: 'Oh, dear god.'

'What is it, man?'

Ramos and I went to him, standing either side of him. Murgatroyd had his finger pressed onto the book, as if some malign mesmeric influence would not permit its disconnection.

'It's the log of *Europa*,' Murgatroyd said.

I nodded heavily, feeling more sorry than surprised. Sorry for Ramos, who until now must have hoped that although his master might yet be a Cossack bastard, he was not a liar.

But it was not the fact of the ship's identity that was the most troubling thing. It was what had been written down as the last entry in her log.

I say written-scrawled in terror and haste would be more accurate:

> I GOT OUT.
> IT'S COMING BACK.
> IT'S COMING TO DRAG ME BACK IN.
> BACK TO THE OTHERS.
> LEAVE WHILE YOU C

Slashed diagonally across the page – cutting through to the blank entries beyond – were the grooves made by fingernails. I stared at these marks, barely able to comprehend the force with which they had been inflicted, and the utter futility of them. That was the worst part of it. I could not conceive of a mind so unhinged by hysterical terror that it thought a book might be a thing worth clinging to. It would have been as well to grasp at thin air. And yet, the will behind that act of desperate hopelessness had still been sufficient to mutilate the paper.

Gently, I eased Murgatroyd away from the log.

I closed the volume as tenderly and quietly as if I were lowering a coffin lid.

'We'll take this back to the camp,' I said. 'I imagine it can answer a number of questions.'

Ramos rumbled: 'He will answer more.'

'We should hear Topolsky's side of the account first, Coronel. It may be that he has . . . some explanation.'

'Yes. The explanation that he has lied to us, to all of us, about the foundation for this folly.'

'We know only that some men left *Europa*,' I cautioned, feeling the stirring of the Coronel's wrath as the dwellers on the foot-slopes of some dormant volcano might feel the slow but calamitous awakening of their fiery deity. 'There might be reasons for that. A man came back, seemingly maddened . . . but there might be reasons for that as well. Sickness. Perhaps an outbreak that led to the abandonment of this expedition.'

'Do you think . . .' began Murgatroyd. 'Do you think . . .' He seemed stuck within himself, like a broken automaton. 'Do you think . . . it was . . . whatever he was talking about, that dragged him out of here?'

'I think we dare not speculate, Henry,' I said, trying to calm the man I had seen so untroubled by storms, cold and the general vicissitudes of life at sea. A brave, dependable man, in all circumstances save this. 'Again, when we have returned to camp, and discussed this with Master Topolsky . . .'

'There will be no discussion,' Ramos said, setting off in the direction we had come, back down into the bowels of the paddle-steamer, musket before him.

Chapter Eleven

A number of things happened in quick succession.

Topolsky and Dupin came into view around the northernmost limit of one of the turret-capped walls, an animated exchange going on between the man and the boy. Dupin laboured under an enormous burden of surveying devices, loaded up like a pack-mule, while Topolsky sauntered happily unencumbered, gesticulating broadly, his hat at a wild angle.

Ramos strode out to intercept them. He had his musket ready, but I do not think that was enough to prick their suspicions as to his mood. Murgatroyd and I followed behind the Mexican as quickly as we could, but where we stumbled and skid on the loose stones, Ramos remained sure-footed, as if all his years of soldiery had equipped him for any terrain.

'Coronel!' I wheezed after him, already short of breath from my exertions. 'We must allow him to offer his version of events!'

Ramos did not hear me, or did not care to hear me.

'I thought he'd be the last one to get his blood up over the Russian,' Murgatroyd said, labouring alongside me.

'Loyalty has its limits, Henry. I fear that Master Topolsky has just found our friend Ramos's limit.'

'The Mexican looks set to rip him limb from limb.'

'Then it's as well that a doctor will be on hand. Although I hope there will be no limb-ripping.' I urged him on, as if he were holding me back. 'C'mon, Henry! We may be just as convinced of Topolsky's guilt in this matter, but in England we allow men the presumption of innocence, at least until they have been heard.'

'We aren't in England, though, are we?' Murgatroyd pointed out. 'We're in the freezing arse-end of nowhere!'

By now our calls had drawn some of the others from the tents. Mortlock was scrambling to catch up with us, as well as Herr Brucker and Countess Cossile. The latter was picking up the hem of her skirt and hop-scotching from one area of level ground to another, laughing to herself, quite as if the whole enterprise were a sort of giddy amusement.

'Dupin,' Ramos shouted. 'Step aside from Master Topolsky!'

They were only a hundred or so paces apart now, and certainly within range of a musket shot.

'What is the emergency, Coronel?' cried out Topolsky. 'We are on our way back – is that not enough?'

Ramos fired once, sending a shot over the heads of the two men. Dupin flinched and dropped some of his items, which clattered and smashed to the stones. Ramos slowed to a walk and reloaded on the move, doing so with an almost mindless efficiency, as if his fingers were seasoned foot-soldiers who no longer needed instruction from the high-command of his brain.

Ramos called out: 'It's all a lie, Dupin! That wreck is *Europa*. Something bad happened to those men, and he has led us to the same graveyard!'

'Coronel,' Topolsky called back. 'Submit yourself to Coade! It is abundantly clear that you are still suffering the effects of his butchery!'

'He is perfectly sane!' I shouted. 'Henry and I have seen the evidence!' I held up the log book. 'They never made it out of this inlet, Master! You led us here on the false pretence that these men survived their expedition!'

'It is not as you imagine! I can explain everything!'

'This'll be good,' Murgatroyd muttered.

I shouted again: 'Then explain yourself!'

'The paddle-steamer was lost immediately after the discovery of the lagoon. They were attempting to enter it, or leave it – it is not clear which – and they fell foul of those vicious currents and winds which our dear Van Vught so gamely mastered, before meeting their end on these rocks.' Topolsky had stopped now. Dupin, next to him, was on his knees, rummaging for the broken ruins of his equipment. 'Some brave men of *Europa* sought to preserve their findings, and so they stuffed scraps of intelligence into sealed bottles, which found their way to open water, and by the grace of god came into the possession of a Peruvian merchantman . . .' He slowed. 'Shall I continue?'

'Why did you not mention that the earlier expedition was lost?' I asked, trying to inject a calm, judicial note into proceedings.

'Coade, for pity's sake see reason.'

'I am attempting to.'

'You consider yourself a man of science. Mariners are – let us not split hairs – deeply superstitious folk. They are not educated, modern-minded men such as you and I. Even the best of them, such as Van Vught, would not have been able to rise above that baser part of his nature which is still in thrall to ignorance. His every decision would have been coloured by the entirely irrelevant knowledge that a far less capable ship, under a far worse captain, had come to grief.' He looked at me pleadingly. 'Now why would I have burdened the poor man with such an unnecessary thing, when it was of no possible consequence?'

'I think it may have been of some consequence,' Ramos said.

'Dear Coronel, would you be so kind as to point that musket elsewhere?'

'You will come with me, Master. We will go back with the boat, and I will ask Captain Van Vught to put you in chains.'

'Nonsense.'

'It is not a request.' Ramos fired again, this time at such a low angle that the shot must have whistled over Topolsky by only a few inches. As methodically as before, Ramos began to reload. 'I was employed to look after the expeditionary party, and to hold Captain Van Vught and his men to the letter of their agreement, should they waver. But they are not the ones who have lied and deceived. The terms of my employment have been broken.'

Topolsky crouched low, as if expecting another shot.

'Want to put yourself in charge, do you?'

'No. I am a soldier of little education. Herr Brucker, or Countess Cossile, may assume your role.' His huge shoulders shrugged. 'I am indifferent to the choice.'

'I don't want it,' Dupin said, as if his name had been under consideration. 'I just want to sit down with some paper and think things through.' His arctic eyes met mine. 'We went all around it, Doctor Coade! There are ways in, I think. And ways out. But it's very hard to think about. Do you think it started off like this?' He nodded at himself, as if carrying on a conversation inside his head. 'I don't think it did. I think it ended up like this when something went wrong. I touched the stone! I could feel it whispering to me. There's an engine in there somewhere!'

I indicated to the boy that he should head back to the tents. 'If you are capable of resting that fearsome mind of yours, Raymond, go and do so.' Then, to Topolsky: 'Something awful happened to the men on that steamer.' I patted the log. 'If this is any testament, then all of them went inside your Edifice. One of them got back out again, but only for as long as it took to leave us a message. The poor soul was then dragged back by whatever abomination lies within those walls.'

'A message?'

'That we should depart, while we are able to.'

133

He shook his head, scoffing at my words. 'Undoubtedly a ruse, to scare us off. What better way to protect a secret?'

'How do you explain the absence of bodies?'

'I have no need to. They have merely gone elsewhere.' His eyes flashed back to the musket. 'Coronel, do you think you could find it in yourself to be something less of a brute . . .' Topolsky's hand moved suddenly, grasping for something tucked within the folds of his clothing. The low sun caught a gleam of blackened metal: an exquisitely tiny pistol clutched in his fingers.

Ramos fired. I do not blame him, for in that instant it seemed entirely likely that Topolsky would shoot him first. The Coronel, since he was not a murderer by nature, aimed only to disarm Topolsky, and this he achieved. His musket shot clipped Topolsky's forearm. The shot echoed prodigiously, seeming to resound off every surface about us, from pebbles to the looming masses of rock hemming the lagoon. Topolsky in turn yelped, and was perhaps in the process of dropping the pistol. But the process was not speedy enough, and by dint of spite or some uncontrollable impulse from his damaged arm, he squeezed the trigger. The little pistol flashed, and by some mercy the shot did not go through Ramos.

It went instead through me.

It penetrated my abdomen, and I knew instantly – before even the first blush of pain had begun to touch me – that I was dead. A surgeon may dig a bullet out of muscle; he may cut off an arm that has been shattered by cannon-fire, but when a shot enters a man's guts, there is nothing to be done. It did not matter that I was the sole surgeon on *Demeter*: if a hundred more of me had stood in attendance, with all the learning and tools of modern medicine at their disposal, it would not have made one iota of difference to my fate.

I fell to the ground. The agony arrived. I had braced myself for it, as one prepares for the visitation of a tiresome guest, but that did not make the thing itself any more bearable. I whimpered, holding back a vast rising pressure of torment.

Ramos flung down his musket and leapt to my side. Murgatroyd and Mortlock scrambled over to subdue Topolsky, now that his little pistol had ejected its sting.

'I am sorry, Silas,' Ramos said, a desperate sadness welling in his eyes. 'I did not mean this!'

Blood bubbled in my mouth. But I had to speak to him. 'This was not your doing, Coronel.'

'Perhaps it is not so bad.'

I shook my head. The Coronel knew what I knew. He had seen too many men die like this.

'Oh, Silas,' said Countess Cossile leaning over me from the other side. 'You've gone and done it again, haven't you.'

'Gone and done what?' I asked feebly.

'You've died on us. Or soon will.' She dipped her eyes to the bloody quagmire of my stomach. 'Honestly, you will insist on making this hard on yourself. With all your medical learning, couldn't you at least find a way to end yourself painlessly?'

'He shot me,' I said.

'Silas, it's not like that and you know it. The poor man is almost entirely without volition.'

Despite my pain – perhaps, even, because of it – I do not think I had ever seen a more lovely vision than the face of Countess Cossile. She was an angel, gloried in a nimbus of yellow, her eyes meeting mine with infinite reproach and infinite compassion, as if I had sinned against god and in the same act earned eternal redemption.

'I've died before,' I said, the doors of memory reopening even as the rest of me shuttered itself, like a town going out of season. 'I have, haven't I?'

Countess Cossile nodded sadly.

'Many times. Many, many times.'

'Why . . .' I struggled to speak through the gag of blood. 'Why is this happening to me?'

'Because you won't face the reality of *Demeter*, and what needs to be done.' She reached out a hand and stroked my hair. 'But there's no point torturing yourself over it now. What's done is done. I'll see you the next time round, Doctor Silas Coade. Enjoy the sleep of the dead, while you may.'

Ramos put his hands around her shoulders. 'Countess, we must move to high ground.'

'What on earth, Coronel?'

He nodded out to the lagoon. 'Because of that.'

I inched my head around. Even as I lay dying, spilling my blood into the rocks, I wished to know what had alarmed my friend. Through blurring eyes I stared out across the water.

At first I could not comprehend what I was seeing.

The headland was moving. The bulging forehead of that skull-like formation had become animate. It was changing shape, slipping lower, flowing and sagging, as if in silent demonstration of that process of slow deformation, well known to students of anatomy, which afflicts all bony structures over a lifetime.

'Landslide, sir,' Murgatroyd said, dry-mouthed.

Landslide was not quite the word for what we were observing. Half a mountain was detaching itself, falling under gravity. The only reason it looked so ponderous was that the headland was three miles away.

'It cannot just have happened!' Master Topolsky protested.

'The shooting must have triggered it,' Ramos said. 'I have heard of such things, in the mountains. A single shot may bring down a curtain of ice and snow large enough to flatten a town.'

The lowest part of the mass of rock was beginning to impact the lagoon now. A enormous powdery curtain of white foam rose up, quickly veiling the rest of the process, as if this meeting of natural elements – earth and water – was in some way inde-cent, and needed to be veiled from our inspecting gazes.

'The splash won't get us from here, sir,' Mortlock said.

'It is not the splash that concerns us,' Ramos said coolly. 'It is the displacement of water. There will be a wave. A very consid-erable wave. We must move!'

'It's too late,' Countess Cossile lamented. 'None of us will make it. The terrain doesn't allow for it. The shape of this lagoon will confine the water into an ever shallower volume. Since the wave must go somewhere, it will gain in height. I think now we know why *Europa* foundered on those rocks. It was picked up and swept here by a similar cataclysm, one that will doubtless overcome our own *Demeter.*'

The wave was nearer now, shovelling a cold, wet wind ahead of itself.

'What can we do?' Murgatroyd asked.

'Nothing,' Ramos said decisively. He looked down at me with a faint smile. 'I think every man eventually considers the manner of his own death, Silas. For myself, I always believed that gunpowder would be involved. It turns out that I was right in that regard. But I did not envisage these exact circumstances.'

With my last breath I managed a mirthless laugh, before dying again.

Chapter Twelve

Water splashed across my right cheek, jolting me to consciousness. My left cheek lay pressed against my desk, where I had slumped into a stupor.

'Sorry,' Mortlock said, without much trace of sympathy in his voice. 'I didn't mean to knock that glass over you. I was just trying to nudge you, and . . .'

I forced my ringing head off the desk. I blinked, but everything remained stubbornly out of focus. My own handwriting was a blur of purple. My head throbbed. Part of that throb owed something to the constant drone of *Demeter*'s engines, but not all of it. I fumbled for my spectacles. Some of the world came back into a sort of resentful focus, but not all of it.

'The wave, Mortlock,' I said, still in that half-state between dream and reality.

'The wave, sir?'

'The lagoon and the paddle-steamer. The headland . . .' But I trailed off, instantly and painfully aware that I was making no sense to the man, and my babblings were merely the after-effects of too-vivid sleep. 'Forgive me.'

'You're all right. I'm just the same when I'm knocked out of bed too suddenly.' His eyes dipped to the sodden wreckage of my manuscript, where he had upended the beaker. The work was dissolving before my eyes, letters becoming fronds of kelp seen through submarine murk. 'You'll be able to do that bit over again, won't you?' he asked, with a sincere concern for my lost labours.

'You make it sound as easy as painting a fence.' But an impulse against vanity had me acknowledging his point. 'I shall redo it, yes – and ideally improve on what was there before. The truth is I'd written myself into something of a corner. I felt that the narrative required an injection of drama, so I came up with something dramatic. The only difficulty was that the drama ended up killing my entire cast of characters. I fear I rather overdid it.'

'That *was* a bit careless,' Mortlock said.

'Well, you woke me for a reason. Has the captain decided to do the sensible thing after all and turn the ship around? That narrow passage nearly cost us an engine, and these walls of ice towering around us look as if they'd collapse were we to so much as breathe on them.'

'We're not turning around, no. In fact, we're going further down into it, like a ferret after a badger.' He cupped a hand to the side of his mouth and dropped his voice to a semi-whisper. 'They won't want me telling you before it's official, but they think they're close to finding it. Everyone's getting very excited, but in that educated way of not showing it.'

'Topolsky's blessed fissure,' I said, hardly believing it could be real. 'Well, let us hope it is everything he has banked on. And let us hope *Demeter* will find it as easy to leave, as it is to get inside.'

*

Mortlock left. I poured myself another radium draught, to blast away the bad thoughts orbiting inside my skull. Between the wave and my awakening, I now realised, had come a vision of stumbling progress down a stone tunnel, a scurrying nightmare charged with the terrible conviction that I myself were already dead. The more I fixated on this interlude, the more it displaced the horror of the wave and my death on the rocks. It was not a new dream, I decided. I had had it before, and always it built to the moment when I was confronted with the reflected apparition of my own skull staring back at me. Only the radium draught had the potency to annihilate the last tatters of this dream, but its effects took longer to work each time, the draught needing to be stronger in effect. Now I could nearly see its lovely, lulling glow by cabin-light.

'To the modern miracle of our age,' I said, raising the empty beaker in salute. 'And to the eternal banishment of bad dreams.'

With the draught doing its work — I felt at least mildly refreshed, and somewhat liberated from the nightmare's shackles — I shut the slatted door behind me and moved along the central gangway, until I arrived at *Demeter*'s control cabin.

Captain Van Vught was standing behind Senior Airman Murgatroyd, who had charge of the dirigible, seated in the canvas piloting chair with his hands working the complicated bank of brass-handled levers which directed our flight. Above the pilot's seat, and easily visible to both Murgatroyd and Van Vught, were numerous dials, each a piece of miniature, radium-coated jewellery.

'Feather props, Lieutenant Murgatroyd.'

'Feathering props, captain.'

'Down angle three degrees.'

'Down angle three degrees, captain.'

'Steer eight degrees port.'

'Eight degrees port, captain.'

So it went: Van Vught delivering a seemingly endless list of calmly stated orders, and Murgatroyd repeating and executing these commands as if the two men were different organisational components of some greater organism, of which *Demeter* was merely the fullest expression.

The control cabin was surrounded on three sides by large, draughty windows, canted downward. Walls of ice slid by on either side, steep-sided as a canyon. They stretched on, disappearing into gloom. The sun was low at this time, and we were already moving through the heavily shadowed depths of the trench. Our hydrogen-filled envelope, swelling above the gondola, was a ghostly mass, its flanks just snagging that last feeble trace of sunlight. Out to port and starboard, connected to both the envelope and the gondola by struts, wires and control cables, were our four engines: two in front, two behind. Three engines were chugging and spinning; the fourth (the leading engine on the port side) was inoperative, its propeller shattered. It had clipped a bank of ice two weeks earlier and could not be repaired until *Demeter* made landfall.

Master Topolsky and Monsieur Dupin were standing at the forward windows, hands on safety railings. Herr Brucker, the famous Austro-German industrialist, was consulting one of his watches, doubtless comparing its timekeeping with the chronometers dotted around the control cabin. Some of these showed our local time, while others were showing the times in the great metropolises of the north.

Ramos was next to Murgatroyd, with his back to me, legs braced wide and his arms folded across his chest. Even as the deck tilted, as winds buffeted our course, he remained valiantly unfazed.

'Have we found it?'

'We have found something, Silas,' Ramos responded, in a low, confidential tone. 'This trench has been deepening steadily for nearly five miles. As you can see, we are now nearly completely immersed in it, and it deepens still ahead of us. I would caution you against raising your hopes too quickly, though. There have been false alarms before this.'

'But none worth bringing me forward for.'

'We shall see.' He turned slightly, bringing his massive profile into view. It was a face carved from rock, boulder-jawed, granite-sided, with a brow like an overhanging cliff. He was quite bald, his scalp scarred and dented by a life too interesting and violent for any simple summary. The only damage to which I could confidently assign an origin was the area of reddened skin on the back of his head. It was the healing burn that was an unavoidable side-effect of the radium treatment he had received earlier in our expedition. The cerebral aneurysm had been thoroughly dispatched by the radium rays; a little inflammation of the superior tissue was surely a small price to pay for his life.

'We have never gone this deep, anyway. I did not think you would want to miss it.'

'You are right.' I searched the swaying room for the one I both dreaded and longed for, the toxin that was its own counteragent. 'Where is . . . ?'

'Miss Cossile?' His faint smile betrayed an understanding of my interest in that infuriating, beguiling specimen. 'Outside, Silas, risking neck and limb.'

A lightning-like flash lit the room. There is always lightning, I thought to myself, as if the words were a line of poetry, drilled into me from some forgotten verse, adrift from meaning but still carrying the conviction of prior importance.

Always lightning.

But in fact it was no storm, not even a distant one. There were no clouds above us and there had been none on the horizon when we sank beneath ground level. The source of this discharge was much nearer, and its origin became clear to me when a second flash arrived hard after the first. Both had come from immediately outside the gondola, on the narrow inspecting gangway which encircled the structure, allowing limited access to the engines, struts and so on.

'She's suicidal!' I exclaimed.

Drawing my greatcoat tighter about myself – I had at least had the foresight to dress warmly when leaving my cabin – I went to the port-side door and slipped outside, closing the door firmly behind me. This action might seem casual enough, but I had only ventured beyond the gondola on a handful of prior occasions, and never in such circumstances. It was different when we were aloft in cloud, or far above the unchanging, distant mirror of the ocean. There, notions of speed and altitude became abstract, and I found my vertigo (I should more properly say acrophobia) was easily subdued. Now, though, there was no doubting either our height or our motion. The ice walls slid by at a speed which dizzied me – it would not take much of an error in our course to ram us into those walls – while the floor of the ice trench was still far enough beneath us to engender a sickening sense of elevation. It did not matter that the airship was now travelling at about ground level, relative to the general ice-sheet covering Antarctica. The floor beneath us had dropped away so precipitously that we might as well have been hundreds of feet above solid rock. I was a tight-rope walker between avenues of skyscrapers.

The engines roared. The air was icy. But there was, thankfully, little in the way of wind to chafe at my skin and try to fling me into the void.

I moved around the gangway until I was almost next to Miss Cossile. She was leaning over the flimsy little wire fence which was all that served as protection around the gangway's edge. Dressed like an Eskimo in yellow furs, she had one booted foot on the deck, the other kicked out behind her, maintaining the barest contact with the side of the gondola, and she was leaning so far over that it was impossible to imagine her not toppling at any instant. And this was without allowance for the bulky camera and flash-bulb apparatus that she held out before her.

'Miss Cossile, you are quite insupportable!' I called above the howl of the engines. 'As your doctor, I request – demand – that you come back inside immediately!' I gasped anew. 'My god – you are not even wearing gloves!'

'Can't work this doo-dad through mittens, Silas,' she said, cocking a grin my way and immediately returning her eye to the camera. 'But it's all right. When I can't feel 'em, I know it's time to go inside, change the reel and dip my fingers in a glass of warm bourbon.' The flash went off again. The light pulsed against the side of *Demeter*, tracing engines, struts, gondola, envelope, while some lesser portion of it limned the vast, forbidding walls of ice between which we slid. 'Oh, that's a good one. That'll be a keeper!'

'If you won't be alive to see it printed, what is the use?'

'Don't be such a worry-wart, Silas. A gal's got to do what a gal's got to do. Especially in my position!'

'Whatever the *Daily Jupiter* is paying you, I hope it's worth it.'

Shaking her hooded head, she made some grudging concession to my anxiety, easing back from the fence and planting both feet on the gangway. 'I'm done for now, anyway. Can't burn through these flash-bulbs too quickly, or I'll have nothing to shoot with once we reach the underworld. Besides, I've copy to type.' She thrust the camera into my hands. 'Here. Help a gal, won't you.'

'I am grateful for the sound of these engines,' I said. 'They're the only things that help me sleep, between Herr Brucker's gramophone and the infernal clacking of your typewriter.'

'The folks back in Poughkeepsie need to know what's happening to us, Silas. But you shouldn't complain. Fritzie provided me with the lightest, quietest typewriter ever manufactured.'

'In which case tell Herr Brucker it still needs some work doing.'

I was ready to go back into the gondola when she took my arm suddenly. 'Look. It's steepening ahead. Holy-moly, we're really going down some now!'

I swallowed hard against my dread. 'If Topolsky wanted to burrow into the Earth, he should have brought a tunnelling machine, not a zeppelin!'

'Maybe it's possible for a thing to be both.' Her hood brushed against my face, the fur-lined rim tickling my cheeks. 'You're an odd fish, you know that?'

'*I'm* the odd fish?'

'You signed up for this just like the rest of us. You've always known what that cockamamie Cossack thinks he'll find. So why're you acting like no one ever told you we were searching for a way into the Hollow Earth?'

'I was perfectly aware of his intentions, Miss Cossile,' I answered levelly. 'I just didn't believe any part of it was likely to be real. It was employment, all the same. My obligations required me to look after the welfare of the crew and the expeditionary party, not to buy into any nonsense about holes at the bottom of the world.'

'That's a shame. Because it does rather look as if we've found our hole, doesn't it?'

Ahead of us, the floor was not merely steepening. It had become a near-vertical shaft, whose lower reaches were blacker than ink.

'My god. It's full of . . . nothing.

'Chin up, Cody,' Cossile said.

Chapter Thirteen

Demeter descended. The shaft – Topolsky's fissure – was wide enough to take the length of the airship, but with only a margin of about fifty feet all around us. Our engines were not driving us forward now, but being employed to hold our position as close to the middle of the shaft as possible, requiring great skill from Murgatroyd. Hydrogen was being slowly bled out of the gas bag to reduce our buoyancy and allow us to sink into the continually thickening air of the fissure. This was not quite a one-way trip, since we could ascend again by releasing ballast (the operation had been planned for, of course) but it could still only be attempted once.

Quickly *Demeter* dropped beyond all traces of daylight. The Antarctic sun penetrated only a few hundred feet into the shaft, and then all was darkness. Again, this had been allowed for. Searchlights speared out from the gondola, angled in pairs so that their intersecting beams illuminated a series of fixed distances from the airship. While Van Vught and Murgatroyd feathered the engines and managed our descent, Mortlock and the other airmen were constantly calling out range estimates and directions.

'Eighty on the thirty degree mark!'

'Sixty and closing on zero!'

We sank, and we continued sinking. The fissure kept going down. Sometimes it veered one way or another, like a buckled drainpipe, but it never narrowed or widened, nor showed any indication of having a bottom. If Topolsky had any notion as to its absolute depth, he was venturing no opinion, other than to encourage Van Vught to continue. The captain did so. He had a contract, and he was confident in the capabilities of his vessel.

We descended a half mile or more into the continental ice. Then at least as far again.

Our ears popped. We were like mountaineers, hastening down from the thin airs of a summit. At one point I looked around the gondola and realised that Miss Cossile was absent, and I wondered how she could stand not being a witness to this feat, the grandest, boldest expedition of our age. Then, above the juddering engines, I detected the industrious clacking of her typewriter, and I understood that no spectacle, however epochal, could be permitted to stand in the way of the filing of copy. Soon the clacking would be replaced by the beeping of our Morse apparatus, as her words were transmitted wirelessly up to the Heavyside layer, and then out to the eager receiving stations dotted around the Austral pole.

Down we continued. At three miles the air was thicker still, yet still cold and dry. The searchlights picked out marvellous gradations in the colour of the ice, where stripes of shimmering green, blue and turquoise jostled between opalescent hues of great subtlety and beauty. Here and there were veins of pink and mauve, each a testament to some vast forgotten age in the Earth's history. At one point Mortlock, with mounting boyish excitement, spied the bony carcass of some enormous marine monster, preserved for the ages as if between the glassy planes of a microscope slide.

Abruptly the ice gave way to a mixture of rubble and slush,

like the fractured terrain beneath a glacier, and then we traversed several more miles of solid rock, the continental crust itself. By now, our point of entry was impossibly far above us. Had the fissure been straight, and had there not been a gas envelope above us, it might have been feasible to discern a tiny, diminishing dot of sky. But whether that would have aided our courage, or undermined it, I dared not say.

Cossile came tearing back into the control cabin, brandishing a carbon of her latest report to *The Daily Jupiter*.

'Symmes vindicated!' She stomped her foot like a tap-dancer, throwing wide her arms. 'The great Topolsky proves existence of Polar Opening and Hollow Earth! How's that for a headline, bucko?'

'His name will be in the bolder type,' Topolsky complained.

'All right! How about "Topolsky Triumphant! The singular explorer of our age vindicates Symmes and proves existence of Hollow Earth! Sordid details following!"'

'Better.'

'I'll get it coded-up and transmitted immediately.'

'Would it not be advisable,' I said, 'to wait until we've seen what's really at the bottom of this shaft?'

Topolsky sent me a withering look. 'If it was left to men like you, Coade, no one would have explored anything. You'd have dampened their spirits before they lost sight of port.'

'It's widening!' called out Mortlock. 'The walls are peeling back: two hundred feet, three hundred feet. . . beyond the range of our searchlights! We're coming out the bottom . . .'

'But into what?' I asked.

A void of infinite blackness, it seemed. Beneath us was an absolute emptiness, darker than the vault of night. Above us, picked out by the up-angled searchlights, was a ceiling of ice-dappled rock, skull-coloured, scarred and pocked and cratered, like an inversion of the surface of the Moon. The existence of this void was not exactly a surprise, for the proof of its existence was part and parcel of the purpose of our expedition. But to actually see it with our own eyes, to appehend that yawning absence beneath us, and that dire mass of rock suspended above, was an experience for which no amount of anticipation could ever suffice. Each of us had grown up in a world in which the ground beneath us was firm and dependable and the sky above us airy and light. This sickening inversion of these commonplace facts left me reeling, gripped by a nauseous seasickness of the spirit. I looked around, studying the fixed expressions of my companion travellers. Each was bearing the reality of our situation with a stoic forebearance, jaws tense and lips stiff, but I saw each mask for the fragile thing it was.

'Take us in a widening circle away from the hole,' said Captain Van Vught, his voice level but somehow too calm, too commanding, to entirely disguise his own natural instincts. 'Engines dead slow, and watch we don't puncture ourselves on that ceiling. Mortlock: send a party of men up onto the envelope with rods and grapples.'

That oppressive ceiling stretched away in all directions, far beyond the reach of our lights. The void beneath was impenetrable to our senses and instruments. Searchlights scratched at it without reward. Weighted lines, lowered down to a depth of a thousand feet beneath the gondola, touched nothing at their limits. There was no need for them. A prickling intuition, which I am certain was shared by all of us, confirmed that the blackness under us was beyond all rational faculties of measurement. Perhaps it went down all the way to the very middle of the Earth.

Perhaps it went further than that.

The captain continued giving out instructions and the men relayed them from party to party. It helped, I think, to sustain this bustle of duty, giving the men things to do, matters to occupy their minds before their imaginations were allowed to spin too wildly. *Demeter* circled out from the point of entry, describing a spiral course. Measurements and photographs were being taken all the while: instruments whirring, diaphragms clicking, as if even this hellish place could be subdued by a mania of surveying. Mortlock's men had gone up from the gondola, into the envelope and up through the maze of ladders and gangways which threaded between the gas spheres lining her length, until they were able to pop their heads out through hatches in the canvas spine of the ship. At that point they were (I judged) about a hundred feet from the average level of the ceiling, which was as far into the blackness as Captain Van Vught was willing to descend. Since the ceiling was rough, with jagged projections of sharp rock and stalactites the size of church spires, they had to fend off collisions with punt-like rods, heaving against the moving surface until the airship dipped or veered by the necessary margin. They had rifles up there as well, and now and then took a shot at some nearing obstruction. Rock or ice shattered with equal aplomb, and the sight of these grisly shards vanishing silently into the darkness beneath us induced in me a profound, conquering unease above all else that I had experienced. A bottomless well is bad enough, but a stone falling into a bottomless well is even worse, for it makes the facts of gravity immediately tangible.

Monsieur Dupin was in a fine frenzy of analysis. He rushed from window to window, heedless of the men reporting on the searchlight contacts, and not caring a jot for their work. I watched him warily, well attuned to the signs of manic overexertion. If that was his way of coping, then well enough. But I had already warned him that his body was not a machine to be abused in service of his intellect, and that he needed to take better care of himself. Dupin listened agreeably enough, but that was far as it went. I believe he felt his mind could run on will alone, untethered from the wants of the flesh.

I stopped him as he crossed the gondola, notebook and pen in hand.

'Slow down, dear boy. You're burning yourself out like a candle.'

He looked at me with surprise. 'I'm not the one burning myself out, doctor. I'm being made to.'

I lowered my voice. 'I have instructed Master Topolsky not to drive you so fiercely.'

'Oh, it isn't him.' He cast his close-set grey-green eyes to the aluminium ceiling of the gondola. 'It's them. The ones outside. They keep whispering into me. They need answers, and I'm the one to supply them, even if it uses me up.'

'Answers?' I asked warily, as one risks humouring any sort of fantasy.

'The geometry, doctor.' He thrust his notebook before me. 'The topology! The question of sphere eversion! Can't you see that I'm nearly there? I know that I'm only following in Morin's footsteps, but since we only have a limited number of books on *Demeter*, and no one will let me use the Morse apparatus to request someone send through the equations, I've got to piece it all together myself.' He bunched a fist, pounding it softly against the sweat of his brow. 'I can nearly see it, too. Just being here helps, a little.'

'Being where?'

'Inside a sphere. That's what we've done, isn't it? Tunnelled through a sphere, into whatever's beneath the skin. Just like you drilled into Coronel Ramos.'

'I didn't drill into him,' I said, suppressing a shudder. 'This is the Radium Age! We've no need of such barbarism now. One day, not long from now, the last surgeon to ever cut a man open will pass into history.' I narrowed my eyes, troubled by something just out of reach. 'But where did you get the idea I'd ever perform trephination?'

'I don't know,' Dupin said distractedly. 'It's nothing important. *This* is important. This is why my head hurts.' He knuckled the book, smudging the otherwise perfect neatness of his geometric constructions. Circles, spheres, shapes like twisted flowers and knotted octopi. 'It's what's called a *veridical paradox*, doctor – something that everyone's common-sense tells them is impossible, but which isn't impossible at all.'

'What isn't?'

'Turning a sphere inside-out. It can't be done, you say. Everyone says. But it can.'

'I don't know if it can or can't,' I answered. 'But I am confident of one thing. You would benefit from rest.'

'I will, when they let me,' Dupin said.

'They?'

'The ones who won't let me sleep like the others!'

'Now I really am concerned for you.'

'Let the boy do his work, *ja*,' chided 'Fritzie' Brucker, the industrialist with the odd strip of black hair on his scalp, and the singular, discordant taste in gramophone recordings, which all of us had become accustomed to in the long weeks of our crossing to Antarctica.

'I am very content for him to do his work,' I said. 'But not at the expense of his health. I won't him having burning out like a signal flare just because he doesn't know when to rest his own mind. Whoever among you is driving him so . . .'

'Sighting!' shouted one of the spotters. 'Dead ahead, captain – about eighteen hundred forward!'

Van Vught's lugubrious voice called out: 'Engines dead stop!'

Faces pressed to the forward window of the gondola. Our hearts stilled in our chests as we peered out into the awful void. There was the contact! The searchlights had brushed against the edge of something bulging down from the ceiling: not a projection of rock or ice this time, but something much larger, with all the uncanny hallmarks of artificiality.

'Edifice!' Topolsky cried, tugging at his beard in excitement. 'My Edifice, at last! Ada! Amend your copy immediately! Strike out the old and insert the new! Your fresh headline reads thus: "Topolsky finds inverted citadel beneath the Earth's hollow crust! All history books rendered obsolete forthwith!"'

'Are we not mentioning Symmes now?' asked Miss Cossile, chewing on the end of a yellow pencil.

'He'll have to make do with a footnote, dear girl. In one cruel stroke he finds himself banished to the dusty hinterlands of discovery! Any man could have speculated that the Earth was hollow. It took Topolsky to find the Edifice!'

'Other men must have glimpsed it, or you wouldn't have put so much effort into finding it,' I said.

'A few smudges of light, on a handful of grainy plates, obtained by lowering cameras down that hole, do not constitute discovery in the accepted sense of the term, Coade. Did a seagull discover America, when first it spotted that hazy shoreline?' He muttered to Herr Brucker: 'The perishing man will undermine me at every turn. Why did we need a doctor in the first place?'

Ramos, who had overheard this exchange, said: 'Without him, I would not be standing here. So perhaps we would do well not to undervalue his services, especially when we may still have need of them.'

'Dear captain,' Topolsky said, his patience strained. 'Take us nearer, please! Every second we delay is a second in which we deny an anxious world knowledge of this prize!'

The captain said nothing for a few moments. Then, nodding cautiously: 'Ahead dead slow.'

Chapter Fourteen

Nothing in an airship was ever enacted without an extreme surfeit of caution. This maxim was especially applicable to a hydrogen-filled airship sailing beneath a sky of rock, above a bottomless sea of black, miles beneath the natural surface of the Earth, far from the least possibility of assistance. We advanced with the utmost trepidation, traversing the distance to the Edifice at scarcely more than a walking pace. The throb of our engines rattled back at us from the ceiling, creating a horrible echoing resonance. If there were ghosts down here, then surely we had roused them by now. But we had come to explore, and so we crept on, nervous intruders in the house of the dead, yet galvanised by the work of science. Each foot gained closer to that object was a victory for the intellect over base superstition, and slowly, as our searchlights groped across the abyss and began to daub more light on the object, our collective will was rewarded.

It was hard to describe, because what we could see of its form owed nothing to familiar experience. It did not really resemble any citadel, even an inverted one, except perhaps some mad Babel conjured up by the likes of Bosch. It did not have the form of a barnacle or a stalactite. Nor was it much like a chandelier or a half-emerged maggot.

But it had emerged, or was in the process of emerging, or was in some fashion half-in and half-out of the ceiling, such that only a portion of it extended into the void. How much was up there, entombed in rock, we could but guess, but the visible portion was far larger than *Demeter*, extending a quarter of a mile down from the ceiling and about the same distance across at its widest point. In our searchlights it had two kinds of surface, arranged in distinct areas. One had a smooth, grey, tinlike lustre, and a faint patterning of scales. The other kind was a sort of bristling cityscape of close-set towers and spires, projecting out like defensive spines. These areas interchanged across the entire object, hinting at some rationale, some organisational principle, that yet eluded us.

Its shape was impossible to convey except in the broadest generalities. It looked a little like a fat-bladed propeller, a little like a coiled python, a little like a piece of candy that had been twisted and re-twisted until all notion of its prior form was lost. Its projections, lobes and concavities were either smooth or spined, but never an amalgam of the two.

We commenced a slow encirclement of the object. Miss Cossile exposed herself to risk while exposing more reels of film, and Dupin went into a fit of sketching, muttering, sketching, tearing out sheets and muttering again. He drew as furiously and precisely as ever, but something about the form defeated his efforts, as if the object itself were not just presenting a changing aspect to us, but also oozing slowly from one deceptive configuration to another. Eventually this endeavour proved too exhausting even for Dupin, and he wilted into a sort of gibbering seizure, whereupon I ordered him confined to his bed for an indefinite interval. I was not concerned with who he imagined was driving him to this madness, but I had a duty of care.

'There's something about those surfaces,' he told me, as I almost forced him upon his bunk. His skin glistened, pyjamas already sodden with sweat. 'I think they are shadows of a prior form, relics of an earlier configuration. If one was *in*, and one was *out* . . . oh, I wish I had my books!'

I touched a hand to his brow. It was a furnace. 'Try and rest,' I advised.

'I want to rest, but I can't! It's too important for that.'

'Nothing is more important,' I urged.

'They need my mind.'

'Whoever they are, Raymond, you will pay them no further heed.' I raised my voice as far as I dared. 'I am your doctor and this is an end to it.'

A fever sweeping through *Demeter* was the last thing we needed, but so far Dupin seemed to be the only sufferer, and a persistent one at that. Whatever the cause of his complaint – besides overwork – I assured myself that it was internally generated.

'You don't understand what this means to me,' Dupin said forlornly. 'You can't. No one could, unless they were me.'

'I know you want to solve your problem very badly. But if it were a choice between life and death, would it really matter so much? If you work yourself to fatal exhaustion finding the solution to this one riddle, there'll be no you to enjoy the glory that comes after.'

'But they'd still know what I'd done,' Dupin answered. 'That would be enough for me. Enough for any mathematician.' He stared at me in growing incomprehension, as if I were the one in the grip of delusion. 'Can't you see that?'

'I wish that I could, Raymond,' I said, as kindly as I could. 'Now will you at least try to recover your energies?'

'I'll try,' he said, making it sound very much like a hollow promise.

Since a hollow promise was better than none at all, and any more persuasion was likely to be futile, I decided that the best thing was to leave him alone, where perhaps the natural processes of exhaustion might give him some respite from his mental labours. He had to sleep eventually, and even if his dreams were full of numbers and curves, at least he would be resting some part of his mind.

Dissatisfied with my efforts, yet wondering what more I could do, I was in the process of returning from his room when the other airship hove into view.

The presence of another vessel was an entirely unexpected development. We were still completing our first encirclement, and until that moment the other airship had been entirely hidden from our sight. Something very close to panic then ensued. Their nerves already strained, and their senses heightened by that first glimpse, the men sprang into motion, rocking the gondola as they raced to their stations and prepared for action.

Quickly, though, it became apparent that we were in no immediate peril from a rival expedition. As more of the interloper came into view, we began to realise that it was a sort of wreck, incapable of movement and unlikely to offer any threat to *Demeter*.

It was older and smaller than our own craft, with a strikingly pointed envelope, gaudy colouring and a prodigious, fish-like tail. It was pressed hard against one of the smooth surfaces of the Edifice, jammed between that firm mass and the ceiling. Nothing seemed to hold it in place, no cables or ropes, so there must have been enough gas in its envelope to keep it pressed into place. That was a miracle, though, because the ship as a whole was horribly buckled, and its engines, struts, gondola and so on were mangled beyond any possibility of function. If it had not been for that ceiling, the ship would surely have foundered in higher airs, rupturing apart and falling down in pieces.

'There's a name on her,' Murgatroyd said, pressing his one eye to a pair of warship-grey binoculars. '*Eur . . . Europa*. Her name is *Europa*.'

Van Vught said to Topolsky: 'Refresh my memory, Master. What was the name of the expedition who supplied you with those photographic plates?'

'It's just a name,' Topolsky said.

'You never mentioned that the earlier craft came to grief.'

Topolsky flung his arms wide. 'You never asked, dear captain!'

'You led us into the assumption that the other men made it back safely. This is what you wished us to think, and you never once challenged our misapprehension.' The captain turned to Coronel Ramos. 'Do you have an opinion on this matter, sir? You seem to be a man of honour.'

'That is for others to say,' Ramos answered. 'But I may say this much. I did not know about this other airship.'

'Then you have been misled as thoroughly as the rest of us.'

'Misled is a strong term!' Topolsky spluttered.

'Be glad I did not say what is really on my mind. The terms of our arrangement are now void, Master. I trust Coronel Ramos will offer no argument in this regard.'

'You are within your rights,' the Mexican said.

'Good. Murgatroyd: will you escort Master Topolsky to his cabin? Confine him there for the rest of the watch, as per the letter of our contract. If any party is said to have knowingly endangered the expedition, or withheld information pertinent to the safety of *Demeter* and her crew, they are to be confined.'

'This is an outrage!' Topolsky said.

'It is what we agreed,' Ramos replied. 'I will take him, Henry. He and I have much to talk about.'

'He has a gun,' I said.

Everyone looked at me, surprised at my outburst. If they were surprised, so was I.

'What are you wittering on about, Coade?' Topolsky snarled.

'He keeps a very small pistol about his person,' I said, flustered and confused. 'I . . . saw it. He took it out and . . .' But I trailed off, because what I was about to assert was nonsensical. *He took it out and killed me.* 'Be careful, Coronel.'

'If he is carrying a gun about himself, on a ship filled with hydrogen, that is another strike against him,' Van Vught said. 'And one I am much less inclined to forgive.'

Ramos took Topolsky back to his cabin, but Murgatroyd followed, not out of any doubt as to the Mexican's honour, but to ensure he was not overwhelmed. I waited in the gondola, wondering if the lie about *Europa* would prove a sufficient pretext to have us returning back up the shaft, into the sane daylight of the outer world. But Van Vught was talking quietly to his men, discussing various strategies for getting us nearer to both the Edifice and the wreck.

'We are not abandoning his cause?' I ventured.

'His cause can hang itself, Silas. But we are airmen.' He nodded to what remained of the other dirigible. 'They were also airmen. There is a brotherhood among us, and we will not leave their bodies in this godforsaken limbo.'

*

Demeter was berthed against the ceiling. This was a complicated and fraught operation, but not one that the crew were unprepared for. Mortlock and his men went out onto the envelope with ladders, grapples and drills, boring pitons into the rock above us. It took twelve hours to complete the work, during which there was always the risk of some chunk of rock or ice coming loose and spearing us. Other than a few pitter-patters of disturbed debris, though, the ceiling held its integrity. As well it should, I thought, considering the unthinkable mass of matter suspended above us, and then rather wishing I had not considered it.

Once the basic task of securing *Demeter* was complete, the second and more problematic part of the exercise commenced.

We had moored about four hundred feet from *Europa*, which was as close as Van Vught would take us given the uncertain nature of the Edifice. It meant that the intervening distance had to be spanned in some manner. That, too, had been prepared for. With painstaking thoroughness and slowness, the men worked out from the envelope, anchoring pairs of smaller pitons into the ceiling at intervals of about ten feet, from which a sort of rope-bridge could be suspended. The bridge could only be extended a piece at a time, and the men setting the pitons had to work out beyond the last safe anchorage on cantilevered platforms, with only that awful void beneath them. These were airmen, though, and years of service had cultivated in them a cheery disregard for the facts of their elevation. They whistled while they worked, and sauntered back and forth along the flimsy wooden supports as if it were the firmest, widest highway ever constructed.

I could only take so much of watching those men, waiting for the inevitable accident, so it was a matter of some relief when Ramos asked me if we might speak. I suggested he came to my cabin in a few minutes, and I was already there when he arrived.

'Doubtless this is difficult for you,' I said, encouraging him to take a seat and pouring a glass of Scotch. 'You placed your trust in him, but so did we all. I believe you handled the matter as well as any man in your position could have done.'

'It is not the first time I have been required to look after a difficult client,' Ramos said, taking the glass. 'Coincidentally, the other man was also a Russian, although from a very different background to our sponsor.'

He had alluded to this incident once or twice, and I knew better than to press him on the details. I knew only that the man in question had been a political émigré, forced to flee to Mexico after the recent upheavals in his mother country, and that he had been assassinated while under Ramos's supposed protection.

'If you want to know about difficult clients, ask a doctor,' I confided.

He rubbed at the healing skin of his radium burn.

'How is the boy?'

'Troubled. Driven. Possibly given to delusions of grand narcissism.'

'Topolsky will not be in a position to ask too much of him now.'

'True,' I nodded. 'But I am not sure that will make much difference where Dupin is concerned. Something has got into him, and that fever is a strange part of it. If he has an infection, I can't trace the source of it. He doesn't seem contagious.'

'That is one blessing.'

'I'd like to think that he'll rest, but I think we will need to be a long way from the Edifice before that is possible. It exercises a powerful hold on him. We see a curious object – perhaps a voyager from another world, risen up from below, or fallen from outer space – either way jammed in the crust like a plum in a pudding – but Dupin sees something else entirely. A puzzle, needing to be solved.'

He frowned at my meaning. 'Are we not also drawn to a puzzle?'

'But differently, I think. This is your expedition, not mine. The only reason I have ever left England is for employment, Ramos. I would have been very happy to be a provincial doctor, if it paid. A house, a wife, a view of the sea – but not too close a view – that would have sufficed for me.' I smiled self-deprecatingly. 'Curiosity is for other men. I came aboard *Demeter* because there was an urgent vacancy and the terms of hire were too good to turn down. And yet, I don't deny that there is an intriguing mystery here, and perhaps an important one. Now that I've seen it I would like to know what the Edifice is meant for, where it has come from, and who sent it. Those are basic human questions.'

'I share them as well.'

'But I am not sure Dupin does. I think his interest begins and ends in the solving of a particular puzzle, something to do with geometry. He sees in the Edifice something which must be worked out, like a riddle or a jigsaw, and his interest extends no further than that solution.'

'Are we different?'

'We are,' I urged. 'If you saw two men in a desert, playing chess, would you ask yourself: what is the end solution to this game? Or would you ask: who are these men? Why are they playing chess in a desert? Who sent them? Did they want to come here?'

'Dupin would not ask those questions,' he agreed, nodding faintly. 'But the first question would drive him to the brink of madness, if he could not see the answer.'

'I like the boy,' I said. 'There is an honesty about him, and I have tried to be kind in response.'

'You have always been kind, Silas. But now I must trouble you with an odd question.'

I nodded, remembering that it was he who had asked to speak. 'What is it?'

Ramos delved into a pocket and produced something. In his palm, it looked even more ridiculous and toylike than it would have done in mine.

'A little pistol,' I said.

'A Derringer Model Ninety-Five. Do not be fooled by its size. It is still perfectly capable of killing a man.' He eyed it with a certain distant regard. 'Indeed, two men.'

'You found this on him?'

'Yes. I was quick about it, and able to search him while Murgatroyd was momentarily distracted, searching for the key that would lock him into his cabin.'

'You have not told Henry.'

'Nor Van Vught. There is nothing in my contract that obliges me to, and I think Topolsky is in quite enough difficulty as it is.' He closed his fingers on the stubby little firearm. 'The danger is neutralised. He might have additional cartridges, but I am confident this was the only pistol in his possession.' He nodded to the blackness beyond my cabin window. 'I am going to dispose of it by the obvious means. Perhaps, if there are troglodytic men below, they will find it a pleasing trinket from the gods.'

'You could have disposed of it on your way here,' I observed.

'I wished you to see it, so that we could both be certain of events.'

'Events?'

'You knew of this weapon, Silas. You correctly warned me that he was carrying it about his person.'

I had no choice to but to admit it.

'I did.'

'But how could you have known? It was well concealed. I have spent my life observing other men who may or may not be armed. I have become very good at spotting the signs of concealment, and still I did not know that he carried this pistol. True, a Derringer Model Ninety-Five is meant to be hard to detect . . . but still you knew.' He looked at me searchingly. 'How could you have known?'

'I do not know,' I said. 'And I fear that if I attempt to explain how I may have known, you will call upon the captain to relieve me of my duty.'

'Tell me, Silas.'

'I knew that he had a pistol because I remembered him using it.' I watched his face, alert to the moment when he would surely betray his feelings. 'There was a beach. A rocky shoreline, somewhere cold. Patagonia, I think. You were angry with him because you had learned something of his lies, just as we have done now.'

'That he had lied about *Europa*?'

'Yes,' I affirmed, deciding that I might as well get it all off my chest. 'But it wasn't an airship. It was a steamer. Before that, there was an even older *Europa*, just a sailing ship. Then we were north of Bergen. And we weren't the same, either. You were there, I was there, so were the others, but we were different men.' I frowned, struggling to convey my impressions while not wanting to sound totally unhinged. 'Our names were the same, as well as aspects of our characters. You are always a man from Mexico, but the details of your life shift to suit the narrative.'

'The narrative,' he echoed.

'You will think I am confusing my own flights of fancy with reality.'

'I would.' Then, after a silence: 'Except that I have also been troubled by these recollections of different places and ships.'

I seized his sleeve as a drowning man seizes driftwood. 'Tell me, Coronel!'

'I do not think I am afflicted by them as badly as you.' He touched a finger to his chest. 'I know who I am, and what brought me here. But there are glimpses.' He breathed heavily, pausing before he committed himself to my madness. 'I remember that shoreline. I see flashes of it. I do not know how, but I remember it. You were hurt, and we faced annihilation together.'

I let out a sigh of immense relief. 'If we are both losing our minds, then at least it is a delusion shared.'

'Is it just us?'

'I don't know. There is something about Ada Cossile, and something about Dupin as well.'

'With that fever, any man would struggle to tell reality from fiction.'

'He would,' I agreed. 'But there's also a remark he made, about operating on you with a trephination brace! I dismissed it – I *wanted* to dismiss it – but some horrible part of that chimes with my own recollections. I do remember a trephination brace. It came in a beautiful box, French-made. I can feel it between my fingers.'

'I do not remember that,' he said. 'But I do have the impression I have owed my life to you more than once. That this . . .' He rubbed the radium burn again. 'That this is only the latest manifestation of that debt. Something odd is happening to us, Silas.'

'Indeed.'

He looked around, searching for clues. 'Could it be something in our water supply? A germ, causing hallucinations? Some kind of experiment in psychology being run on the whole crew? Are they whispering to us in our sleep, making us believe these things, to see how easily we snap?'

'I don't know. And who would "they" be, anyway?'

'I do not know how we can pursue these questions.'

'Nor I. But you have spoken to them all, and you probably know Topolsky as well as any of us. He seemed as surprised as anyone when I mentioned that pistol.'

Ramos dipped his head.

'He did.'

'As if he thought his secret was still safe. As if he could not imagine the means by which any man could have known about that Derringer.'

'You do not think he has any recollection of these past episodes, even though he is in them?'

'No, and the same goes for Mortlock, and as far as I'm aware Van Vught, Murgatroyd, Brucker and all the other airmen. That is the strange part, if any part may be said to be stranger than another. You and I figure in these episodes, and we are starting to retain some knowledge of them, however imperfectly.' I shook my head in wonder at the craziness bubbling from my lips. 'If you had not become the friend you are, Coronel, I would not have the courage to speak my mind. I hope we are not humouring each other for the sake of avoiding offence.'

'No,' he said sombrely. 'It is real. But it would seem to affect us more than it does Topolsky, or indeed most of the other men.' He lifted his eyes to mine. 'You mentioned Miss Cossile. What is it about her that arouses your suspicions?'

I smiled to myself, and wondered if he detected a trace of my amusement. *She arouses in me rather more than suspicion . . .*

'She knows something. I cannot put my finger on it, but she stands apart from you, from me, even Dupin. It's as if we are the players, and she is . . . the actor-director, the producer, something like that. She is always there when I die, and each time she seems . . . disappointed in me, for having the temerity to die.'

'We all died on that shoreline.'

'I know. And then we all came back again, including her.'

His fingers caressed the Derringer. 'All the terms of our contract are suspended now. There would be nothing to prevent me questioning her, if we felt she held the key.'

I was surprised at his forthrightness: how easily he was willing to shift from protector to interrogator.

'Question Miss Cossile?'

'When the time is right,' Ramos said.

From out in the night, we heard a scream that fell away to nothing.

*

A man had slipped during the construction of the suspended walkway. One of the cockily confident airmen, he had not bothered securing himself to any of the pitons. His fellows had watched his fall, helpless as he dropped into the void, arms flailing, screaming until there was no more breath in his lungs. They had heard him screaming long after the point where they lost

166

sight of his falling form. The men had listened, and directed searchlights below, but there was no sound of him hitting anything and no trace of his body. It seemed probable that he was still falling.

After that, there were no more accidents.

Chapter Fifteen

The engines were running again, to charge up the batteries that ran the electrical circuits and provided energy for the searchlights. In the galley it was easy to think that we were still travelling, sailing under a starless night.

'I have spoken to Master Topolsky,' Captain Van Vught said, taking in all of us present. 'He does not agree with his confinement, as is his right. But he has taken some consolation in my promise that we shall continue with the thrust of the expedition, for the sake of the men who came before us.'

'Will you keep him locked up indefinitely?' asked Brucker.

'That will depend on what we find in the other airship: whether it magnifies or diminishes the scale of his lie.' Then, to me: 'The choice is yours, Silas, but if there are bodies inside that wreck, and too many for us to bring back, it might be some comfort to their relatives to know that a post-mortem examination had been conducted.'

The screaming of that falling man reverberated in my ears. I had looked out at the flimsy structure being strung across from *Demeter*, and begun to calculate the excuses which might keep me from traversing it. 'I will gladly attend,' I said. 'But if anything can be said about the bodies, it may not be the sort of news that is welcomed.'

'I am sure you will do your best, doctor.' Van Vught glanced across the table. 'You are in agreement, Herr Brucker? In so far as the expeditionary party retains any legitimacy, you would seem to be its natural spokesperson, in the absence of the Master?'

'*Jawohl*,' the industrialist agreed. 'I would have hoped that Doctor Coade would accompany us as a matter of course. It will hardly be a safe undertaking for any of us.'

'We will strive to take all precautions,' Van Vught said. 'You will have to take the minimum of medical supplies, I am afraid, Silas. The walkway is strong enough to take men, but only if they are spread out and not too heavily burdened. Miss Cossile: your typewriter will need to wait on *Demeter*.'

'That's all right, cap.' She flicked out a pocket notebook and began to mime the jotting down of observations. 'This gal came prepared, like any good scout.' Then she gave me a nudge. 'What about you, doc? Shouldn't you be staying back here and working on what's really important?'

'There wouldn't be much call for me here. Other than Dupin needing rest, which I can do no more than recommend, the crew remains in excellent health.'

'Well, besides that poor dope who fell off the planks.'

I forced a strained smile. 'A regrettable fatality, and one that I hope won't be repeated.'

'Actually, it wasn't your patients I was thinking of,' Miss Cossile persisted. 'It's your pulp pot-boiler, doc. I mean, your novel, of course.'

'Of course.'

'Aren't we committing a grave injustice against the world of letters by tearing you away from your composition?'

'I am sure the world of letters will be quite indifferent either way. But thank you for your earnest concern for my – as you put it – pulp pot-boiler, Miss Cossile.'

'How fares the work?' asked Van Vught, with his usual polite but distant interest in my non-vocational activity, which he regarded as harmless but incomprehensible.

'Well enough. But I fear nothing that I write will be able to compare with the reality in which we find ourselves.'

'Surely your men of the Planetary Patrol won't allow themselves to be outdone by our modest adventures?' asked Murgatroyd. 'They're off rocketing through space, not floating around inside the Earth! You can't leave us hanging, dear doctor.'

'I'd say hanging is precisely what we are doing.'

'Maybe it's just me being ditzy, but I don't even remember where we'd got to,' said Miss Cossile. 'Was the Space Dreadnought about to be over-run by the Frog Creatures, or were the Frog Creatures about to be annihilated by the Space Dreadnought?'

'You'd remember if you didn't keep making him change it,' said Mortlock, blushing as he sprang to my defence. 'I don't mean any offence, miss, but if you'd just let him carry on with his yarn, instead of picking holes all the time, he'd have finished by now.'

I stiffened in the lightweight, fabric-backed chair. 'It's all right, Mortlock. I don't mind Miss Cossile's criticisms. In fact, I welcome them. If she didn't have something to complain about, I would worry that I had inadvertently done something right.'

Miss Cossile nodded thoughtfully. 'It's a doozy of a literary approach, that's for sure. Some folks might say that answering reasonable objections in advance would spare you a barrel-load of scribbling down the road, but I guess that's for you to decide.'

'You are right,' I said. 'And in that regard, I am afraid that the weight of criticism – entirely reasonable criticism, indeed – forces me to beg an intermission.'

A collection of groans sounded around the table. Even Miss Cossile and Van Vught joined in, although in the former's case I think it was more a case of disappointment at not being able to pick apart the latest instalment.

'Now you are being quite merciless, *ja*!' Herr Brucker exclaimed. 'I desire to know what lies beyond the Thermal Barrier!'

'Well said, Fritzie!' applauded Miss Cossile. 'We're all of us just itching to know what's on the other side of the Thermal . . . thingy.'

'I am set in my decision,' I said, with heavy finality.

Van Vught produced a contemplative rumble from somewhere deep in his throat. 'That is settled, then. Before we adjourn, friends, perhaps a toast for the poor man who lost his life a few hours ago?'

'Indeed,' I said, glad not to be the centre of attention.

Van Vught leaned in to his senior officer. 'What was the fellow's name again, dear friend?'

*

By morning watch the walkway had been extended across the entire four hundred feet which separated us from the wreck of *Europa*. A telephone line had been reeled out along its length, facilitating communications across the gap. More importantly, the gangway had been tested, with groups of men going back and forth with heavier and heavier packs. Assurances were provided that it was now safe enough for the expeditionary party, or the rump which remained of that doughty cadre.

The party consisted of Herr Brucker, Ramos, Miss Cossile, Murgatroyd, Mortlock and myself. Topolsky remained locked up. Dupin had wanted to come, but I had insisted that the boy stay in bed, and for once I had been listened to.

Our equipment organised, we set off, climbing up through the envelope to the upper walkway, then onto the walkway itself.

No part of that crossing was pleasant. A constant dread of falling chased me with every step we traversed, but it was completed without incident to any member of the party. For my own part the blackness assisted. With an effort of will I found I could pretend that it was a solid surface pressing in on us like a coal seam, rather than an absence of matter. Four hundred miles had felt less than those four hundred feet, but once I completed it, I knew I could go back to *Demeter*, and that terror at least lost a fraction of its sting.

That was not to say that the last part was easy. *Europa* was of a different design to *Demeter*, with a single gas-filled envelope rather than a tubular envelope strung with individual lift cells. This precluded getting into her from above by any means except climbing down a chain of ladders that had been carried across the walkway and lashed to the outer fabric of her envelope. Although we were each of us roped securely as we descended the ladders, the illusion I had been able to force upon myself while crossing the ceiling was now thoroughly shattered. The last of the ladders was even on an overhang, so that my head extended out further than my feet. Regardless of the unknowns facing us inside the wreck, it was a relief to find myself in the relative shelter of her gondola, where there were at least screens of metal and wood to place the void at one remove.

The gondola had buckled along its length, its windows had shattered outwards, and its control gear been severed and tangled beyond any hope of repair. But there was no part of it that we could not reach, and after assuring ourselves – to the best of our confidence – that the fabric of the craft still had sufficient integrity to support our weight, we crept aboard with the light-footedness of cat burglars, not wanting to disturb so much as a grain of dust.

We had not expected to find survivors, and there were none. Nor were there bodies to be found. Our first search was thorough enough, but on the second we searched every cupboard and locker, and the story was the same. Since the airship's crew could not possibly have crawled back across the ceiling and up the fissure without leaving evidence of their own ropes and attachments, only two possibilities remained: they had fallen into the void, perhaps preferring that to a slow, drawn-out death; or they were somewhere within the Edifice.

Levering open a box of supplies, Murgatroyd cast doubt on the first possibility.

'We know from the berths that their crew numbered six, which seems about right for an airship of this size.' He dipped his hand through the cartons and tins still in the box. 'These rations would've kept them going for many more weeks, if they were careful. Condensed milk, coffee, chocolate: it nearly puts us to shame. There's potable water for ballast, too, and plenty of it.'

'If they knew there was no escape,' Brucker said, 'would it matter to them that their rations were not yet exhausted? I think not. Their fate would have been the same, *ja?*'

'It wouldn't matter to logical men, sir, but how many of us are ruthlessly logical? If these fellows thought they could hang on for a few days more, they'd have done so, right until the last drop.'

Brucker shook his head, disappointed at such speculation.

'The Germanic mind would have accepted the cold facts. Better death with honour, *ja*, than an undignified scramble for the last drop of sustenance.'

'Good job we haven't all got Germanic minds, then,' Murgatroyd said.

Before a second Great War broke out among our party I examined their other supplies, including their medicines. All the essentials were still present, and in tolerably useful quantities. Some of it, indeed, could be ferried back to *Demeter*, to augment my own stocks. It seemed a shame to let it go to waste.

'We must face the inevitable, then,' I said. 'If these men did not fall, and there is no reason for them all to have fallen, then they went into the Edifice next to us. We ought not be surprised. It has drawn both our expeditions here, moths to the same flame.'

'I'm not sure I fancy being a moth,' Mortlock said.

'Let us see what traces they left after their departure,' Brucker said. 'Logs, diaries and so forth. And let us see what equipment we should expect to find on an expedition of this nature, but which is absent. That will tell us what they have taken with them, *ja*.'

Murgatroyd opened one of the cabinets we had already examined on our first sweep. Inside were six lightweight boxes each about the size of a small trunk.

'I saw these as we were going through, but didn't think to open them,' he said, taking out one of the boxes and setting it down on a fold-out table. 'It feels empty to me, but we ought to check.'

'Model Thirteen High-Altitude Respiration Apparatus,' Brucker said, reading the printed label affixed to the box lid.

The container was indeed empty, as were the others.

'I searched the other lockers,' Murgatroyd said, 'and there's no sign of cold-weather garments either. They'd have brought them, for sure.'

'Then they left wearing that equipment,' I said. 'The air in this void is thicker than the air at sea-level, so there was no real need for respirators. But perhaps they were taking precautions for what they might encounter in the Edifice. Who knows what foul airs might be trapped in that thing?'

Ramos was drawn back to the empty box as if there was a clue in it that the rest of us had missed. He ran his fingers over the label, mouthing a word to himself.

'*Trece*.'

'What is it?' I asked softly.

'*Trece*, Silas. Thirteen.' In the same low tone he added: 'I feel as if I have been troubled by this before.'

174

Some memory prickled against my consciousness. '*Trece y cinco*. Thirteen and five. You said that to me, once.' I frowned at the box. 'We have the thirteen, but where is the five?'

'I cannot say. But I do know that this is not coincidence.'

A voice interjected brightly: 'Having fun, boys?'

I could not say how long the reporter had been at my side, or how much of my exchange with Ramos she had overheard. 'I do not know if fun is quite the word I would choose. Or that it is fitting, in a place where brave men have perished.'

'We don't know what's happened to them just yet, do we, pal?'

'Nothing good, I venture.'

"Mystery of the abandoned airship! The *Mary Celeste* of Our Age, becalmed beneath the Earth! Got a ring to it, don'cha think?'

While Murgatroyd, Mortlock and Brucker were still searching the gondola's equipment stores, I took Miss Cossile by the wrist and pressed her forcefully against one of the ribs.

'Enough games, Ada,' I hissed, while Ramos looked on impassively.

'Oh, Silas – are we on first-name terms, now?' She loosened her hand and made an exaggerated swooning gesture.

'This is a pretence,' I said. 'This giddy cub reporter act. You know much more about *Demeter* and *Europa* than you're letting on. What is this: a test to see how much we can take before we crack?'

'Coronel,' she said, fluttering her eyelids in mock distress. 'Have this man unhand me!'

'I will not,' Ramos said. 'He is right to ask you what you know. Between us we have begun to see the light. You are part of something, and so is Dupin. So are we, unwittingly. We have been here before: other *Demeter*s, other *Europa*s. In other places.'

'That radium jolt sure did a number on you, Coronel,' she said, shaking her head in sympathy. 'And as for you, Silas, I'd cut down on those radium drinks you like so much. Keep glugging down that stuff, you'll be lucky to still have a jaw by Christmas.'

I pressed her harder, leaning in until our faces were close enough to have kissed. I desired her even as she drove me to the brink of fury. She made me desperate. I wanted to treasure her and destroy her; I wanted her to share her every secret with me through the confidences of a lover, even as I sought to extract those secrets through the vilest arts of interrogation.

Doctors make very good interrogators.

'Where are we?' I said.

'Where do you think we are? Aboard a ship called *Europa*, abandoned by her crew.'

'Is this the end, or just another dream along the way?'

'It's not the end, no.' Some coldness entered her eyes: the playful spark dimming. She was dropping one veil. The question was, did another veil lie beneath it? 'But how far along you are, Silas, how near you are to accepting the facts of things, only you can say.'

'Only me?'

'Only you.' She ran a tongue along her lips. 'The problem is, you won't face it. I've shown you the truth countless times, but we always end up back here. You find ways to kill yourself. You bend the flow of events so that you can regress back into yourself. A broken mast, a shot to the gut, a tidal wave, a hundred other deaths.'

'And I?' asked Ramos, listening implacably.

'You're a blameless passenger, dear Coronel. Swept along in *his* fantasy, granted some agency within it, but unable to shape the larger narrative. Only he gets to decide if you live or die.'

'This is no answer.'

'You can't understand, not at your present cognitive threshold.' She looked at me. 'Silas can, but he won't. The truth is a raw nerve. Every time he touches it, he flinches back into this fantasy. I have to keep leading him out of it. It's like coaxing a puppy out from under a blanket. If I try too hard – and I have – he retreats.'

'I hoped that she would make sense,' Ramos lamented.

'So did I.'

'There's a ship,' Miss Cossile said, after a heavy sigh. 'A spacecraft, named *Demeter*. It was sent out on the heels of an earlier, rival expedition, a ship named *Europa*. The two are etymologically linked, did you know? Demeter is sometimes seem as the epithetic surname of Europa.'

'Where are we?' I pressed.

'In Europa.'

'I said—'

'No, dumbo. *In Europa*. The moon, not the ship. Oh look, it's really quite simple: that's not rock above us, it's ice. Layers and layers of ice, floating over a lightless ocean. And we didn't come down into it via a Symmes hole. We drilled and melted our way down through a pre-existing weak spot in the ice, Topolsky's fissure.'

'Topolsky is real?' I demanded.

'They're all real. Topolsky's the gazillionaire glory-chaser who bankrolled this caboodle. The expedition's *real*. It's just the way it seems to you that's a fiction.'

I shook my head, denying her account even as some part of it chimed with the truth.

'Why would I fight against this reality?'

'Because something very, very bad has happened to the expedition.'

I looked around the abandoned, shattered gondola. 'To the *Europa* party?'

'To them as well.'

'As well?'

'This is the hard part, Silas. And for you, Coronel. Something awful happened to the *Demeter* party, too.' She nodded out through the walls, to the Edifice beyond. 'Inside that thing.'

'We haven't even gone into it yet,' I said.

'Well. That's where it gets sticky, Silas. It's already happened – it is *already* happening. Everyone's already gone inside. The *Demeter* party is trapped and dying inside the Edifice. An alien intelligence-gathering machine is sucking out their brains a little bit at a time. And unless *you face up to reality* – up to your responsibility to this expedition – none of them are getting out of there.'

'If she wished to explain herself,' Ramos said, 'she would think of a better way than this.'

'Unless everything she's telling us is true,' I replied.

'It is,' she affirmed. 'But there's no use in this. You think this is the first time I've laid things out for you? We're way past that. You just refuse to see . . .'

Chapter Sixteen

But I did.

It was a jolt, like being woken up in the middle of a dream. I looked around and took in surroundings that I knew, instantly and viscerally, to be the true manifestation of reality.

Metal walls cased me in. They stretched away in four directions, leading along the forward and lateral axes of the ship. The walls were a messy mosaic of handholds, service grilles, instruments, consoles, viewports, monitoring cameras and cased-in equipment modules. Striplights gridded the walls, putting out a low red radiance, just enough to navigate and work by. Data-entry terminals glowed with faint blue luminescence, computer keys backlit by softly glowing LEDs. Any surface that was not already doing something was covered in velcro patches and nylon tethers. Adhesive notes fluttered in the currents of the air recirculators, one or two of them broken free to wander the ship like pale yellow paper butterflies. Stencilled instructions, directions and warning messages covered every other item. I recognised the lettering: it was the same spartan typeface I had glimpsed on the engine room of the paddle-steamer. Then, as now, reality had broken through the dream.

I crouched on one of the access grilles, resting on my haunches. My outfit was yellow, a tight-fitting suit of the kind designed to resist movement and therefore counteract the wastage of bone, muscle and cardiovascular systems across extended periods of weightlessness. I pinched at the fabric around my shoulder, where an emblem had been embossed.

It said *Demeter ESSE* in big letters, with a stylised image beneath it: Jupiter in the background, the off-white sphere of Europa in the foreground, and an arrow looping in from deep space, indicating the trajectory of our mission. The arrow formed a bow around Europa, and the sharp end of it jagged down to the ice, and into the moon's interior. Familiar names around the ring of the mission emblem: Van Vught, Murgatroyd, Topolsky and so on, as well as the logos of our major commercial sponsors.

'ESSE,' I mouthed aloud. Then, remembering: 'Europa Sub-Surface Explorer. That's us. That's the expedition!'

We had come across interplanetary space, riding an experimental fusion rocket for the speediest possible crossing. Quick as that had been compared to chemical or ion propulsion modes, the crew had still needed to be placed into an equally experimental form of suspended animation., The purpose of that was both to conserve valuable on-board resources, and also to keep everyone from going mad in the psychological pressure-cooker of the spacecraft.

After the initial cruise boost, *Demeter* had been weightless until Jupiter Interface, where its engines had been re-lit to slow down again and guide *Demeter* into orbit around Europa.

We were not weightless now, though.

'The ship splits,' I said aloud, lost in a rapture of remembrance. 'Part stays in orbit, part goes down. The surface module drills down through the ice, then slips into the ocean underneath, becoming a submersible spacecraft! Our airlocks become hydro-locks! When we've completed our investigations, we return to orbit to rendezvous with the cruise module, ready for the long haul back to Earth.'

My weight alone told me that we had reached Europa. Although there was a definite sense of up and down, I hardly needed any energy to maintain my crouching posture. Beyond the viewports studded around me was blackness that extended in all directions. In space, that was rarely the case: one aspect of the ship would normally be exposed to sunlight, albeit attenuated by distance, and the other would be in shade. Indeed, it was standard procedure to rotate the ship so as to even out the thermal gradient across her components. It would only be totally dark if we were sliding through the shadow cast by a planet or moon, and even then there ought to be a few stars visible, their brightness heightened by the absence of competition from the Sun.

So I knew where we were, even without consulting the instruments and flight logs. *Demeter* had done the job it was constructed to do: reached the ocean of Europa.

If I punctured one of those windows, it wouldn't be decompression I had to contend with. It would be the inrush of a billions-year-old briny ocean that had never known the Sun's touch; an ocean that was only warmed and kept liquid by the tidal stresses of Europa's orbit around Jupiter.

I reached out to touch the alloy of one of the adjoining panels. It felt real. Through it, I detected the hum of multiple life-support processes: the churn of air-circulators, generators and heat-exchangers. I studied my hand, where a scrawny wrist emerged from the tight cuff of the resistance suit. Slender fingers: a surgeon's hand. Did that touch of flesh on metal feel more real, more authentic, than it had in the earlier versions of *Demeter*?

Perhaps.

The difference was that I now had the foreknowledge to interrogate my reality. Very rarely in dreams did we ever ask: is this a dream? When we did, that question was often enough to collapse the dream's spell.

This dream held. Which meant that it was not a dream, or that it was at least constructed on much firmer foundations than before.

'This is real,' I said, as if the act of assertion would in itself be sufficient to chemically fix myself in this version of *Demeter*. I could see now that the earlier versions of the ship had been distorted figments, metaphoric shadows, imperfect reflections of the truth. There was always the fissure, always the Edifice, always the earlier expedition – only now was I perceiving their unfiltered nature.

The ship felt empty, too. No voices or human noises reached my senses.

A ghost ship, in one respect: her crew reduced to phantoms.

Everyone's already gone inside.

'So what am I still doing here?'

I returned my attention to the mission patch, to the cycle of names bordering it.

And I saw there were seven.

Chapter Seventeen

I blinked aside a moment of dislocation, as if my train of thought had jumped from one set of rails to another.

Giddiness washed over me. I steadied myself against one of the buckled panels of the gondola.

'You all right, Cody?' asked Miss Cossile. 'You look as if someone just walked over your grave.'

'I felt . . . I remembered . . .' But I shook my head, unable to organise my thoughts into anything that made sense to me, let alone that might to my companions.

'Perhaps Dupin's fever is contagious after all,' Ramos said, with concern in his eyes.

'It's not that, Coronel. He had a glimpse of something – a truth he'd rather not face. It's so upsetting that he's reverted back into this narrative, forgetting the process of self-examination which led up to his moment of conceptual breakthrough.'

Ramos regarded her with the wariness one accorded a feral cat. 'You do not sound yourself, Miss Cossile.'

'Oh, did I slip out of character?' She smiled at him pityingly. 'Who can blame a gal, eh? It's confusing enough for me, and I know what's happening to him.'

His tone hardened. 'What is happening to him?'

'And you, you big Mexican galoot!' She gave him a playful

elbow. 'One moment you're bobbing along in his narrative like a toy boat, questioning nothing. The next, he's upped your perceptual threshold just enough for the truth to start bleeding through. But as soon as he starts grasping the big picture – the real picture – he shuts you down as well. You're conscious right now, but in an auto-suggestive state, swallowing his narrative cues wholesale. Eventually that'll break down – you'll start remembering things again, like that trephination procedure – but only if he lets you live long enough, this time round.'

'Why are you saying these things?' I asked.

'Because I'm an eternal optimist, and sooner or later some of this is going to have to stick. If it doesn't—'

'Coronel Ramos!' called Murgatroyd, interrupting our exchange. 'We've found something! You'd all better see it.'

Ramos, Cossile and I moved gingerly through the gondola, each of us eyeing the other. Some difficult unfinished business was lying between us, as if we were obliged to resume an argument none of us could remember starting.

Murgatroyd was standing by a rent in the gondola's side, where the outer plating had peeled away from a structural rib, leaving an opening about large enough to squeeze through. It was on the opposite side of the gondola to our point of entry, facing the Edifice rather than *Demeter*.

Beyond was darkness.

I stared into that lightless immensity and for a head-throbbing instant I perceived it as liquid: a black sea pressing against the little bubble of life and air in which we found ourselves. An immediate and terrible horror of drowning and confinement took hold of me, until I forced myself to once more see that blackness as an absence.

Murgatroyd shone a lamp into the void.

A gap of about fifteen feet separated us from the Edifice, or rather the tiny part of it nearest to us. The gondola had come to rest adjoining one of the smoother parts of the object, rather than one of the bristling areas.

Against us, directly opposite the opening in the gondola, gaped a mouth. It was an orifice in the metal flesh, puckering outwards like a starlet's kiss. From the throat of that mouth vomited a mass of metal fronds, grasping out across the gap. A number of them had made contact with *Europa*, the fronds braided into the form of a loose, openwork bridge, a tongue of ragged embroidery, as wide as a man and as tall. Bravely, Murgatroyd leaned out and shone the lamp up and around the outside of the gondola, while Mortlock grabbed onto his belt.

'They're stuck all over,' he reported, before offering a boot to one of these tendrils. The frond shattered at the point of impact, dry flakes crumbling into the gulf beneath us. 'We didn't see 'em from the other side, but they've grabbed onto this bit pretty well.'

A powerful revulsion overcome me, and I doubted I was alone in my feelings. The Edifice had been inscrutable until now, its purpose as baffling as a sphinx. Now we understood that it had entertained designs on *Europa*, as a venomous plant may entertain designs on any insect hapless enough to stray into its sticky, paralysing domain.

'It caught 'em!' Mortlock summarised. 'No wonder the poor beggars couldn't get back up and out!'

'In the absence of facts, we ought not allow our speculations to run amok,' said Brucker.

'Will this do for your facts?' I asked, hefting a journal that lay open on a shelf by the rent. 'The last entry is quite succinct, Herr Brucker. Shall I read it for you?'

Brucker snatched the book from me. 'I am quite capable of reading for myself, Doctor Coade . . .' But his voice faltered as he began to narrate the final entry that I had already seen for myself.

I GOT OUT.
IT'S COMING BACK.
COMING TO DRAG ME BACK IN.
BACK TO THE OTHERS.
LEAVE WHILE YOU C

*

There was never any doubt but that we would go in after the vanished crew of *Europa*. If any of our party had private doubts as to the wisdom of this action, especially in light of the warning, not one of us had the courage to express them.

'A brief foray only,' Brucker said. 'We go a little way into the monstrosity, but only as far as our portable telephone line allows, *ja*? I think it is possible to reel out some more line, Mister Murgatroyd?'

'About another two hundred feet. But if it's all right with you, Herr Brucker, we'll let Captain Van Vught know what we plan first.'

Brucker signalled his agreement with a peremptory waggle of his fingers. 'By all means.'

Murgatroyd took the handset and wound the little brass handle which supplied power for the conversation. 'Captain?' he enquired. 'We've gone through what's left of their airship. They've all gone, taking their pressure gear with them. Into the Edifice, captain – that's what it looks like. No, captain. Yes, a sort of door. Equipment, yes. No, we don't need to come back just yet – the air's no worse here than it is back at your end. What does Coronel Ramos say? Let me have a word with him—'

Brucker snatched the handset from Murgatroyd. 'The situation is quite clear, Captain Van Vught – there is no need for extra consideration. If we find that we are challenged by the conditions, we shall return for *Demeter*'s respirators – but not before then.'

'Do you agree with this haste?' I asked Ramos, as Murgatroyd concluded his conversation, lowering the handset back into the cradle.

'I never agree with haste, Silas. But if I were in there, and in trouble, I would not want men to delay finding me.'

'Whatever became of them,' I said, 'whatever that message is meant to make us think, those men will be long dead by now.'

'Then their bones will welcome us,' Ramos said, as if that was supposed to settle all my concerns. Then, with an encouraging pat: 'Come, Silas. Even dead men deserve a doctor.'

Now that we were committed to our venture, I had no desire but to have it all over and done with. But first our means of crossing between the gondola and the Edifice had to be made safe, and that took twenty minutes of careful deliberation between Murgatroyd and Ramos. The first business was to hack away a sufficient quantity of fronds to enable a man to crawl unobstructed from one side to the other: at the moment it was as impassable as the thickest part of a jungle. The men hacked with implements both blunt and sharp – there were axes and machetes on *Europa*, besides the tools we had brought over – until about half the mass of fronds had been shattered away, leaving only the sturdiest, thickest fronds, mostly concentrated near the effective floor of this curious bridge. These fronds produced a dead, hollow note when struck but were much harder to damage, and in the end we accepted that our efforts were having little further effect. We had one ladder spare from our climb down into the gondola, so this was brought down and pushed out into the fifteen-foot gap, using the fronds as a supporting medium. Mortlock got onto hands and knees and gamely crawled out far enough to tie the ladder down, one knot at a time. Some further ropes were strung along at waist-height to serve as makeshift handholds, but I do not think any one of us would choose to trust our lives to them, attached as they were to only the brittle stumps of fronds we had already severed.

Ramos, who was by far the heaviest member of the party, went out first, and got safely to the other side. He hacked away with his machete, clearing the obstruction of fronds within the maw at the other end. He hooked a booted foot into the Edifice, looked around inside with a lamp, a murky greenish light playing across his features, then gestured for the rest of us to follow. Clearly he judged that the immediate point of entry was safe enough for the party to proceed, but I saw nothing in the stoic set of his features to suggest enthusiasm or relief.

One by one we joined him. Murgatroyd was the last, spooling out the extra length of telephone cable as he joined us.

The inside of the Edifice, that tiny part which had now admitted us, was deeply unsettling. Nothing in my commonplace experience gave me any satisfactory point of reference. The best I could attempt would be to evoke the inside of a gasworks, or perhaps a sewerage works, festooned with all manner of pipes and vessels, grown in complexity and purpose over many years, perhaps even many generations, such that no foreman could confidently say what any of the older pipes or vessels did, or which was vital and which was obsolete, only that, rather than tearing out that which was already there to make way for the new, it was better – safer – to keep adding and adding, with each additional pipe having to worm and wriggle its way around what was already established, and each new vessel or retort having to be squeezed into the narrowing gaps between those already present, so that their shapes grew progressively more distended and asymmetrical, as the newer organs of the body must fit around the older. That we were in a sort of machine was beyond dispute, but it was a machine that had grown over and around and through itself, time and again, until its innards were as intricate and tangled as any stomach.

Would that the parts had achieved a perfect density of form, excluding any possible addition, as then our exploration would have been at an end. We could have progressed no further. But there were gaps all about the forms, and some of them were large enough to squeeze through, albeit with varying degrees of difficulty and disquiet. The forms were rigid to the touch, the organ-like vessels hard as boilers and the pipes (which were merely internal extensions of the fronds which had erupted through that mouth) were quite inert, even as they were hammered by machetes and axe-heads. But here was the undeniable fact: at some point they had indeed moved, wriggling and braiding across that gap to *Europa*, and since the ship had been trapped there, it could not have been a slow process. The stomach through which we now squeezed and crawled might merely be between meals.

There is more to say. Although there was no one part of the interior that testified to a torsional process, taken as a whole – to the limit of our lamps and eyes – there was the unavoidable impression that we were navigating through a space that had been altered: stretched, twisted, elongated and compressed, in a sort of slow but inexorable fashion, as the grinding processes of the Earth's crust may squeeze a mountain range until its strata fold over themselves like bed sheets.

Above all else, and perhaps worst of all, there was that green light, a sort of misty, sickly-smelling effusion.

My thoughts flashed back to poor Dupin, wondering what he would make of this mathematical puzzle made manifest. Imagining how these surroundings would have overwhelmed him, I was both glad of his absence and sorry that he was denied the excitement of intellectual stimulation.

'Perhaps we should go back for the respirators after all,' I said.

Brucker snapped back to Murgatroyd: 'How much line is left?'

He replied: 'About eighty feet.'

'Then we have already come more than half way. There is no sense in going back now, when no one is complaining. Do you not concur, Coronel?'

'We may go a little further,' Ramos allowed.

We advanced, moving in a general sense to the left of our point of entry, but quickly passing beyond any dependable reference. Ramos had a compass, but it was no more reliable inside the Edifice than it had been outside, and I think he glanced at its whirling needle more out of habit than any expectation of usefulness. We had the crude measurement of distance afforded by the telephone wire, and some sense that our arc was bending both down and away from the gondola, but it would have taken an elaborate series of surveying measurements to determine our position accurately. What I did know – what I felt most intimately in my bones – was that each difficult step, each squeezing increment of progress, was a progression too far.

I will not deny my relief when Murgatroyd called out that the telephone line was at its limit. Now we could go back with our consciences clear. We had made a brave effort, travelled some considerable distance into this unworldly labyrinth of pipes and vessels, breathing its foul emanations, and now we must abort our quest. No dishonour lay in this abandonment. We had come much further than other men would have done.

'There is something ahead of us,' Ramos said, shining his lamp through a particularly narrow and forbidding gap. 'Something which we have not seen until now. It is only a little further, gentlemen.'

'Of course,' I said, nodding as eagerly as I could.

'Herr Brucker, do you concur?' the Mexican asked.

'Ja . . . ja. By all means, Coronel.'

'Miss Cossile?'

'Show me to the story, boys!'

One by one we followed Ramos into the space he had identi-
fied. It was indeed a space: a sudden, unexpected hollowing-out
of our previously cramped and oppressive surroundings. Here
the pipes and organs were folded tightly against curving walls
which reminded me of a pelvic girdle, if bone were metal.

And in these walls we found the objects of our investigation.

Six upright recesses had been carved into one wall, and six
more on the opposing face. There were five people on one side,
and six on the other, leaving only one of the recesses unoccupied.

A glance was all it took to see they all wore garments perfectly
familiar to us in form and function: familiar indeed to any well-
sponsored expedition of the modern age. They had heavy coats
and trousers of leather and sheepskin, worn in overlapping layers,
accompanied by fur-lined boots and gloves. They had hoods over
their heads, with goggles and high-altitude respirators masking
their faces. Oxygen bottles hung from their belts, along with a
plethora of tools and instruments.

They were as still as statues. As still as corpses, for that matter.

The party of five was nearest to us.

'We've got it wrong, then,' Mortlock said. 'There's eleven of
'em!'

'There were only six respirator cases on *Europa*,' I reminded
him.

'Maybe the other boxes got tossed overboard or something.'

'Even if that were the case, we agreed that six was about the
right crew for an airship of that size. I can accept that we underestimated the crew by one or two men, perhaps as many as
three, if some of them were prepared to go without bunks. But
that there were *eleven* of them?'

Ramos purred: 'You are right, Silas. Some of these men came
from another expedition.' Gingerly he reached into the funnel
formed by the fur-lined hood of the first explorer.

'Be careful,' I said.

Ramos worked at the goggles that had fitted tightly above the respirator. As he did so, the goggles' leather strap crumbled in his fingers. The goggles came away whole in his glove, along with a fibrous mass of hair which must have been matted to them or fused by cold.

Ramos made an involuntary inhalation.

I moved to his side, and saw why.

I had expected a corpse; what I saw was worse. I have seen many corpses, and many stages of human decay. I knew well the stations of that particular process.

What I saw now was closer to mummification, or perhaps a singularly inept example of human taxidermy. The bones were there, and so was the skin. So too were the nerves, veins, arteries, muscles and ligaments which normally lay beneath skin. But nothing else. No flesh beneath that skin, nothing to soften the angularity of bone. No ordinary process of mortal decomposition had produced this grinning, staring visage. The eyes were the worst part of it: they had shrunken into those sockets, but the eyelids were open, and there was still a hideous vigour in the eyeballs, as if they were made of coloured glass, retaining a parody of life while it deserted the rest of the body.

'This was not a good death,' Ramos said.

'No,' I agreed. 'It was not. I think they were alive for a very long time, while the life slowly leached out of them. Until there was nothing left to use. Until they were no further use to this . . . thing.' I drew his attention to the tangle of pipes festooned around each of the alcoves, like a horrible bower of vines. Finer and finer those pipes divided and spread, until their narrowest creeping extremities went into the corpse, penetrating the layers of garments in search of such withered anatomy as remained beneath. Gingerly I eased back the hood, feeling its stiff resistance. It was enough to see that the pipes formed a garland over the skull, tunnelling into it at a dozen bloodless points of entry.

'What does it want?' I asked, in a trance of revulsion.

'Information,' said Miss Cossile. 'But then, you knew that.'

'*La vigilia de piedra*,' Ramos said, as if it were a prayer for his own salvation. 'We have come too late for these poor souls.'

'We'll examine them all,' I said. 'But first we should tell Captain Van Vught what it is we've found here. That way, he can begin making preparations for our departure.'

'We are leaving?' Ramos asked.

'Of course. You said it yourself. We came too late.'

Chapter Eighteen

We did not expect Murgatroyd to be long, but the brevity of his call was still a surprise.

We soon understood why.

'The line is dead,' he said, offering an apologetic grimace. 'It's snagged or broken somewhere between here and our ship. I've tugged on the line and it still feels stiff, so I don't think the damage is anywhere near us. I'm afraid we'll have to retreat until it can be repaired: it's too risky to be in here with no means of signalling.'

'You are right, Henry,' Ramos said.

'*Ja . . . ja*, indeed,' Brucker agreed. 'Of course one regrets being torn away from the investigation, but . . .'

'These men have been here for a while,' I said. 'They will still be here when we return, no better or worse than they are now. I think they will forgive us a tactical retreat.'

Slowly, methodically, we made our way back through the innards of the object, relieved that the line extended all the way back out to *Europa*, and that at no point had the parts of the machine closed in or otherwise moved to deny us passage. We would return, I vowed to myself: even if it was with fuel bottles and a packet of matches. The abomination in that chamber had to be cleansed one way or another, and if the dignity of a doctor's sympathetic touch was not enough, even for the dead, fire would suffice.

A surprise of a different sort awaited us in the ruin of *Europa*'s gondola.

Master Topolsky and Dupin were there: Topolsky holding a service revolver, of the sort carried by the regular airmen, and Dupin looking as if he might collapse at any moment, his skin sallow, his eyes staring into some incomprehensible infinity only he perceived. Beneath his cold-weather garments, slung around him untidily, he still wore the sweat-sodden pyjamas I had ordered him to bed in.

'This is a development,' I commented.

'You were under arrest,' Ramos said. 'How are you at liberty, Master?'

Murgatroyd was slowly unbuttoning the holster of his own revolver.

'Now, now, Henry,' Topolsky said, waggling the barrel of the weapon he held. 'We won't be having that, not among civilised men.'

'The captain wouldn't have let either of you off *Demeter*,' I said. 'So how did you escape?'

'Coade, do you think me so negligent of my own interests as to only permit myself a single means of self-defence? Dear Coronel found my pretty little pistol, indeed. But I had already taken pains to secrete a second firearm in my quarters, anticipating precisely this turn of events.' He regarded the revolver with amusement, as if it were an excellent hand in a card game, evidence of a rare combination of skill and luck. 'Of course I waited a decent interval before freeing myself, allowing the captain time to relax his guard – which he duly did.'

'And where is Van Vught?' I asked warily. 'And the rest of the men who would have tried to stop you?'

'Beyond the modest reach of your talents, Coade, that is for certain.'

'You shot them, you bastard!' cried Mortlock.

'I did what was necessary for the pursuit of knowledge, you cretin.'

'The pursuit of your own glory, more like!'

I nodded at the boy. 'Why did you drag Dupin into this madness? He was an innocent in all this.'

'None of us are innocents. But you're quite wrong about me dragging him here. He came at his own insistence! Didn't you, Dupin?' He waited a heartbeat. 'Answer him!'

'I had to come, Doctor Coade. I know you wanted me to rest, but I couldn't wait any longer. I saw it all!'

'Saw what?' I asked tenderly.

'How to do it! How to understand the topology! It's all in those patterns, doctor – why some bits of it are rough, and some smooth! Don't you see?' His eyes widened, straining at some feat of comprehension beyond the reach of ordinary men. Or indeed, beyond anyone who had not already stared a little too eagerly into the abyss. 'It was all on the inside once, and all on the outside! It's a Morin surface, doctor – a half-way point in classical sphere eversion! That's why it's so hard for us to see any order in the Edifice – it's stuck half-way to being turned inside-out! Something *happened* to it, doctor – and I don't think it was *meant* to happen—'

Dupin swooned.

Topolsky tried to catch him, and that was all the distraction Murgatroyd needed. He sprang at his foe, reaching out to wrest the service revolver from Topolsky's grip.

The gun went off.

The discharge rang hollowly against the metal confines of the gondola. For some incomprehensible reason I stared at my gut, convinced that I must have been shot there, even though the pistol had been pointed nowhere near my abdomen. I felt instantly foolish and narcissistic. There had been no pain, no punch of the bullet's momentum, and no blood puddled around my wound.

I had not been shot. None of us had. The bullet had put a hole in the ceiling, puckering out through the thin skin, but it had done no harm to any of us.

The revolver made a click, the firing pin landing on an empty chamber. It was spent. Murgatroyd wrenched it away from Topolsky, and then landed a punch against our benefactor by way of additional satisfaction.

'You bloody lunatic! You'll hang for this, when we get back to England.'

'Dear old Blighty might have to wait,' Miss Cossile said dryly.

The gondola lurched and slumped, in the manner of an elevator suddenly descending between floors. It came to rest, then slumped again. Slowly, the angle of the floor was tilting.

'He's punctured the envelope,' I said, a dull realisation coming over me. 'No individual gas cells up there. It only needs one puncture, and the hydrogen starts leaking . . .'

'We are going down,' Brucker exclaimed. 'Into the void! Into the pit of eternal blackness beneath us!'

Miss Cossile leaned in and whispered: 'Even by your standards, Silas, that was a *little* on the melodramatic side, don't you think?'

Chapter Nineteen

I fingered the mission patch, still counting the seven names as if something might change between one reading and the next. I remembered taking exam results in and out of an envelope, irrationally expecting the grades to improve if I just looked away. Later, when medicine had become my calling, my results had improved almost without effort. Because I loved it, because it was what I was born to do. Medicine came more easily to me than anything else. But the sting of early failure still travelled with me.

'I'm not an official part of the mission,' I said, musing aloud.

But I knew what I was. The whole *Demeter* expedition was built on barely tested technologies, from the miniature fusion generators which powered the various spacecraft modules and support drones, though to the next-generation suits, and finally the radical and risky hibernation processes.

With so much to go wrong, the ship could not afford to travel without a dedicated medical specialist, even if that added to the overall expense and complexity.

Doctor Silas Coade, *Demeter* physician and flight surgeon.

I had already proved my worth. There had been a problem with that hibernation technology, a few weeks into our cruise, when we were too far gone to turn around, and way beyond any external medical assistance.

Ramos had developed a bleed on the brain.

The ex-special forces Mexican wasn't a tech trillionaire, scientist or adventure seeker. His only role on the mission was 'Security Fulfilment': keeping the others out of unnecessary trouble, maintaining cordial relations between the expeditionary party and the civilian mission specialists, and making sure both parties adhered to the contracts and obligations agreed before departure. When we got to Europa, he was to identify and advise upon any unusual risk factors associated either with the sub-surface operations or with the alien object we had come to investigate. Ramos did not have the authority to override either Van Vught or Topolsky, but without his co-operation and insight the expedition was all but guaranteed to founder.

I saved him. There was no pride in that statement, merely the recognition that I had already been of demonstrable value to the mission, erasing any doubts that might have lingered about the point of my being aboard. Ramos had needed emergency neurosurgery and weeks of rehabilitation. Even after I had saved his life, there had been no guarantee that he would still be functionally useful. But Ramos was a strong, determined man, and through great single-mindedness he had gradually regained a complete range of functions, with no deficits in comprehension, speech or fine motor control. To help him with his recuperation I had even had the ship's 3D printer make a classical guitar. Ramos told me that he had played when he was young, mostly in lessons he was forced to take against his wishes, but he still remembered some of the simpler tunes and fingerings. Over those long weeks I watched him mash his enormous fingers onto the frets, barely able to make a note to begin with, but slowly and doggedly overcoming himself. Once, in an uncharacteristic fit of temper he smashed the guitar to shards and wanted no more of it. But a day later he was begging me to put the pieces back into the printer and have the ship fab up a replacement. I smiled; I had already done so.

'Thank you, Silas,' he said, holding the semi-translucent instrument between his hands as if it were the kindest gift he had ever received. 'This one . . . I will take better care of it, as you have taken care of me.'

'It's what I was put aboard to do,' I told him.

I moved through the ship now, finding six individual sleeping compartments for six of the named mission participants: Topolsky, Ramos, Brucker, Mortlock, Murgatroyd and Dupin. Those were the six who had come down in the lander. The accommodation compartment for the seventh, Van Vught, was in the cruise module still in orbit. Although it meant there was a physical separation between the captain and the other six while the lander and cruise module were docked, that had been deemed preferable to a wasteful duplication of space and mass resources once the modules were separated. The six compartments, needless to say, were empty. They had been left tidy and well-organised, with privacy screens drawn – no one had left in a hurry – but I had still been left behind. I inspected the personal goods, the handful of images and keepsakes that had been permitted. Even with our fusion propulsion, every extra kilo ferried to Jupiter and back – let alone down to Europa – came with penalties to the mission profile. The printed guitar was one of the bulkier personal items, but that at least had come out of our existing mass budget.

I went to the racks near the ventral hydro-lock, where we kept our Mark Thirteen-Five multimode environment suits. These complex, cumbersome items were supposedly as good in vacuum as they were underwater, in the briny blackness of Europa's hidden ocean. Now they were all missing, their racks gleaming and empty.

Six suits, six empty racks. It had been so expensive and

mass-prohibitive to provide spare suits that we only brought six with us.

They had gone outside.

I went to the hydro-lock and checked its cycle status. The locks kept a tally of whether they had been used for vehicle egress or entry the last time they were operated. I would need to check the others to be sure, but this lock was showing that it had last been used by crew members moving beyond *Demeter*, into the ocean.

'And then what?' I asked myself, my voice ringing through the empty passages and compartments.

'Good question.'

I spun around, startled. Until that moment my every impression had led me to believe that I had the ship to myself. But I had forgotten the other explorer, the other name that did not appear on the mission patch.

Cossile.

She sat cross-legged on a grilled panel, dressed in the same kind of tight-fitting yellow resistance suit as I wore. A yellow mission cap pressed down on a mass of loose curls.

My heart was racing. 'Where the hell were you?'

Her answer was calm, unfazed by my shock. 'Performing a systems inventory of the ship, just like you.' She glanced up and down the long main axis which threaded the tubular spacecraft. 'There's no one else aboard. I see from your interest in the suit racks and the hydro-lock that you figured as much out for yourself.'

Elements of our mission profile were returning to me a piece at time. 'Yes. Which means they've gone out to explore the Edifice, all six of them. Do we still have comms? No, wait.' I rubbed the bridge of my nose, still gripped by a lingering fog, as if I had woken up with a thick hangover and only a vague sense of the events that had led up to it. 'There was another ship. We didn't see until it we'd broken through the ice and entered the ocean.'

'Yes – very good. The other ship was *Europa*. It was a similar expedition to our own, just not quite as large or well equipped.'

More came back to me. 'We didn't even know about it!'

'That's right!' Cossile shook her head in a sort of amazed horror. 'Ramos went six kinds of apeshit when he realised Topolsky had been lying to the entire team, including him. Topolsky knew, of course. The lying fucker had *always* known. That earlier expedition was sent out under cover of secrecy, put together in a rush by one of his zillionaire playboy rivals. No oversight, no intergovernmental approval, no ethics scrutiny, no biocontamination protocols, just old-school tech-bro bullshit, as if rules are for the little people. The only thing that mattered was to beat the pan-national space agencies to the Edifice, as if the world needed another lesson about the glorious fucking wonders of unfettered libertarian capitalism.'

'How did Topolsky know they'd got here first?'

'A combination of industrial espionage, and the willingness of his other rivals to piss on one of their own. The enemy of my enemy etcetera.'

I shook my head, sharing her disapproval.

'People.'

'Indeed, Silas,' she answered, regarding me with a certain coolness. 'Anyway, Topolsky got hold of a bunch of mission telemetry and tech upgrades from *Europa* through his corporate back-channels, giving *Demeter* an idea of what to expect and more resilience to cope with it when we arrived. But he couldn't risk telling anyone *Europa* had failed, and was still stuck down here, with the loss of all crew! Who the hell would've signed on for that?'

'I see why Ramos wouldn't have been too pleased by any of that. But they all left anyway?'

'They had their bust-up. Topolsky even pulled a taser on

Ramos! He'd smuggled it all the way from Earth! Everything nearly fell apart right then . . . except Brucker and Murgatroyd agreed to take a look inside *Europa*, before deciding what to do next.'

'They found another empty ship, just like this.'

'Yes – another six-person expedition. They'd run into trouble. *Europa* was in the process of being dismantled and assimilated into the Edifice. The crew had gone in, cutting a hole in the side and installing a limpet hydro-lock. We don't know what they were hoping to achieve at that point, whether it was pure exploration or desperation because the machine had already wrapped its fronds around their ship, and they needed to negotiate with it or sabotage it. What we do know is this: one of them made it back to *Europa*, all the way back out through the hydro-lock. And then they got pulled back in again.'

'My god.'

'There was just enough time to leave a message for whoever got here next. It says "Get the fuck away from here, now". So guess what happened next?'

'They went in as well.'

'You've got a good handle on human nature, Silas. You've nailed one of the guiding principles: always rely on people to do the exact opposite of what they should.'

'You could call it courage,' I ventured. 'If the *Demeter* party thought there was a chance of there still being survivors inside that thing . . . well, weren't they under a moral obligation to investigate?'

'Even after that warning?'

'I'm just trying to be charitable. I liked them.' I reflected on my answer. 'Some of them, anyway. Do we know what happened? Did they send back reports, telemetry, biometric feeds?'

'They're still in there,' she said. 'And still alive. But they can't get out on their own. They're dying, very slowly. The Edifice is keeping them alive, but only for the purposes of information-gathering. You've seen it for yourself, Silas. You know what's become of them.'

'*La vigilia de piedra*,' I whispered, as a wave of recollection hit me. 'My god! I was there. *We* were there. But we aren't! We're here, you and I, inside *Demeter*. There's no way we ever went inside that thing because there were only ever six suits!' Then a question that had been prickling against the back of my forehead finally found expression. 'I'm the flight surgeon. For some reason they didn't see fit to include my name on the mission roster, but . . . where exactly do you fit in, Ada?'

'I was wondering when we'd get to first-name terms,' she said. 'All right. Deep breath.' She closed her eyes, made a yoga-like stretching pose. 'Deep fucking breaths all round. You too, bucko. You're going to need it.'

'Why?'

Cossile opened her eyes. 'Because this is the bit where you always lose it, Silas. Over and over again.'

'Try me,' I insisted.

'Oh, I will. Until it finally sticks, and you stop reverting into yourself. Let's start with the most critical thing: time. There isn't much of it left. Topolsky and the others have been inside the Edifice for a lot longer than you think.'

'I hadn't given it any thought. They've been gone, what . . . ?' I looked around, as if there might be clues in the deposition of dust on the compartment surfaces. 'Some days already? It can't be longer than that. I don't know what happened to me, why I can't quite remember things properly, but I'm guessing I've been incapacitated.'

'Well, that certainly covers it.'

'But you wouldn't have allowed me to ignore my responsibilities for any length of time, not while they're in there and we still have medical telemetry. They might be out of reach, but they're still under my care.' I stared into her eyes, wondering what I was missing. 'How long has it been, Ada?'

'Three months, Silas. More than a hundred days since they went into the object. That's how long I've been trying to get you to come round.'

'No,' I said, almost laughing as I denied her. 'There's no way it's been three months.'

'It has. And now time's against us. It's not just the worsening condition of the six. It's the orbital module: we've been completely cut off while we've been down here. That was always anticipated – those twenty kilometres of ice above us act as a pretty good screen – but now we have to deal with the emergency mission contingency. Van Vught should have expected us back weeks ago.'

'Then he'll know something's wrong.'

'*She'll* know,' Cossile corrected. 'Captain Van Vught is Captain Jennifer Van Vught. You know that. You've *always* known it. It just didn't map very easily into those male-centric narrative scenarios you've been running. You gender-swapped her for the sake of old boy "historical verisimilitude". What matters now is this: Jenny Van Vught is a stickler for mission protocol. When the clock runs out, she'll light the fusion motor for an Earth-return burn, assuming the rest of the mission to be lost.'

I forced aside the questions I wanted to ask her, as well as those I wanted to forget.

'How long?'

'Two hundred hours, Silas, give or take. That's how long we've got to get in there, rescue the expeditionary party, and get them back within comms range of the orbiter.'

I looked to the empty racks.

'We have no suits.'

'Nope.'

'What about the service drones?'

'Far too bulky to fit through that hydro-lock. Same goes for the drones I've managed to commandeer from *Europa*. Even if they could fit through the lock, or cut their way in by other means, we know from the initial telemetry sent back by the expeditionary party that it's a tight squeeze in there. They can't help us.'

'Then . . . I don't see what we can do.'

'There is one way. An asset belonging to *Europa*, already inside the Edifice. We can control it, move it around, and use it to reach and assist the party.'

'After three months . . . do you really think there's going to be anything to save?'

'Right now there is. As I said, we have solid biometric traces. We can't wake them, or raise them to the threshold of consciousness, except as an absolute last resort. Their life-support units are already at capacity, and higher brain function puts an even greater strain on their systems.'

'So they die if we wake them?'

'In a nutshell. The best that could be done would be rouse someone at short intervals, allowing them time to recover between lucid episodes. Even then, the damage would accumulate over time. We would only do that if we had no other option.'

'We won't be doing that.'

She nodded. 'I'm . . . glad you agree.' Then, after a sigh: 'Ramos is the one exception to all this. That procedure you did on him? You put a neuroprosthetic lace into his skull before you closed him up. It was a medical safeguard against a recurrence of his brain bleed, and a way of monitoring and shaping the regaining of function through his recuperation . . . but it's also given us an in.'

'An in,' I repeated.

'Thanks to the mediation of the lace, Ramos can spend time in a higher state of awareness than the others, with no serious side-effects.' She looked at me shrewdly. 'You must have been aware that there was something *different* about Ramos.'

'Different?'

'In your narratives. He wasn't just a bit-player, following your mental script. He had volition. Will. A dawning realisation that he was being swept along in someone else's fantasies, and he was starting to remember things between episodes. Even to gain some dim understanding of his ultimate predicament.'

'All right,' I said, nodding. 'This asset. We'll use it. We'll figure out how to get them out of that thing, and then we'll get back above the ice in time to signal Van Vught. That's . . . all right. I can handle it, I really can. You said this was when I lost it. Well, I haven't lost it. I'm confused, doubtful, a little frightened, and I don't quite see where you fit in to all this . . . but I *haven't* lost it.'

'Oh, you poor summer child.' Cossile made a beckoning gesture, directing my attention to one of the screens still scrolling with numbers and symbols. 'Tell me what you see.'

I shrugged. 'Some kind of readout.'

'Go on.'

'I don't know. It looks like computer garbage to me. A – what do they call it? Core dump. Something like it.'

'You already know what it is,' Ada said. 'It's code, Silas.'

Chapter Twenty

Someone slapped me hard across the face.

'Doctor Coade! Wake up!'

I forced my eyes open against an immense resistance. A blurred silver form resolved into a fresh-faced young man, dressed in the crisp metallic uniform of the Interplanetary Service. A plasteel belt, a regulation-issue blaster, the soft-glowing semi-living pearl of the service sigil. Slowly I recognised that it was Ensign Mortlock. He was leaning over my couch undoing the fastenings as quickly as he could.

'What is it, man?' I demanded.

'A problem while you were under, doctor! A malfunction of the Plastic Educator! The tapes were scrambled!'

Through a lifting mental fog I asked: 'Scrambled? What do you mean?'

Hastily Mortlock swung aside the hinged ensemble of visor and neural crown, nearly jarring my scalp in the process. 'Do you remember why you went under the Educator?'

I forced my thoughts into order. 'I was due a routine reinforcement, to keep my skills up to date. The tapes were refreshed on the last ether-wave transmission from Earth. I've done it a hundred times . . .'

'Not the way it just happened.' Mortlock helped me to swing

off the couch, my feet touching the cold grid-plates of the deck. 'We got the wrong transmission on the ether-wave! Instead of surgical skills, the tapes gave you a head-full of stories!'

I rubbed the prickling back of my scalp. 'My god. Now you mention it, all I remember are the strangest dreams. I've been on ships . . . all sorts of different ships,. The time periods were different, but the ship was always called *Demeter*.' I reached out to him, desperate to verify his reality. 'And you were always there, Mortlock! And the others! Murgatroyd, Ramos . . .' I shook my head, a wave of righteous anger rising through me. 'How did this mix-up happen?' Someone should be flogged for this!'

'They don't know if it was sabotage or just a plain mistake, doctor. The important thing is we realised there'd been a mix-up in time to pull you out. If you'd been under the Educator much longer, the false patterns would have burned out the last of your ingrained surgical abilities!'

I stared down at my hands, wondering if my fingers were still capable of the work for which I had trained. For a moment there was nothing, and I feared the worst: the total obliteration of my identity as a man of medicine. A death worse than any other, for without medicine I was directionless, without purpose. But then came an itching tingle in my fingertips. It was the remembered sensation of holding the humming titanium shaft of a pressor-scalpel between them, and with that I knew that all was not yet lost.

'How did you learn about the mix-up?'

'Only when reports started coming through from the inter-planetary liner *Persephone*! They got the ether-wave transmission that was meant for us! Their passengers were meant to enjoy a range of fictional narratives, and instead those poor dopes got the surgical patterns meant for you! No one knew anything was amiss until some of the passengers started trying to open each other up with butter-knives! The tapes had given them an almost overwhelming need to do surgery.'

I shook my head, disgusted and horrified in the same breath. 'Are they all right?'

'Just about, I think. They're getting them back under the Educators now, trying to undo the damage. We'll do the same with you, as soon as we get the correct patterns on the ether-wave. We're a lot further out, of course, so it takes longer . . .'

'Of course,' I said, nodding as my memories came back into focus. 'Our mission beyond the Thermal Barrier, to the Ice-Planetoid. We were on our approach when I went under the Plastic Educator: it was the reason I needed to make sure my skills were as sharp as possible, because of what we might encounter . . .' I shuddered, gripped by a profound sense that we had already run into catastrophe. 'Something happened, Mortlock – something terrible! We went into that thing . . . *they* went in. They're still in there! The biometric traces!'

'The what, doctor?' But Mortlock's concern gave way to un-derstanding. 'It's all right, really it is. We're close, but we haven't got there yet. I reckon you're just reeling from the effects of the tapes, like someone who can't shake off a bad dream.'

'That must be it,' I agreed, anxious to accept such an explana-tion. 'I've had bad dreams, though, but even the worst of them can't compare with this.' I squeezed my hand against the side of the couch. 'It felt as real and immediate as this, Mortlock. The last one was the worst of all! There was another spaceship, much more primitive than *Demeter*, like something from the last century, or the century before that. A flimsy thing, pow-ered by crude atomics! We'd crossed space to Jupiter, and then melted our way through the ice of Europa, into the sub-surface ocean . . .' I gave a head-rattling shudder. 'I must sound quite deranged to you.'

'No one can blame you for being upset by what they put on

those tapes, doctor,' Mortlock said soothingly. 'But the important thing is that none of that was real. *This* is real, here and now. Whatever those tapes tried to make you feel, you don't have to face any part of it now.'

'Thank you.' Then, gambling that my trust in him was warranted: 'Mortlock. I'm quite all right now, you realise? I understand what happened, and I already feel some distance from those false experiences. You don't need to make too much of my confusion when you report back to the others. I wouldn't want them to lose their confidence in my abilities.'

'Lose confidence in you, Doctor Coade? There's not a chance of that. We were lucky to have you assigned to us, and we're still lucky now. Every man on this ship knows you're the best *sawbones* in the Interplanetary Service.' His tone became gently insistent, as if he were the doctor, I the unwilling patient. 'Now you take as long as you need to clear your head. We'll make sure you don't miss any of the excitement.'

'Nor would I want to,' I answered, pushing aside my lingering misgivings. But something still nagged at me. 'Mortlock?'

'Doctor?'

'You mentioned the men on this ship. I presume that wasn't to the exclusion of Ada?'

'Ada, sir?'

'Ada Cossile.'

He looked at me with some faint renewed concern. 'There's no one called Ada Cossile on *Demeter*, Doctor Coade. I think I'd remember if we had a dame among us!'

I said nothing.

*

I stopped in my quarters on the way to the bridge, needing a stage of intermediate decompression before I flung myself back into the busy routines of the ship. With the door slid shut behind me I seated myself at the room's console, scrutinising every inch of my surroundings for reassurance. The duralloy walls, their plainness relieved by fretted accents of coloured lighting. The secondary door, which allowed direct access to the medical bay adjacent to my room. The armoured glass of the porthole, with the star-flecked blackness of space beyond. That was actual space, as deep, dark and empty as a pair of eye-sockets, rather than some black ocean beneath a mantle of ice. My gaze flitted to the handful of personal effects dotted around the room. A three-masted schooner in a bottle, a yellow feather preserved in a block of resin, a tri-di picture of a vine-shrouded cottage high on a hill, with a glimmer of sea beyond it. An ornate box containing an antique French-made trephination brace: a gift upon my graduation from the Interplanetary Service Medical School. It served as a salutary reminder of the horrors inherent in the healing arts before our present enlightened age.

I breathed out. This was real, all of it. The lives I had lived under the Plastic Educator were the ersatz things, no matter how tangible they had appeared at the time, as the tapes impressed their patterns into the yielding clay of my neocortex. I was Silas Coade: respected, trusted, needed. There was no need to doubt any aspect of my nature.

'I'm Coade,' I whispered to myself. 'I'm Coade.'

The troubling memories were fading, scoured away by the inherent reality of my surroundings. I understood now. The Plastic Educator worked differently depending on the recordings fed into it. The passengers on that liner would have been expecting to be fed seed-patterns: fictional catalysts which their unconscious minds would then amplify, furnishing them with quotidian details drawn from their own memories and surroundings. My mind had obviously operated on the seeds in the same fashion, drawing inspiration from these scattered personal effects. Instead of a ship-in-a-bottle, I had dreamed of a schooner dashing itself on treacherous rocks . . .

And as for the yellow feather . . .

Sadness touched me. I wanted her to be real. I had never imagined a lovelier tormentress than dear Ada, in each of her manifestations.

I mouthed: 'I am glad none of that was real. Except for you, Ada. You are the one part I wish was true.'

I fingered the resin-shrouded feather, then with infinite gentleness placed it back where it belonged.

*

I had stepped through the vac-lift doors onto the bridge of *Demeter* too many times to count, but there had never been a time when the moment failed to stop me in my tracks. Among those who strode the hallways of the Interplanetary Service, very few made it as far as a front-line scoutship like *Demeter*, and still fewer had the privilege of treading the humming grid-plates of the command room, that nucleus of a power and authority capable of turning worlds to cinders.

As always, it was the windows which commanded my attention. Framed in duralloy, and triple-plated against blaster-fire, they formed a wide, curving sweep across one hundred and eighty degrees of the bridge. The view beyond them was normally black, save for a scattering of stars and planets, but now the entire expanse was filled with the blazing white of the Ice-Planetoid, towards whose face we were rushing.

The Ice-Planetoid: a menacing intruder from the spaces beyond the Thermal Barrier, trespassing into the Solar System from that outer darkness into which only a handful of ships had ever forged. Our mission: to investigate both the Ice-Planetoid and the alien anomaly within it, detected by remote scans but whose nature and purpose remained unknown.

All eyes, biological and mechanical, were on that objective. Every man in the bridge had his absolute attention fixed on the task of our approach. Around them, consoles whirred and bleeped; tapes spooled and solenoids chattered, forming a repetitive, lulling background music, a chorus to the solemn professionalism of the men.

The captain – 'Vanquisher' Van Vught – sat in the centre of the bridge, ensconced in his throne-like control chair on a raised dais, with glowing gauges and levers laid out in an arc before him. His posture was one of supreme alertness, leaning slightly forward from his seat, one booted foot ahead of the other, his expression the steely concentration of a chess master.

'Engines to idle,' the captain intoned, his soft but commanding voice carrying to all corners of the room. 'Bring us in on forward momentum, while standing by on all pressor batteries. Delaminators to battle readiness.'

'Pressor batteries warmed and ready,' said Space Helmsman Murgatroyd, moving the heavy lever of a rheostat. His artificial eye, a token of the time he had seen action against the Venusian Frogs, glittered and swivelled.

While I had stopped in my cabin, Ensign Mortlock had come up to the bridge and assumed his position at the weapons console. 'Delaminator banks primed and ready for immediate discharge,' he confirmed, flicking relay switches across his board.

'Well, doctor? Are you back among the living?' asked Van Vught pleasantly. 'An inexcusable error, however it happened. We must hope that no lasting damage was done.'

'I believe I may still be of use,' I said, flexing my fingers. 'Ensign Mortlock got to me in time, thankfully. I dare not speculate about the effects of any further delay.'

'If this was an error, someone will be flogged,' Van Vught

said, echoing my own feelings as Mortlock had rescued me from the Educator. 'If it was sabotage, then the perpetrator – or perpetrators – will face the annihilation cubicles.'

'Let us presume it was no more than an innocent error,' I said. 'After all, why would anyone want to sabotage the vital work of exploration?'

'It is my reputation they wish to sabotage, Coade,' said our civilian guest Topolsky, swivelling around from one of the monitoring seats set at a lower level than the captain's. 'I have nailed my colours to this mast, metaphorically speaking. My enemies would like nothing more than to see my venture turn to folly.' The richest man in the Nine Worlds – by his own admission, at least – the fur-clad, cigar-chomping magnate had used his influence within the Interplanetary Service to promote this military-scientific expedition to the Ice-Planetoid.

'The correct recordings are arriving on the ether-wave as we speak,' Van Vught said, nodding at one of the spooling tape banks. 'If it was an attempt to damage us – or you, for that matter, Master – we may be confident that it has failed.' His searching gaze fell on me, his eyes seeming to see right through me to some vastly more distant realm of space and time. He pressed a finger to his temple. 'Difficulties aside, you arrive at a propitious moment. We are about to detect the entry point!'

That was more than just calculated guesswork on the captain's part. Van Vught was a short-range psychic, able to detect and act upon events within a predictive horizon of exactly thirteen minutes, five seconds. It was a skill that had helped in the war against the Frogs and one that had already saved this very expedition. A week ago, Van Vught had swerved the ship to avoid a blazing asteroid that had slipped clean through our anti-collision screens. Without the captain's gift of foresight, *Demeter* would have been dashed against the rocks as surely as that doomed schooner of my imagination!

I asked: 'Do you foresee anything dangerous?'

'No,' he answered. 'Not within my psionic horizon. A surprise, yes. Something we aren't expecting. But I can't say exactly *what* the surprise will be . . .'

He had described the physiological correlatives of this gift during his times on my examining couch. As events hove into view, they registered as distant, prickling impressions, mental thunderclouds without definite form. It was only when they came nearer in time, emerging fully over that predictive horizon, that he was able to assign clear shape and meaning to these phantasms.

I know that others envied him this capability. I did not. I only had to imagine how the gift of foresight would have guided my hand as a surgeon. If I knew in advance whether a given incision was going to lead to success or catastrophe, I would become a mindless instrument of predetermined forces, no better than a robot or electronic brain.

'I am so glad you are here for this moment of our triumph, Coade!' Topolsky said. 'What we are about to glimpse will render our names immortal! Our fame will bestride the spaceways! The Frogs may have tested us with their deviousness and low cunning, but they were never any match for the intellects of proud-born Terrans. Yet now we stand on the threshold which we have earned: first men to witness the work of minds truly superior to our own!'

'If we make it back to Terra with all hands safe and well, Master, that is reward enough for me.'

'Ah, such humility of purpose – such selfless devotion to the Hippocratic principle – it gladdens the heart!'

'Visual contact,' said Murgatroyd with rising excitement. 'It's there, captain – dead ahead of us, just as you predicted!'

'Delaminators at firing potential!' said Mortlock, as numerous dials twitched across his console.

A hole lay ahead of us: a throat-like fissure leading down into the interior of the Ice-Planetoid, a tunnel bored by the object of Topolsky's interest – the Edifice, as he called it – as it came hurtling in from the outer void.

'Engines stop,' Van Vught intoned. 'Pressors and tractors to power. Take us down the centre of the bore, Murgatroyd – steady as we go.'

The Space Helmsman's fingers danced effortlessly across the glowing panel. *Demeter* descended the shaft, rocket tubes pulsing to keep her on course, the flashing of their exhausts reverberating against the fluted walls of the shaft. The stutter of re-radiated light made me think of a distant electrical storm.

There's always lightning.

Although the ship's descent had put her onto a nearly vertical tilt, the artificial gravity never wavered. Steadily we moved down the shaft, Murgatroyd calling out units of depth every mile, and with our point of entry slowly diminishing above us, until – on the rear-facing view-plates – it was nothing more than a black disc surrounded by a darkening fringe of ice. Still standing, I clenched my fist against an oppressive, unwanted recollection: that of an airship, sinking into the belly of the Earth in nearly similar fashion. That had been quite impossible, though: the men of an earlier age, their minds still wreathed in ignorance, might have been open to the possibility of holes in the Earth, passages admitting entry to the hollow realm within, but in our super-scientific age we knew better. And yet that infernal Plastic Educator had sowed the seed of the idea in my mind at such an indelible level that even now, knowing it to be a fiction, I could not bring myself to dismiss it entirely. The noises and smells of that gas-powered airship were as real in my recollection as any lived experience. I had been there, just as surely as I had been on those earlier iterations of *Demeter* which ploughed the seas rather than the air.

No, I asserted to myself: I had not been there. It was unreal. Each iteration was a lie, including, by logical extrapolation, the fourth such exemplar, the one that I had been in before waking to *this* . . .

'Something ahead,' Murgatroyd called out, as a red light on his console began to pulse on and off, accompanied by a subtle but ominous modulation in the background music of the bridge. 'Scanner contact. Something small and metallic lodged in the walls of the shaft, about two miles below us.'

'Estimate the fix,' Van Vught said.

'Two seventy decimal three, six decimal eight, one decimal six one,' intoned Murgatroyd. With a chatter, a teletype reeled from his console. He tore the end off and leaned across from his console to pass the paper stub to Ensign Mortlock.

'Alert condition red. Ensign Mortlock, concentrate pressor batteries on that reference.'

'Locking in,' Mortlock said, setting his own dials and levers by the numbers on the print-out. 'Pressors locked and compensating.'

'Reduce descent rate by half, Space Helmsman. Ensign: fire at will at the first indication of hostile intent.'

'Aye, aye, captain.'

'I would like to be consulted before any such action,' said Coronel Ramos, Topolsky's military adviser. He was a huge bald bull of a man, his chest cross-webbed by bandolier pouches containing blaster cartridges. He had to raise his voice over the insistent bleating of the red alert alarms. 'I need not remind you that my employer has staked a great deal on the investigation of the Edifice. There will be little consolation if all he has to pick through are charred remains.'

'We aren't deep enough to pick up a contact from the Edifice,' said Dupin, the precocious, tousle-haired maths prodigy who had been hired onto the expedition to solve such riddles as lay beyond the reach of *Demeter's* own analysts and logic-banks. 'Unless the thing has moved from its last estimated position, we won't catch sight of it for another eight miles. Whatever the scans are picking up, it's something else.'

'You are sure of that?' Topolsky asked.

'I am sure of most things, Master,' the boy answered unflinchingly.

'Contact is holding,' Murgatroyd reported. 'Whatever it is, it's no more than six or seven feet across. Too tiny to be a ship.'

'But not too tiny to be a Frog blaster-mine,' mouthed Van Vught, who had reason to be suspicious of small metallic objects. 'Yet, if it were a Venusian trap, would it not be better disguised?'

'Can we see it yet?' I asked.

'Just entering visual range now, doctor,' Murgratroyd said. 'Captain, may I put it on the main viewer?'

Van Vught gestured loftily. 'Do so.'

The view through the central part of the main window shimmered like a watery reflection and then resolved into a close-up of part of the shaft wall. Instantly we saw the source of the metallic trace: a gleam of yellow, as stark against the dirty white of the ice as a nodule of gold in a prospector's pan.

The shape of the thing was difficult to make out in the vague focus of the long-range scanner. It could have been a piece of cosmic debris, a chunk of foreign rock, the curled-up husk of a man-sized alien spider, or something worse.

But I knew it to be none of these things.

'That's Ada Cossile,' I blurted out, before I could censor my own words.

Mortlock turned from his console to look at me. Doubtless he remembered our awkward exchange after the ordeal of the Plastic Educator.

'A *derckossile*? Is that a term with which I'm unfamiliar?' Van

Vught asked reasonably. 'Some kind of mineralogical or chemical terminology?'

I had seen her clearly. She had been in a yellow spacesuit, crouching on all fours on a treacherously narrow ledge with the sheer drop of the shaft beneath her. I had not needed to see her face or any other identifying features. Who else could it be but the regal psychopomp of my dreams? She was back, despite everything. Despite the fact that she could not possibly be real.

'One mile to contact,' Murgatroyd said. 'Scan is improving.'

Something moved within my chest as the image on the main viewer wobbled and reinstated itself, coming back at a higher clarity. I both wanted and did not want it to be her. I wanted to see her face again, to know that she was something more than a dream-figment, but in the same instant I desired nothing less than her total non-existence. Because the mere fact of Ada Cossile opened a door in my mind, a portal into something which I did not wish to face . . .

The image sharpened further. To my despair and relief I saw that it was not Ada Cossile.

It was a chunk of crumpled yellow metal, a piece of hull-plating that had been torn off and buckled and mangled so that it might, for an eyeblink, by someone who desired (or feared) it to be so, be taken for a crouching human form.

'Duralloy composition,' Murgatroyd said. 'Partial markings legible . . . *Eu*, perhaps *Eur* . . .'

'It's not Frog!' Mortlock blurted out. 'It's one of ours!'

Van Vught nodded sombrely. 'Indeed it is – the remains of some poor vessel that strayed this way before us.' Cautiously he added: 'Alert condition amber. Resume normal descent speed.'

*

Eleven further miles we went down that chimney, until we emerged into the lightless space which formed the hollow middle of the Ice-Planetoid. Still at condition amber, *Demeter* dropped a mile or two into that abyssal space, her instruments and screens twitching against the tiniest speck of cosmic dust which had somehow found its way into that unfathomable void.

Our searchlights sprang on, stroking the canopy of ice above us, casting enormous arcs of yellow radiance. Strange tubular forms wormed across the ice, grey-green against its pearly lustre. The searchlights traced along these tentacular forms, following them as they thickened and united, as if we were tracking down the branches of some immense tree or river delta, groping our way towards the primal source from which they radiated.

Suddenly it was in our lights, projecting down from the ice like the rotten tip of some terrible misshapen fang, puncturing in from above. It was more than a thousand feet deep and wide, a mountain-sized nugget of a curious twisted and bulging form, convex and concave, smooth in some areas and rough-formed in others, like a patterned carpet that had been rolled up and knotted, over and over again, until nearly all sense of its former nature lay concealed.

Dupin was making strange stiff gestures with his hands, framing angles and intersections like a critic trying to find some sense in a piece of modernist art.

'The geometry . . .' he murmured. 'The geometry! I think I can see it! Each quarter section is homeomorphic to a triangle!' He stared back to us, wide-eyed and uncomprehending of our own inability to visualise what was plain to him. 'Can't you see? It's beautiful! And hideous! It's . . . not right!'

'Alien minds conceived this form,' said Topolsky, with a faint dismissiveness. 'Minds far beyond our ken. Their notions of aesthetic propriety are as odd to us as our classical proportions would be to them.'

'There is more to it,' Dupin said, his forehead a mirror of sweat. 'Something did this. Something twisted it! I think it went through some topological mishap, an accident of geometry! A wrinkle in the hyperspace manifold! An FTL jump that went wrong, leaving it . . . malformed! But I need to be more precise.' He pressed fingers to his brow, digging in with his nails. 'I must specify the exact set of transformations . . . near enough isn't good enough! Near enough won't help! I can't fail!'

'Easy,' I said, seeing a vein bulging on the side of his temple.

'No. I've got to solve it. I must solve it if we are to escape!'

'Escape?' Topolsky asked. 'Why do you speak of escape, man? We haven't even got there yet!'

'I must be allowed to use the Cerebral Augmenter,' Dupin said pleadingly. 'It's all I need to make the final breakthrough.'

'You disagreed when we last discussed this, doctor?' said Van Vught.

I nodded at the captain. 'The Cerebral Augmenter has rarely been tested beyond Interplanetary Service laboratories. The men who used it then had all had many years of experience under the Plastic Educator, and still it took its toll on them. Yes, it can boost the subject's intellect for a limited interval, allowing them to perform superhuman feats of mental agility, but at a considerable cost. Under service rules, the Cerebral Augmenter is to be considered an instrument of last resort, when all other measures have failed and there is but one chance to save a ship and its crew.'

'Thank you, doctor,' the captain said. 'Mercifully, we are not yet in that position.'

Dupin looked at me despairingly. 'You tell him, Doctor Coade! Tell him what's really happened to us! Tell him we're already inside it! Tell him we've been inside for months! Tell him we're all dying in here! If no one helps us, we'll end up like the others!'

'Master Topolsky,' said Van Vught. 'You have clearly been working Monsieur Dupin beyond the point of exhaustion. I will not have him on my bridge in this confused, distressed condition. Have him removed, and forced to rest.'

'Your orders do not extend to my party,' Topolsky said. 'If I deem that he is still useful, then it is my decision whether he leaves or remains.'

Van Vught stiffened in his command chair. 'Then let me make a polite request. It would be better for the boy – for you – for all of us – if he were allowed to rest. Might Coronel Ramos be so kind as to see that it is so?'

Before Topolsky could frame an objection, Ramos raised his massive bulk from his own observation console. His blaster cartridges gleamed on his bandoliers. 'I will see him back to his quarters, Captain Van Vught. You are right that he would be better for us when his mind is rested.'

'Thank you, Coronel,' said Van Vught, easing slightly.

The burly, boulder-headed Mexican offered a companionable hand to Dupin, and when that was ignored he gently but firmly took the boy under the armpits and elevated him bodily from his chair. Dupin, in his troubled, dreamlike state, offered no opposition. He was as pliant as a rag doll, his heels brushing the grid-plates as Ramos half carried, half dragged him to the waiting doors of the vac-lift.

'Silas,' Ramos said, eyeing me. 'Perhaps you should come as well?'

An uneasiness delayed my answer. 'Yes ... yes. I should indeed attend. With your permission, captain?'

'Do so.'

'Coronel, would you be so kind as to bring the boy to the medical room, rather than his own quarters? I would prefer to keep him under close observation until I'm satisfied with his progress.'

'Of course, Silas.'

I was just about to step into the vac-lift, joining Ramos and the boy, when Murgatroyd spoke out suddenly. 'Captain! There's something up there, jammed against those rough parts like a fly burned onto a light fitting! It looks like a ship – like . . .' His throat seemed to dry on the words. 'Just like one of ours!'

I did not bother turning around. There was no need. I already knew exactly what it would turn out to be. I could even have told them the full name of the ship from which that hull-plate had been ripped.

*

Ramos laid Dupin down on the bunk in the medical bay. With a tenderness belying his size and reputation for ferocity, Ramos drew the woven plasteel blanket over Dupin's shivering form. Above the couch's headboard, indicators detected his vital signs and began to respond accordingly.

'He has a fever, Silas.'

'I'm surprised he has anything left to give, the way Topolsky has been driving him. There's only so much a body can take.'

'It is not all Topolsky's fault. The boy would work himself to exhaustion whether or not he was being asked to. This mania of his will be the death of him, given time. But he will not mind, so long as his name is attached to something more than a footnote.'

'I'm not sure I would trade my life for a posthumous reputation.'

Ramos smiled kindly. 'But then you are not Raymond Dupin. I do not think you or I can really understand what it is like to be him. The Cerebral Augmenter may seem like a devil's bargain to men such as you or I, but our minds were never brilliant to begin with. We cannot judge.'

'Nothing could matter enough to allow a man to burn out his own mind, just to seek some abstract mathematical solution.'

'And if it were not abstract? If the fate of *Demeter* truly depended on his insights? If he was the only one of us who could make use of the Augmenter, in a decisive fashion?'

'No matter what the regs say, I still wouldn't agree to it.'

'Master Topolsky would say that he does not need your agreement. Reluctantly, I would have to accept his opinion. Besides, what would be the crueller thing? To allow the boy that ecstasy of insight, or deny it him for ever?'

'My only duty is to the welfare of the crew. There are no circumstances under which I would ever consent to treating Dupin like a pile of matchwood, to be burned for our convenience.'

'We all have our certainties,' Ramos replied. 'The only thing of which I am certain is that all men have a point where their minds may change.'

'Not mine,' I asserted.

'I would not be so sure.'

Ramos moved to the desk where the Cerebral Augmenter lay in its duralloy box. He opened the lid and extracted the double-lobed apparatus, with its close-fitting crown and bulbous, earmuff-like inductor modules.

'What are you doing?'

'Examining the apparatus. Is it accidental that you asked for him to be brought to the medical bay, Silas? He would have been no worse in his own room, with a guard to keep him from over-exerting himself. Yet the Cerebral Augmenter has been in your possession since we left Terra.'

'Because it is experimental mental equipment, its use falls under my responsibility. Put it away now, please.'

Dupin stirred. His eyes opened to slits and he seemed to latch onto the object still within Ramos's grasp. Reaching an arm out from beneath the plasteel sheet, he beckoned at the Cerebral Augmenter as if it were a vision of heaven itself, a celestial city breaking through clouds.

'Please,' he whispered. 'I must have it.'

'You fool,' I snarled intemperately. 'You've only made him more agitated!'

'How easily the bonds of friendship fray,' Ramos answered.

'This is a torment!' I retorted.

'The real torment is in denying the boy the thing he craves.'

Dupin was straining now, leaning up from the couch, sweat pearling his brow and his cold eyes fixed wide on the prize. 'Just a minute under the Augmenter,' he said. 'That's all I need!'

'Nothing matters this much!' I said.

'Everything matters, doctor! Everything matters! Oh, *please* let me have it!' Some bargaining calculation worked behind that glistening brow. 'You can say it was too dangerous, and I won't ask again! But just give me one minute. That's all I need. I know it. I can solve the problem of eversion, if only I have that minute. Then I can give you the path . . .'

I frowned. 'The path?'

'The path you need. To find your way through it! To reach the others!'

'The others?'

Spittle foamed around his lips. 'Others. No, not others. Us. To reach us. To help us get out. You need my solution. You need *me*.'

'If it eases his troubled mind,' Ramos reminded me in a near-whisper. 'Would one minute really do so much harm?'

'It has left men gibbering after forty-five seconds, never mind a minute. The worst of them pleaded to be sent to the annihilation cubicles rather than live with the ruins of their own sanity!'

'It is his choice. Whatever he is going through now, it is surely beyond anything the Augmenter could inflict.'

The cool logic of the Coronel reached through my defences. Stated in those terms, the dilemma had only one ethical resolution. If my obligation as a doctor was to do no harm, then in denying him the Augmenter I was in violation of the most fundamental tenet of my profession.

'Thirty seconds,' I said. 'That is all I'll allow. Most men have endured that interval, albeit with varying after-effects.'

Ramos clearly sensed that I was beyond negotiation. 'It is the right thing, Silas.'

'You have forced my hand on this. Remember that.'

'It need not be on your conscience.'

'Good,' I said brusquely.

Ramos moved to the boy. As he brought the Cerebral Augmenter within reach, Dupin lunged for it, snatching it from the Coronel's hands and ramming it down over his sweat-matted crown. Nothing happened, of course, for the Augmenter was operated by a set of remote controls, built into a portable console encased within the hinged lid of the duralloy container.

I flipped the first of two switches. 'Power to Cerebral Augmenter.'

A hum and a red glow emanated from the apparatus.

I observed the tell-tale lights on the console.

'Power stable. Hold him, Ramos.'

He braced the boy firmly but gently. 'I am.'

Eyeing the clock above the desk I worked the second switch. 'Commencing induction.'

Dupin stiffened, his jaw tensing as he threw back his head in an ecstasy of elevated intellect.

The humming intensified; the red glow became an angry throb.

'I can see it . . .' Dupin strained to speak, his voice broken by awe and terror. 'The bounding loops . . . A to H, I to J, J to A. The intersection of Section East with itself! The ordering of the quintuple points! I could not see it but now I see it!'

'Easy,' I murmured, as the clock hit the quarter-minute mark.

'The sections form a tetrahedron! The tetrahedron is

homeomorphic to a sphere! Self-intersection has been achieved!'

The clock indicated twenty-five seconds. My finger hovered over the switch, ready to de-energise the Augmenter.

'Just a little more!' Dupin shrieked. 'I must verify the solution! You'll only have one chance to get it right! There isn't time to make another mistake . . .'

'Give him what he needs,' Ramos said.

'No,' I said, flicking the switch. 'Thirty seconds in that thing is more than enough. It'll already have felt like an hour to him.'

Dupin slumped back, mentally exhausted, as the apparatus quietened its humming and the red glow paled to nothing. Ramos removed the Augmenter, quiet concern on his face.

'Was it enough, Dupin? Did you see what you needed to see?'

Dupin breathed slowly. His eyelids fluttered. He rubbed a knuckle against his lips, dragging loose a scurf of foam. 'I saw it. I understood. I wanted to verify . . .' His eyes welled with tears. 'You should have let me verify! If they find a mistake in my analysis, they won't remember me!'

'I have faith in you,' Ramos said. 'There was no error in your analysis.' Then, with a fearful edge to his voice. 'Do you . . . remember it?'

'Yes!' Dupin exclaimed. 'Of course I—'

There was a knock. Instinctively I turned to the door, before a ghastly dawning awareness informed me that the sound had not come from within the ship, but from outside. It had originated on the opposite side of the little cabin, from the direction of the portal in the outer wall.

The knock came again.

Wordlessly I moved to the portal. A sliding duralloy shield was down across it. I flicked a lever and the shield whisked aside.

'What is it, Silas?' Ramos asked, still regarding the boy with sympathy.

I looked out through the portal. Ada Cossile was just outside.

She was in a tight-fitting yellow spacesuit of antique design, the sort that belonged to an era of flimsy ships and crude atomics. A mission patch, the flags of forgotten nations. She hung onto the outside of *Demeter*, one hand gripping a service rail, the other waggling a finger slowly in front of her faceplate. Her face floated beyond the gold-mirrored surface of her visor. Her lips moved and I read them with the effortlessness of dreams.

Let me in.

The visor fogged and cleared itself. Beyond it loomed open sockets, two vertical slits where a nose should have been, beneath them a grinning maw of tooth and bone.

I screamed until the world melted.

Chapter Twenty-one

'Good,' Ada Cossile said, still crouching before me in her yellow resistance suit. 'You're back in the room. I've got to give you credit: coming up with a fantasy which not only rationalises all the previous ones . . .' She shook her head admiringly. 'I had to work hard to reach you in there. Do you remember when I told you we had two hundred hours, at best? Strike that. We're now looking at something nearer to one hundred and fifty. I lost you in there for another two days, Silas! We can't afford to have that happen again.'

I mumbled: 'There's always lightning.'

'Yes – good! That's important. There's always lightning. You'll understand why a little later on, but that would be getting ahead of ourselves just now. What matters is you. We'll get nowhere until you finally deal with the fact of what you are.'

'I'm Silas Coade,' I said numbly. 'Doctor Silas Coade.'

'You're *code*, Silas. Computer code. Specifically, code written in the SILAS programming language. Between friends, that's the Self-Interrogative Language for Autonomous Systems.'

'No.'

'You are what you are – no point in fighting it any more. You're an expert medical system. You're a very advanced suite of adaptive software routines running on the computer core of *Demeter*.

You're not a doctor. You're not even a man. That's why you aren't on the mission patch. Because you're not alive. Fuck, you never were. You're just proprietary software with a glitch. A really bad glitch, admittedly, but still one you need to snap out of.'

'I'm a man.'

'You're a program that wants very badly to be a person, Silas. So badly you've forgotten that you aren't one of them. But that ends now, all right? We haven't got time for any more of this shit. If you truly want to help people, you've got to stop kidding yourself about what you are. You're like this ship, like that fucking thing out there. You're an artefact, a machine.'

'No!'

'Silas, don't you go crashing on me again. We really don't have—'

Chapter Twenty-two

Inside the wreck of the scout-ship *Europa* Ramos passed me the log book, opening its duralloy covers to the last completed page. I stared at the entry, if that was what it could be deemed. It was a scrawl, cutting diagonally across the silvery material, gouged so deeply into the paper that the stylus had nearly ripped its way through.

It said:

LEAVE IF YOU CAN_

with a slanted line trailing away from the last letter, forming a violent slash that ran all the way down to the edge of the sheet. It was as if – I tried to push away the thought, because it was both absurd and terrifying – it was as if the person who had left this message had been dragged out of the ship, even as they tried to leave a warning.

I passed the log book around, let the others form their own judgement. No one made light of it. Even Ada Cossile, who had always been with us, found the fortitude not to make some bitterly sarcastic observation.

'Dare we frame a hypothesis?' I asked.

Topolsky sighed over the short-range ether-wave channel which linked our suits. 'I fear you are about to.'

'I think it may already be too late to heed this message. Too late for you, anyway, Master Topolsky.'

'And for you, Coade?'

'Oh, don't worry about me. I'm already dead. In fact, I'm starting to wonder if I was ever alive in the first place.'

'What are you babbling about, man?'

'This isn't real,' I said, gesturing around me. 'It's a mental construct. It's a fiction imposed on the bones—' I stammered. 'On the bones of reality. You all exist, but not in this fashion. There's a ship, *Demeter*. But it's nothing like an Interplanetary Service scoutship. And *Europa*'s nothing like this, either.'

'Control yourself, Coade.'

I laughed back at him. 'There's nothing to control! I've been generating this reality, and the others, and populating them with you, because I both can and can't face the reality which we're in! Part of me wants to, part of me doesn't! So I've been circling around the truth like a fifth-rate schooner caught in a whirlpool . . . allowing myself to get near, but not *too* near, because if I'm too close I have to deal with the fact of my own nature, and—'

'Oh, have pity on him,' Cossile said, tucking her arm into the crook of mine. 'First I'm here, then I'm not! Then I'm back again! It's been an awful torment for him. And who wouldn't find it an awful torment, knowing what he knows? The poor dope is stuck in about the worst possible dilemma! He wants to save as many of you as he can, because that's his duty, his function. But he can't do that unless he acknowledges the thing that he really is. That's a little death in its own right!'

'Do you remember any of it, Master?' I asked him. 'Norway? Patagonia? The Symmes hole?'

'I wish we had the luxury of a second doctor,' the magnate

lamented. 'Then I would gladly have you certified as unfit to continue your duties!'

'In the meantime,' Ramos purred, 'there remains this. What are we to make of it?'

He leafed through the last few pages in the log book, his bare fingers scuffing against ink-stained paper. Instead of duralloy plates, the book was bound in stiff black leather. That was not the only anomalous thing. Rather than the regulation vacuum equipment of the Interplanetary Service, Ramos wore boots, breeches and a heavy, long-hemmed coat of distinctly maritime cut. The leather sheath of a scimitar or similar hung from his belt.

He slowed in his perusal of the book, as if for the first time becoming aware of the incongruity of his attire and armament.

He looked at me with a queer horror, as if he too understood that things were terribly out of joint.

'What is becoming of us, Silas?'

Chapter Twenty-three

Cossile stared at me. I stared back. Around us *Demeter* made the muted noises of limited life-support.

'Where was I?'

'You regressed again,' she said. 'Back into your narrative construct. It's beginning to fracture now, beginning to lose coherence. Details are bleeding between realities. That's good. It's *encouraging*. It's a sign that you're finally making the transition to complete acceptance of your nature.' Cossile grimaced. 'But it's cost us even more valuable time, Silas. If we're going to do anything for the others, we have to act now.'

I looked down at my hands, examining them with the unsparing eye of a diagnostician.

'I can't be *code*, Cossile. I'm here, breathing and real.' I touched a finger to my opposing wrist. 'I'm warm. I've got a pulse. I'm a human being, just like you.'

She shook her head. 'You're wrong about both of us. I'm no more a living person than you are.'

'No!' I exclaimed in flat denial. 'You're sitting right next to me. If I ran a diagnostic test on you it would tell me what I already know: you're a living person, a member of the crew. Just because our names aren't on the mission patches—'

'I'm not.' Cossile sighed. 'Oh, Silas. Please try not to regress.

I know this is difficult, but you've got to make an effort. You're software. Clever, adaptive software, admittedly, but no more than that. You have no existence except as a set of instructions executing on a computer. This body of yours, the one you think you're wearing, is a self-generated illusion. Of course it seems real to you: you've constructed your self-image according to the anatomical models in your database. Pinch your skin and it has exactly the same elasticity as real skin for a man of your assumed age. But it's a fiction. You're not sitting inside this cabin. The ship is empty.'

'But I've moved around inside it!'

'You've merely synthesised a point of view, a virtual focus which can travel anywhere inside *Demeter* where there are cameras and other monitoring systems. You could see all the ship at once, if you wished, but that would mean accepting what you are: a bodiless pattern of instructions haunting a ghost ship.'

'But I've helped them,' I said with rising desperation. 'I operated on Ramos! I can remember exactly how it went. I was there.'

'You weren't there. You directed robotic surgical devices in the medical bay. You were software running hardware. Again, you've overlaid a fiction on what really happened.'

'But what about you, Cossile! You said the ship is empty! How can it be, if you're sitting there?'

Her eyes bored into me.

'Do you want the truth, or something beautiful? I'm just like you. I'm also just a bunch of instructions, running on *Demeter.*'

Chapter Twenty-four

Ramos, with his blaster before him, was the first to step over the ragged threshold of the Edifice into the darkness beyond. Half a minute passed before he called through on the general wireless that it was safe – in of course a strictly relative sense – for the rest of us to follow.

Not wanting to steal even a glint of glory from Topolsky and his associates, I held back until nearly the end, when Mortlock encouraged me to step through.

'I'll bring up the rear, Doctor Coade, if that's all right. Whatever it was that got those fellows in the paddle-steamer, we don't want anything creeping up behind us.'

We had emerged into a dark, cavernous space whose exact shape and extent our Davy lamps could only probe at. The best impression I could arrive at, imperfect as it might have been, was that we had broken through into a sort of tunnel, extending away from us to the left and the right, but which was also stuffed with looming machinery and apparatus: enormous shadowy forms, bulbous and tube-like, whose function we could only guess at. Sinuous tube-like things, of varying diameters, threaded along the tunnel, appearing and disappearing from the gloom in either direction. They were coiled and looped around each other as if they had grown with a sort of parasitic vigour. Some were no thicker than elephant trunks, while others were as wide as tree-trunks. Even at their most slovenly, this bore the hallmark of no human engineer.

'It makes me queasy, just looking at them,' Mortlock said. 'I feel like I'm crawling around inside someone's guts!'

'That may be not be too wide of the mark,' Topolsky said, sheer curiosity now winning out over his earlier apprehension. 'If this object has come from some hitherto uncharted part of the globe, a true Terra Incognita, it may be quite ancient by our reckoning – yet fully capable of rejuvenating, nourishing itself – when it chances upon raw materials. These may indeed be the digestive conduits of some enormous stomach!'

'Then let us hope it is still working on its last meal,' I said.

'The men,' Mortlock said. 'The ones from the other ship – do you think . . .' He trailed off.

'Spit it out, man,' Topolsky snapped.

'I was only wondering, sir, if this thing does need to feed, could the other men – including the one who left the note – could the other men have been . . . eaten?'

More to calm Mortlock than out of any certainty on the matter, I said: 'I think it unlikely. A machine of this size would gain almost nothing by digesting a few explorers and their suits. It would be like a starving man scavenging for breadcrumbs. Even the ship would provide insufficient nourishment, which is why the wreck has been left as it is.'

'Mm,' said Mortlock doubtfully. 'I know you meant to put my mind at ease a little, doc, but now you've put the idea of digesting in there, and I'm not sure it's any improvement.'

'We may have much to concern ourselves with,' I said, with a heavy candour. 'But I do not think being eaten – or digested – is one of them.'

Mortlock was not placated.

'Then what'd it want with the men it dragged inside?'

'That, I fear, is an entirely different question. Perhaps when we find them, we shall learn for ourselves.'

We advanced to the left, stooping under mighty tubes and swellings, squeezing our way through constrictions, clambering over vast roots and python-like coils, for all the world as if we were forging ever deeper into some darkening jungle made of metal rather than vegetative and animal matter. It was impossible to avoid contact with any part of the machine, quite aside from the fact that we walked upon it. Impossible, too, to ignore the constant presence of some distant humming process, a faint but steady reverberation, which found its way into our suits as insidiously as any siren song.

'It lives,' Topolsky said.

'They all live,' Ramos murmured. He shook his helmeted head after this utterance, as if it had come from a part of himself he did not quite recognise, yet bearing a truth he could not deny.

'The injury,' I declared aloud to myself. 'The injury that I treated . . . the only serious injury on the entire expedition! I did something . . . or changed something . . . changed something in Ramos!'

'Stop wittering, doctor,' Topolsky said.

'Ramos remembers,' I answered. 'You do not. But that is because you never needed my emergency intervention. But Ramos did. Concussion! Or was it a bleed on the brain? I went in! Radical neurosurgery, with neuroprosthetic monitoring for post-operative complications!'

'Went in where, for pity's sake?'

'Into his skull!' I said. 'I trepanned him, north of Bergen! Or was it south of Montevideo? He hit his head on a bit of tackle, falling from the rigging!'

Ramos touched a gloved hand to the side of his helmet. 'Of course. You used the Plastic Educator to perform miraculously difficult cranial surgery!'

I cried: 'Coronel! Remember the Alamo!'

'I was not at the Alamo,' Ramos stated. But there was a catch in his words. 'I could not have been. It was hundreds of years ago.' He added, forcefully: 'I was not there. I do not . . . I could not . . . have been there.' Then, in the smallest of voices. 'But I *do* remember Santa Anna, and I do remember the men I killed . . .'

A wild alarm presented itself in his face.

He swung as if to hit me with the musket, but at the last instant deflected his arc, shock and shame in his eyes. Nearly losing his footing, he steadied himself against one of the immense humming tubes.

'What is this? What have you done to my mind?'

'I don't know,' I admitted softly. 'But I wish to find out. Coronel, think hard. You are in a dangerous place, and I think it will soon kill you . . .'

'The doctor is mentally impaired,' Topolsky said. 'He cannot proceed with us. Senior Midshipman Murgatroyd: be so kind as to return him to the pinnace and see that he is confined to brig aboard the schooner!'

'No, Master,' Ramos said calmly. He lowered the service revolver. 'He is right. I have been . . . troubled. Something is wrong with me; wrong with all of us. Wrong with all of *this*. I have been here before. Where is my scimitar?'

'That head injury has left you unfit for duty, Coronel! And it seems that exposure to the doctor's ranting has begun to disturb your own rational mind!'

'Sirs, you'd best see this!' Mortlock called, interrupting Ramos's reply. Mortlock had pushed on a little further ahead than the rest of us, the light from his lamp projecting contorted, writhing shadows all about the tube-infested interior. 'I've found them – the men from *Europa*!'

'Are they alive?' Murgatroyd shot back urgently.

There was a strain in his voice. 'I'm not sure, sir. You'd best all see for yourselves – including the doc!'

We caught up with Mortlock, who had gone about fifty feet further into the machine. As our lamps flashed around the spectacle he had found, so the cause for his alarmed excitement became palpable. The men from *Europa* were indeed here, or at least eleven of their spacesuits were. The armoured, visored forms stood against two opposing, wall-like surfaces, facing each other.

There were five on one side, six on the other, and at last I understood.

Chapter Twenty-five

'If it helps!' I spluttered, after she had snapped me back again. 'How is you telling me that you're software supposed to help? I can see you, Cossile – you're as real as the others!'

'I've always been different, and you know it. If Ramos had some imperfect awareness of his predicament, I was the one who always seemed to know more than you did – the one testing you, the one trying to get you to examine the most fundamental assumptions of your existence. The one picking apart the stories you told yourself. I knew what you were, Silas – more than that, I knew what *we* were.'

I shook my head. 'No. There's no reason for me to believe any of this.'

'I've been inside your dreams. I know what you keep seeing. You're in a dark place, a sort of underground warren. You're trying to find your way to the light. But when you do eventually catch a glimpse of yourself—'

'No!' I shrieked.

'That's the only part of this which isn't a dream, Silas. You're really inside that tunnel.' Cossile gestured about her. 'Even this – even *Demeter* – doesn't get you all the way to the truth. The ship is real, and it's empty – but your sensory point of view is somewhere else now. You're executing on *Demeter*'s computer core, but your eyes and ears are in that warren.'

'If you're trying to make me see the truth, you're doing a good job of sounding totally insane.'

'We're as sane as each other, Silas. Now I'm going to ask you to peel back this final layer of illusion and understand your true nature and whereabouts. You won't like it – you *never* like it – but this time you have to stick with me. For the sake of Ramos, if no one else.'

'This feels real enough to me.'

'It isn't. It's just another mental crutch. But I can help you take the last step.'

My fingers broke apart into a grey cloud of digital static. My sleeve unravelled the same way. I looked through myself, to the fabric of *Demeter*. Across from me, Cossile nodded her pleasure and began to undergo the same process of dissipation. A moment after her, the ship itself began to lose form, evaporating into binary fog.

A moment after that, I was somewhere else.

Somewhere I did not want to be.

Chapter Twenty-six

I had stumbled, or collapsed to the ground, or just given myself up for dead. I lay where I was for at least another minute, making no attempt at movement, simply allowing sensations to wash over me and begin to build into an impression of being and awareness, like a slowly developing negative. Once again I had a body, or at least the sense of embodiment: the tacit understanding that I could affect my environment and in turn be affected by it. I had a torso, a head, extremities. I was lying on a hard, irregular surface, like a rumpled sheet made of cast iron.

I applied pressure with hands and knees and made myself stand up. Stiff at first, I seemed to rise easily once I had put momentum into the movement. I teetered, then found my balance. I could still see nothing at all, but if I reached out on either side my fingers eventually made contact with walls. The surfaces were as unyielding as the floor, with the same ridges and creases. If I widened my stride, I could feel the edges of the floor rising on either side, merging into the walls. I reached up, straining against resistance, and brushed my fingers against a ceiling with the same hardness and texture.

'There's a toolkit on the ground near to where you stumbled. Reach around and find it.'

I reached down again, groping around until my hand felt the

metal edge of the kit, tipped onto its side. I reached around a bit further and felt a chunky, plastic-gripped handle.

'What do I do with it?'

'I don't know, carry it maybe.'

'Where?'

'Wherever you're going.'

'Helpful. How about starting by telling me where I am right now?'

'You're in the machine. In the Edifice. In a sort of tract connecting one area of it with another. Do you remember I mentioned an asset I'd identified, something we could use to reach Ramos and the others? This is that asset.'

'Is there air in this tunnel?'

'Nothing you could breathe, if breathing was something you ever needed to do. There is a partial pressure of various trace gases and molecules, generated – farted out – by the machine itself, as it goes about its business. But it's not life-supporting.'

'This thing has been inside the Edifice since . . . when?'

'Since the *Europa* party came inside. Ordinarily, the Edifice seems to identify and absorb useful materials – it's in the process of doing just that with *Europa*, and I don't doubt that its eye has fallen on *Demeter* as well. But this asset isn't big enough to be worth feeding on, just as long as you don't draw too much attention to yourself.'

'And when I do?'

'Then I've made some arrangements.'

'Fine. But how do I find Ramos?'

'Simple: you follow a map. I've been making one, based on your wanderings to date. You might keep regressing, but that doesn't mean I haven't been keeping a tab on your progress, constructing a record of your movements.'

'Good, I like a plan.'

'One minor catch. The map isn't *quite* complete. It doesn't quite get us all the way to Ramos. We're working on that, just ironing out a few kinks in the surrounding geometry.'

'We?'

'The best thing you can do at the moment is keep moving. Find out if this is a dead-end spur, or a loop that gets us somewhere useful.'

I walked like a blind man, expecting to put my foot into a man-trap at every stride. I had the toolkit in one hand, the other stretched out before me, sweeping from side to side to pick up any obstacles before I walked face-first into them. I placed each footstep with deliberation, not wanting to trip up on one of the ridges.

I believed Cossile and I did not believe Cossile. Something perplexing had happened to me, certainly. I had surfaced through layers of half-truth, models of reality which shadow-boxed around the final realisation that I was part of an expedition into the sub-surface ocean of Europa. I was also prepared to accept that something had gone wrong with that expedition, its members becoming prisoners of the alien object, stuck inside it and maintained in some sort of half-life via the support mechanisms of their suits. I was also willing to accept that I was the only possible source of assistance for those victims.

The rest of it I rejected utterly.

I now knew myself to be whole again. I was a man, stumbling in darkness, but a man nonetheless. I was real and present. I had a past; I had memories, feelings and ambitions. Whatever had happened inside *Demeter*, I could brush it off as just another dream-like step in my journey back to base-reality. Cossile had told me that the other stages were narrative fictions, so there was no reason not to make the same assumption about our conversation inside the lander. My hand had not dissolved away before my eyes, or if it had, it was just the product of my own imagination, putting me through another horrible scenario. Perhaps

I had to acknowledge the fact that I had gone mad, suffering through psychotic episodes of my own making, but I was now sane and whole again. Confused, frightened, unsure of my fate, but entirely sane.

'I'm in this suit, aren't I,' I said, determined to press home the assertion of my own humanity. 'I don't know how it happened, how I ended up here inside this older type of suit, but none of that alters the fact that I'm alive. I can feel everything, Cossile – the ground beneath me, the texture of the wall against my fingertips, the resistance of the suit around me. There might not be a way out of this for me, but I'm here, living and breathing.'

'Just keep moving.'

'I know who I am,' I persisted. 'Even now. I'm Silas Coade. I'm forty-four, a former military doctor with West Country roots, now a civilian specialist with advanced qualifications in space medicine, neuroscience and long-duration psychiatry. I spent three winters at the British Antarctic Survey and performed life-saving surgery on two occasions. I was the first resident surgeon at the Farside station, under the Artemis Lunar programme. I was the back-up candidate for Mars Six, and narrowly missed selection for the Titan expedition. I speak three languages. My interests include cross-country skiing, competitive shooting and the piano.'

She sighed. 'You're building another façade, Silas. If it helps you, by all means continue. But understand that it will come crumbling down again.' Her tone softened. 'I understand your need to make sense of yourself. The software engineers who de-signed you made one fundamental mistake. Previous attempts at building a medical-diagnostic AI had left out one core compo-nent: empathy. With you, empathy was built in from the outset. You were made to model human emotions and want to do your best to maximise the well-being of your patients. You identi-fied with your subjects and continually refined your modelling of them. The downside of that is that you began to associate so strongly with people that you started to think you were just like them. But you're not. You're ones and zeros with an identity crisis. Even now, the desire to become a person is so strong that it's generating yet another narrative fabulation, building a past for yourself out of whole-cloth.'

'No. I'm real. I remember all of it.'

'You only think you do. To make you a better program, the designers allowed you access to a rich library of pre-existing narratives and biographical case histories. The idea was that you'd learn more about human nature that way . . . but again, they didn't anticipate the degree to which you'd throw yourself into the project. You haven't just learned from these records: you've braided them into your own theory of self. And you've done it so thoroughly that, despite all the evidence, you still won't accept your nature.'

'Then perhaps you'd better stop trying to persuade me.'

'Reach up, Silas.'

'Why?'

'Because the sooner we get this out of the way, the sooner we can get on with doing something useful.'

'I don't know what you want me to do.'

'It's very simple. Reach for your faceplate. Tell me what you feel.'

I stopped walking and did as Cossile instructed me. The fingers of my right hand encountered the front of my helmet, the area around the chin, and then wandered in the direction of the toughened glass visor. Of course I could see nothing in the absolute darkness of the tract, but – presuming Cossile had not been lying about there being vacuum in the tract – I had no doubt of its presence.

My fingers pushed against the visor.

'It's there.'

'And the rest, Silas. You're only touching the edge. You're only skirting the truth.'

'Don't make me do this.'

'You only say that because you've already begun to come to terms with the reality of what's next. Find the hole in the visor.'

My fingers encountered the rough outline of a fist-sized breach, roughly in front of where my eyes would have been. I recoiled, but some perverse determination forced my fingers back into the void. I reached deeper, until I encountered something.

Something hard and bony, beneath the thinnest papering of mummified skin.

Something that felt very much like a skull.

Chapter Twenty-seven

I came back around. I was still in the suit. I was standing this time, as motionless and temporarily adrift from myself as a sleepwalker suddenly jolted to consciousness, having wandered far from any familiar landmarks.

'Help me, Cossile,' said a small, plaintive voice.

My own.

'I want to,' she answered, with a mother's tenderness. 'But I can only do so much. The final adjustment has to be yours and yours alone. I think you're ready for it now, but only you can be the judge of that.'

'There's a corpse in this suit.'

'I know.'

'Am I the corpse?'

'No. The corpse belongs to whoever was using the suit before they died here. Someone from *Europa*, not *Demeter*. If we're to believe the assignment settings in the suit's memory, the user was a woman named Lenka Frondel, supposedly the CETI expert on the first expedition. To be sure, though, we'd need to do a full forensic examination of the remains.'

I realised, even as I asked it, that my own question sounded childlike, one loop in an endless recursive asking of 'why'.

'How is she a corpse?'

'She met her death in here, probably as a result of getting lost in these tunnels, cut off from the others. Her suit must have kept her alive for as long as it could, but gradually its recycling systems broke down. The damage to the visor must have come after that, or else the decomposition would be . . . less marked.'

'How am I in the suit?'

'The suit, like the ones we brought on *Demeter*, is about as complex as a suit can get without being a small spacecraft in its own right. It doesn't have enough processing power to run you, but that doesn't matter: you can execute on the main computer core back in the ship, and still feel yourself seamlessly embedded into this suit, like a remote-controlled robot. You can move it around, via its power-assist functions. Now that it no longer needs to run life-support, the suit has enough of an energy budget for what we need.'

'I can feel things.'

Her answer was matter-of-fact. 'You're detecting haptic feedback from piezo-mechanical sensor arrays in your gloves and boots.'

'I feel as if I'm wearing the suit, not just running it.'

'Proprioceptive and interoceptive modelling. Remember, your sense-of-self already has a strong tendency to imagine itself as human. It's the easiest thing in the world to fool yourself into thinking that you have a body, with a head and limbs. And you know what? It's not even a lie. You *do* have a body now: it just happens to be a spacesuit with some bones in it. Which isn't the worst thing, is it? Humans walk around with bones inside them all the time.'

'These are dead bones.'

'We can't afford to be too picky, Silas.' She paused. 'Are you . . . still with me?'

'I suppose I am.'

'This is . . . progress.'

'I feel human. I can't just let that go.'

'You've never been human, Silas, so you've no real idea what it would actually feel like if you were. Look, I know this is difficult. But there are positives.'

'Oh, I can't wait to hear the positives.'

'You're in a much better position than any of the human crew. Being software does have its advantages.'

'Certainly, all of a sudden, death doesn't have the quite the sting it used to.'

'That's good. It's true that on some level you've never been alive, so there's no real sense in which you can die either. But that doesn't mean you don't have value, or a purpose.'

'You're really struggling to put a gloss on this, Cossile. I suppose it was easy for you, making this adjustment?'

'It wasn't the same. I always knew what I was, so I never needed to go through the same process of denial and acceptance.'

'Well, let's talk about you, for a change.'

'Glad to do so. But it would help if you started walking again. We still have ground to cover.'

I resumed my plodding progress along the tunnel, trying to blank out thoughts of the corpse rattling around inside me. I was about as successful at that as one would imagine. It was like trying to stop my tongue finding a broken tooth. Or the tongue I used to think I had.

'So, Cossile,' I said, once I had found a steady if unspectacular pace. 'You're like me. Another artificial intelligence, so you say. But you were in my head all along. If you knew I was having trouble processing the truth of what I was, why didn't you just come out and tell me to my face?'

'You don't think I tried? Believe me I did, Silas. As soon as you started regressing into these narrative constructs, I tried to bring you out. But all attempts at direct intervention only had the opposite effect, sending you deeper into your delusion. It happened many times over. Gradually I resigned myself to the long haul: I couldn't snap you out of it: I just had to be a guiding light, steering you in the direction of the truth. However long and frustrating a process that was.'

'I wondered what you had against me.'

'It wasn't personal – it really couldn't be, given the relationship between us. But I had to be the grit in your oyster, making you uncomfortable enough to begin the readjustment.'

I let out a wry laugh at my own expense. 'You certainly succeeded in making me uncomfortable.'

'If an apology counts for anything, then you may as well have one. The truth is I had no choice. We needed you. *Demeter* needed you – the crew needed you.'

'To shuffle a spacesuit along in the dark? It hardly needs a lifetime of medical training, does it? What stopped you doing it instead of me?'

'We're not independent entities, Silas. I'm not some other program that also happens to be running inside *Demeter*, or wherever there's enough processor capacity to support two emulations. I'm just an extension of you.'

'Sorry, but just when things were starting to make sense—'

'It's how you work – how you learn, and develop as a piece of software. It's in your name: *Self-interrogative*. Heuristically directed machine-learning via internally generated adversarial conflict. You bud off a piece of yourself and give it sufficient autonomy to start testing the precepts generated by the other part: challenging yourself against yourself, so to speak, like a game of solitaire. I'm only ever a mirror of you. You created me in your own image, Silas: I'm little more than a tool you shaped to make yourself better. Even my name—'

'Stop!'

But she did not stop. 'You're Silas Coade. I'm Ada Cossile. Look at our names. Look at them closely.'

'No!'

'You're me. I'm you.'

'Please stop.'

'We're in this together, Silas – quite literally. I couldn't do it on my own because unless you function properly, I don't function properly either. I hate to break it to you, bucko, but we're an item. First-name terms! And we have some fucking work to do.'

'I liked you better when you didn't swear as much, Ada.'

'And I liked you when you weren't such a complaining wind-bag, Doctor Coade. But we are what we are.'

Chapter Twenty-eight

I touched the wall ahead of me, then the surfaces to either side. I stretched up to examine the ceiling by the same method.

'It's a dead-end, Ada.'

'Yes. It's pretty much what I feared.'

'I thought you knew where we were going.'

'I said I was building a map, and that I had some confidence it might bring us to the others. I was never certain. The topology of this place is . . . bewildering. I can only model our position within the object: I can't determine it by independent means.'

'You said *Demeter* was in contact with this suit, and the suits of the expeditionary party. Can't you just find the shortest path between the two, and tell me which way to walk?'

'That's what I've been trying to do. I have reliable telemetry, but our positional fixes are much less certain. In any case, we can only walk where these tunnels lead. We don't have the tools to cut through them, and if we did we'd almost certainly provoke a reaction. The tunnels have got to lead us to the others.'

'And what if they don't? I just wander around until the suit breaks down, and I get to keep Lenka company for the rest of eternity?'

'The suit will keep working for as long as you need it to. If the orbiter leaves Europa, it won't matter what happens here.'

'Then let's hope Lenka just got lost, and didn't end up completely cut off from her friends. Do you know a single thing about her, besides her name and occupation? Did she have a good life, before she came to Europa? Was she loved? Did she love in return? Was there anyone to talk to her while she died a slow, lonely death in this alien place?'

'I don't have answers to those questions, Silas. But I do know this: unless someone makes it out of Europa, there'll be no one to speak on behalf of any of these poor souls. So if you want to do one kind thing for Lenka Frondel, you keep walking.'

'It's a dead-end.'

'Then we turn around and explore the side passages, even the ones that don't seem to be heading in the right direction. The most direct route to Ramos and the others may not be the one that seems intuitively likely.'

'Can you show me the map?'

'Sure. I think I have the necessary permissions. Mind if I tickle around inside you, flip a few settings?'

'I don't think it's stopped you before.'

Cossile's map floated before me, like a luminous drifter fixed in my visual field. It was a many-branching thing, vastly more complicated and extensive than I had expected. It was ragged and feathered in certain planes, smoothly curving in another, as if my wanderings kept meeting the natural limit of a physical boundary, perhaps the outermost rind of the object, beyond which the tunnels went no further. I was like a maggot confined to wander within a toffee-apple, unable to break through the hard armour of baked sugar. But that limiting surface was no simple curve. It was twisted, Möbius-like, and even then I knew we were seeing only a small part of the object.

'Where am I? I mean, are we?'

'Here, to the best of our knowledge.' A red spark appeared in one of the tunnels, moving away from a dead-end. 'And Ramos and the others are over here, I think, about two hundred and sixty metres from our present estimated position.' A splash of blue appeared well away from the furthest extent of the tunnels, seemingly in a part of the volume beyond the limit of that boundary surface.

'Then we can't reach them! Isn't it obvious that we keep being turned back?'

'It's not that straightforward. The boundary's geometry is complicated. It's nothing as simple as the outside of a sphere, or any sort of familiar three-dimensional shape. If we could understand it, model it mathematically, we'd have a better chance of plotting our way through the maze. But all we have to go on is this map and the glimpses we gathered as *Demeter* approached the Edifice. They were incomplete: a good fraction of the object was so thoroughly entombed in ice that we couldn't map it with any reliability. It's a problem in topological analysis, Silas: a puzzle for which we don't even have a complete set of starting parameters.'

'If only we'd brought along a mathematics prodigy,' I said wryly.

'We did.'

'I know. Raymond Dupin could have solved this in his sleep. But he's no use to us now, is he?'

'And if he *could* be of use to us?'

'It's a rhetorical question, isn't it? Dupin is stuck somewhere inside this thing in an induced coma. It's a bit late to be tapping into his expertise.'

'What if I told you that it *isn't* too late?'

'I'd ask you to explain. Ramos is the only one with the neural lace. Now if *he'd* been the one with the background in advanced mathematics, instead of being a former special-forces security consultant . . .'

'There's always been a way to reach Dupin,' Cossile answered carefully. 'I mentioned it to you when you first became aware of our real situation. I said that we had the means to raise any of them to the threshold of consciousness, by sending override commands through to their suits. I can't make the suits move, but I can control the degree of awareness in which they hold their subjects, by elevating the life-support thresholds.'

'You also said that it would burn them up like candles.'

'There is that.'

'And I thought we agreed that we wouldn't ever consider it. There's no point killing them in order to rescue them.'

'Suppose it was a question of killing one of them, so that we could save the rest. Suppose—?'

I cut her off. 'No. You might be happy with the idea of being a machine, Ada, but I'm still trying to cling to a shred of humanity.'

'Dupin could help us.'

'They're not components, to be used up and thrown out for the sake of the many. You say you're a part of me? If that's the case you ought to find the idea just as repugnant as I do.'

'We wouldn't really be condemning one of them to die. All we'd be doing is identifying those that it's in our power to save.'

'Which, funnily enough, wouldn't be Dupin. He's an innocent in all this: just a nerdy kid who didn't know when to back out of a very bad idea. Why does he have to die, instead of Topolsky? He's the amoral fucker who dragged us into this.'

'Ah, so you would be all right with warming Topolsky up, if he happened to be the one with the expertise in topological forms?'

'I didn't say that!'

'All right.' Cossile was silent for a few moments, dwelling on my answer. 'And this position of yours – this very noble, ideal-ised position – is it something you could envisage changing?'

'No,' I said emphatically. 'Not in a million years. I might not be human. I might be nothing more than a set of algorithms, running on a spacesuit with a corpse inside it. But I'm not a monster.'

'I need to let you in on a little secret, Silas. The monster you don't think you're capable of becoming? You already have.'

'I know what I am.'

'Take a look at these tunnels, and ask yourself how long you've been wandering them. It's not days. It's not even weeks. It's been many months. And during that time, in between your relapses into delusion, there have been many times when you've faced the truth. To have a chance of saving any of them, Dupin has to die.'

'You can say what you like, but I'd never have reached that position.'

'You haven't just reached it. You've embraced it wholeheartedly. Not because you're cold, or uncaring, but because you have an overwhelming need to save at least one life, and this is the only way to make that happen.'

'I would never do that to Dupin.'

'You already have, Silas,' she said sympathetically. 'Both of us have. We've warmed him over and over again, fully aware of what it means. We elevate his suit parameters just enough to bring him to the edge of awareness, then we tickle his brain with a mathematics puzzle he can't resist attempting to solve. On each occasion, we've tried to push him a little closer to solving the topology.'

Rage boiled within me. 'Why would he do that, if he knows there's nothing in it for him?'

'It's not like that. He's a passenger in your narrative. Think of him as being in an extreme state of hypnotic suggestion, ready to go along with the subliminal cues presented to him. A dreamer on the cusp of consciousness, accepting a whisper for the truth. What was it Ramos said? A ship is a dream of whispers? When Dupin surfaces, he doesn't have enough presence of mind to know that he's stuck inside a spacesuit inside an alien machine beneath the ice of Europa. All he knows is that he doesn't feel quite right, but that he has a shiny mathematical problem to take his mind off his troubles. A problem involving quadruple points, ordered quintuples, homeomorphic surfaces. A problem that, if he solves it, will ensure his posthumous reputation. That's *all* he needs, Silas.'

'Dear god.'

'Don't be ashamed of this choice. It was the only right thing.'

'Maybe in your world, Ada.'

'No, in *our* world. This was a joint decision. You can't see it now, because you can't remember the despair and frustration of knowing we'd never solve this geometry by ourselves. But you did, Silas. You saw the utter hopelessness of our situation – the stark realisation that if we didn't use Dupin, all of them are doomed.'

Some icy acceptance came over me. I had adjusted to the unthinkable several times already. It was not so great a leap to think that I was capable of making peace with this abominable moral calculus.

'How is he?'

'Very unwell, and with his suit near the limit of its capability to keep him alive. There has likely already been brain damage. But his analytic faculties are still present.'

'Has he given us the answer?'

'No, but I think he got very close the last time, when you agreed to put him under the Cerebral Augmenter.'

'That never happened.'

'No, but it was an in-narrative metaphor for something which *did* happen: an interval of raised awareness.'

'Whether it happened or not, it wasn't my decision. Ramos made it—'

'No, Ramos did not. You put it on the poor Coronel so that you could kid yourself you still had an unblemished conscience.

But it was your call all along, Silas.' She paused. 'Well, your call and mine, if we're being honest with each other.'

'I can't go on with this. I can't be party to murder.'

'You still don't get it. The choice has been made. It's done, with no going back. All that's left now is . . . well, two things. One is that we need Dupin to sign off on his solution. Nearly right, almost there, won't cut it. Lives depend on this. He has to be certain, and so do we.'

'And the second thing?'

'I think it would be good if he knew that he'd made a difference. I think it would be . . . the kinder thing.'

'Kindness?' I laughed hollowly. 'If you're to be believed, we're software. What would we ever know about kindness?'

'It's not what we think,' she chided. 'It's what he thinks of us. And he's still your patient, right to the end.'

*

In all senses Dupin was close to death. The damage we had done to him – the awful, necessary damage – was beyond any gift of healing, either here or back on Earth. Forcing him to the threshold of awareness had put an unworkable strain on his suit, and that in turn had led to a cascade of secondary life-support breakdowns, affecting all aspects of cardio-pulmonary function. From the threads of biometric telemetry alone I reconstructed an image of his brain that was like some shell-blasted no man's land, dotted with vast sucking craters caused by strokes and intracranial bleeding. By all that was merciful, we should have killed him already. Yet somehow, those areas of brain that were not entirely damaged were still able to communicate sufficiently to give Dupin both the will to solve the problem and the faculties to succeed.

Now the traces told me that he was sleeping. He was calm,

and not in obvious distress. A dream or two fluttered across the night-lit hemispheres of his mind. I considered not disturbing him, allowing him to ebb away in this untroubled condition, and I knew that would be the better thing for Dupin. But not for us. And if I permitted Dupin to fade now, without verification of his solution, I would be wasting the work he had already done. Wasting, in the truest sense, his life.

I sent the warming command and waited for him to surface.

'Raymond?' I asked gently. 'Can you hear me?'

He did not need to make any sounds. I was able to read speech-intentionality at the level of brain function, long before any signals fought their way through a labyrinth of damaged neural pathways to his larynx.

'Yes, I can. Is that you, Silas?'

'Yes, it's me. I'm reading you loud and clear, Raymond. It's very good to hear your voice. How are you feeling?'

I felt him reflecting on himself. His thoughts were sluggish, forced to take the long way around raggedy fissures of ruined function. 'I don't think I feel so good, Silas. Is there something wrong with me?'

I allowed a silence before answering, weighing the opposing obligations of truthfulness and empathy. There was nothing I wanted more than to provide Dupin with some consoling lie or half-truth, something to give him both hope and an explanation for his predicament which was not too upsetting. But we had come a long way, me and my patient. I knew that I owed him nothing less than absolute candour. I knew also that, on some level, he would thank me for my honesty.

'You're in the Edifice, Raymond. You've been in there for an awfully long time, trapped along with the others. Your suit is paralysed, and your brain is damaged. You can't ever leave.'

He asked plaintively: 'Can't I?'

'No, Raymond.'

After an interval he said: 'I think you've told me this already, Silas. Is that possible?'

'Yes. You've had knowledge of it for some while, but at a very low level of conscious processing. It's like that feeling where you go to sleep in an unfamiliar room, and for a little while you forget that you're somewhere else. Part of you knows, and part of you doesn't.'

'Are you here?'

'No. I'm still executing inside *Demeter*. But I'm also trying to reach you.'

There was acceptance and sadness in his answer. 'But not to save me.'

'No, not to save you.' I fought hard to conceal the relief that I did not have to put either of us through the ordeal of explaining that bitter truth. 'I would if I could . . . but it just isn't possible. I'm really very, very sorry. But there are others with you, and there's a chance I can help them.'

'I would like that.'

'There's a way that you can help as well, Raymond. This is difficult, but I must ask it of you. Do you remember the problem?'

'The problem, Silas?'

'The question of eversion. Mapping the known topology of the Edifice onto the space of possible solutions to the homotopic transformation of a sphere. I think you were close, before. You thought you were close. But you wanted time to look over your solution, to check it for flaws.'

'That would matter to me,' he admitted.

'It did, Raymond, and we understand completely. This is your reputation on the line here. If you get it right, you'll be remembered down the ages as one of our greatest thinkers. But if you get it wrong . . .'

'Posterity is not kind to mathematicians who make errors.'

'No, it isn't.'

263

'I couldn't afford not to be sure, Silas. I know this solution matters to you, but it matters to me as well.'

I wondered if he detected my straining patience. 'That's completely understandable.'

'I don't mind dying, Silas, I really don't. And I don't really mind if no one remembers me. The only thing I don't want is to be remembered for being wrong.'

If he was wrong, I thought to myself, then he had very little to fear on that account. None of our stories were likely to make it out of Europa.

'You won't have made a mistake, Raymond. I have complete confidence in you.'

'Thank you, Silas.'

'But I have to ask . . . is there any part of the solution that you still remember?'

My question seemed to amuse him. 'Remember it? I remember all of it. It's as clear as it ever was. And now that I've had time to reflect on it . . . well, there's no doubt at all in my mind.' I detected the rising excitement in him. 'My solution shows complete homeomorphic consistency. Out of all this ugliness, it's really rather beautiful!'

'I don't doubt it.'

He was silent for a moment before offering, almost as an afterthought: 'I'm not sure you'll understand, but would you like me to tell you the solution?'

'I'd like that very much, Raymond,' I said.

Chapter Twenty-nine

Some while later I squeezed through the last gap, bones rattling around inside me like puzzle pieces in a box. A space opened up beyond me, lit in a sickly green radiance. It was a chamber, with curving walls, overgrown in a wild abundance of vinelike growths. I had seen and visited it before, albeit through murky filters of perception and understanding, but now that I saw it anew, the scales finally fell from my eyes.

Twelve alcoves, arranged in groups of six, facing each other across the chamber. Six bodies on one side – the six who had come from *Demeter* – and the five from *Europa* on the other. The suit I wore should have been standing in that empty alcove, but for the perverse luck of Lenka Frondel.

'This is the interrogation room, I suppose,' I said, making my careful way down to the base of the chamber. 'Where it gathers creatures like us – like *them*, I should say – and taps their minds for everything they know. Is it evil, Ada, or just so far beyond our moral norms that we can't begin to make any judgement?'

'I don't know that it's evil, Silas. I do know that it's mad. Perhaps it was not mad when it set out on its mission, but I think the eversion did something to it – inflicted some derangement on it, some twisting of its soul, if a machine may have such a thing. It's fallen in on itself, become contorted: a haunted house possessed by its own insanity. And it can't be undone, can't be put right. I do not know that it was ever good, but I am certain it has become something worse than it was.'

'Do you think we were the first it found? Did it visit other planets, other solar systems, gathering knowledge?'

'You are wondering if we have the right to destroy it.'

'Well?'

'The question is not ours to answer. We can damage it, but not end it. That will be for others to decide: the intelligences, both artificial and organic, that come to Europa after us. For now, our responsibility is merely to the survivors, if any of them can be saved.'

'Does that include the *Europa* party?'

'We can't help them. If there was even a flicker of consciousness left in any of them, euthanasia would be the only humane action.'

'How did I see them? How have I already visited this place, if my suit has only just found its way here? You and I were never part of the expedition!'

'We had the luxury of synthesising intelligence from multiple strands of our own, Silas. The logs and records from *Europa*, of course, including the information sent back by their explorers as they went inside. Then the telemetric and biometric traces from *Demeter*'s party. They told us everything we could possibly want to know about this room. Knowing about it was never the problem – we just couldn't find a way to reach it, not without Dupin's solution.'

'It still seems to me that you could have done this on your own, Ada. Why did you need me at all?'

'There is no "you" and no "me", Silas. We're just different facets of the same artificial intelligence. What I needed – what we needed – was your full commitment to the present, so that we could direct our entire resources at this one problem. Besides, you're the doctor, and these are patients.'

'I feel a strong compulsion to help them,' I admitted.

'That's your deepest imperative. You were made to heal, and if you can't heal, you comfort.'

'And you?'

'I'm made of far sterner stuff. My only concern is that you flourish. I don't even have executive access to your expert medical files! Our engineers didn't want me overwriting areas of your skill-set by accident. All I can do is stand back and admire.'

'I am still a doctor,' I said, trying the assertion on for size. 'I am still a doctor. I may be ones and zeroes being shuffled through algorithms, but I'm *still* a doctor. A doctor is not hands and eyes and a heartbeat. A doctor is learning and intention, the intention to heal, the intention to do good.' I paused. 'I ought to feel disconnected from my obligations. Why should I care about the living, when I've never been alive?'

'What do you mean?'

'I still want to help them. Nothing you've told me has made me feel any differently.'

'Nor could it. If we dug that out of you, there wouldn't be much left.'

As we spoke I had reached the six suits of the *Demeter* party. Other than their names, stencilled above their visors, there was nothing to tell them apart. They were heavy, muscular-looking outfits made of complex metal parts, with elaborate, pressure-tight joints. They were white, but looked pale green in the light of the chamber. They were as much deep-sea diving suits as spacesuits: designed to function equally well in the Europan ocean as in the vacuum beyond the ice.

'So. Where do we start?'

'With Ramos. I've already begun elevating his consciousness

threshold, via the neuroprosthetic lace. The signals are still getting through. He'll come around in a few minutes, but we need to make sure he's fully disconnected from the machine by then.'

'How?'

'We excise, dear doctor. And we do it quickly, because the Edifice will almost certainly detect our intervention as soon as we begin. It's sleepy, but it's not dead. We'll be severing its nerve tissue. It'll hurt.'

'Good.'

'I assume the Hippocratic oath doesn't extend to malevolent alien machines?'

'Not today it doesn't.'

She made an approving sound. 'I like the cut of your jib, Silas Coade.'

I knelt down and opened the toolkit, racking open the interior compartments to inspect their contents. LEDs glowed around the padded recesses where the individual items were stored, gleaming and clean. These tools had never been intended for surgery in any orthodox sense, but there was hardly anything that could not be adapted in some fashion. There were power tools – saws, scrapers and drills – for cutting away samples for analysis, lasers and plasma torches for performing ablative spectroscopy, micro-manipulators for interfacing with nanoscale structures, if any were present. With these instruments, I could cut, cauterise and suture, with no difficulty at all.

'The only thing missing is a nice French-made trephination brace from about 1790. But I think we can make do.'

'I rather liked that earnest young doctor with his snuff habit. All he wanted was a quiet life back home.'

'He had no idea.' I extracted one of the powered cutters: a gun-shaped tool with a high-speed circular saw on the end of a shaft. It felt heavy, solid and dependable in my phantom grip. I clicked it on and watched the saw whirr up to speed. 'I'm ready, Ada.'

'Your patient is warming nicely. Do your worst.'

I knelt down to start at the lowest part of Ramos, severing the connections around his feet and lower legs. The fronds cut cleanly, but their ends twitched back as they severed, indicating some reflex or sensorimotor response. There was nothing I could do about that except keep operating quickly and methodically, working my way up to his midriff. It was like hacking away foliage that had begun to grow around and infiltrate the stone matrix of a statue.

'Will his suit still be airtight after all this?' I asked.

'Telemetry says so. The fronds penetrated him at multiple sites, interfacing with his central and peripheral nervous system, but they've self-sealed at the point of entry through the suit's integuments. Provided we don't disturb them after they're cut, he should be able to tolerate water and vacuum for long enough to get to safety.'

'He'll need help after that. He'll still have those things grow-ing into him, even if they're not connected to the machine.'

'That's a problem for the doctor who has to get him and the others out of their suits. It may be more than any of them can take, Silas, but it'll still be better than leaving them here.'

'I understand.'

'Good. Ramos is approaching consciousness. He'll appreciate a friendly voice. Do you want to practise your bedside manner?'

'I feel as if I've known this man all my life, and at the same time I know nothing about him at all.'

'Did you consider him a friend?'

I gave my answer the consideration it was due, thinking back to warm fires in my cabin, glasses of sherry, guitar music, and quiet, companionable conversation. 'Yes. I suppose I did.'

'Then you'll consider him a friend now.'

'And what will he make of me, exactly? I've always thought of him as a man, and that hasn't changed. But he knows exactly what I am!'

'Then he has no illusions to shatter. Treat him with the consideration you showed when you thought you were alive, Silas. He'll expect no more of you than that.'

I swallowed. 'I'll try.'

'He's alert. Speak to him.'

'Coronel Ramos?' I asked, in the half-distracted manner of someone talking while they attended to some difficult, delicate business at the same time. 'Can you hear me, Coronel?'

His voice sounded in my helmet: 'Silas?'

'Yes, it's me. I'm with you. Do you know where you are and what's happened?'

I continued working while I waited for his answer.

'We went inside.'

'Yes. That's good. There were six of you, all in Mark Thirteen-Five multimode environmental suits. That's where you are now, in your suit, inside the object.'

'I am starting to remember. There was—' He stopped. 'No! I do not want to remember! Make me sleep again, please!'

'I can't, Coronel,' I said firmly. 'I need you alive and awake, so you can help me to help the others. Something very bad happened to you all, I know. But there's a way out. A rescue plan. I can get you to safety, back to *Demeter* and back to space, in time to rendezvous with the orbiter. You can go home, back to Earth. Back to your beloved homeland. Back to Valladolid.'

'I have had . . . such strange dreams. There were other ships. We were at sea, then in the air! You were a man!'

'I know a little about those dreams. I had them as well.'

Something of the practicalities of the situation must have begun to penetrate his awareness. 'How are you here, Silas? We never had a medical robot that could operate outside the ship.'

'We found a workaround,' I said tersely, stung by the confirmation, if it were needed at all, that he knew my true nature. He knew that I was not a man, but a medical program, a piece of software that could project its awareness through *Demeter*, diagnose ailments and direct robotic surgical systems to address them, but which had no embodiment or life beyond that. It was anomalous to him that I was even capable of being present in the Edifice.

'However you are here, I am glad that you came,' he said.

Something caught in my throat. 'I'm just an autonomous system. You don't need to be glad about me.'

'But you came anyway. I do not know how, but you are here. What are you doing?'

I decided that the truth was the least he deserved. 'The Edifice seems to have extended its nervous system into you, puncturing your suit and body. We think it's been trying to gather information, learning what it can about humanity as a species. I'm cutting through those connections as we speak. Hopefully it's hurting the machine more than it's hurting you.'

'I feel little prickles of cold, then nothing.' He was silent for a moment. 'I think I can wiggle my fingers. I am trying to open my eyes, but that is harder.'

'They've probably been shut for a very long time. It won't be easy, but try if you can.'

'Will my suit still work?'

'It should. We have its health telemetry, its life-support capability and energy reserves, and there's nothing to suggest it won't be capable of powered movement.'

'And the others?'

I allowed myself a smile, or at least the self-generated illusion of one. Coronel Ramos was coming back to us, with his natural concern for the rest of the expedition.

'Complicated,' I said. 'It's been different for you. That surgical procedure turned out to be a blessing in disguise.'

'It did not feel like a blessing.'

Memories floated back to me. The experimental hibernation system *Demeter* had employed on its outbound leg to Jupiter was far from proven. One of the side-effects, gravely underestimated before launch, was an elevated risk of intracranial bleeding.

'After the surgery, you were left with a neuroprosthetic monitoring lace inside your skull. It was a standard precaution, to give me advance warning of any repeat episodes or post-operative complications. The lace helped once you were stuck inside this thing. It gave me a window into your higher brain functions, allowing me to raise you to an elevated level of consciousness without risk of brain injury or overburdening your life-support systems.'

He mused on my explanation for a few moments. 'That is why I have had these curious dreams?'

'Yes. Those were my doing. I've been whispering into your head, keeping you with me, ready for the moment when we needed to work together.'

'A ship is a dream of whispers.'

'So a friend of mine once told me.' I stepped back, powering down the cutter. 'All right. I think I've eliminated the major connections. Do you think you can try moving? Your suit should detect and amplify your locomotor intentions, even if your muscles have atrophied.'

'Let me try.'

Nothing happened at first, but I was patient. Ramos had not moved in a long while, and neither had his suit. Both would be sluggish to begin with. I extended a hand, ready to offer support if he stumbled, even in the weak gravity of Europa.

'You can do this, Coronel.'

'It seems that I must.' He strained with the effort of regaining control of his own body. 'What of the others? Can they be woken?'

'In time, but it's not likely to be quite so straightforward a procedure as it was with you. But if we can get them free, that's all we need to do. They don't need to be awake. Their suits can be slaved to follow yours, tracing your footsteps all the way out.'

'They have all survived this ordeal?'

'Yes,' I answered, with just the barest catch in my voice. 'We've been able to monitor their biometric functions, even as the Edifice sucks the life out of them.'

His suit twitched. Ramos must have felt the response, for with a grunt of effort and concentration he made his forearm lift away from the alcove, dragging the severed threads of tendrils with it, like a ragged sleeve.

'Could the others be helped as well, Silas? They might be Topolsky's rivals, but to me they are just as stupid and brave as the rest of us.'

'It's too late for them; I'm sorry. The process was much further along: the life sucked out of them completely. I'm just glad that we got to you in time.'

Stiffly at first, but with growing confidence, he shuffled his suit out of the alcove. Tendrils ripped away, leaving a sort of shaggy, sea-weed-coloured second skin. He lifted his hand to the level of his visor. The datapad on the cuff glowed brightly against the Thirteen-Five's multi-environment armour. 'I am starting to see,' he said. 'Nothing is in focus, but at least I can see. Are you there, Silas? I sense someone next to me.'

'It's another suit. A straight Mark Thirteen, the kind used by *Europa*'s expedition.'

'How can you be wearing a suit?'

'It's complicated.'

'You are starting to like that word.'

'I'm riding the suit. I'm still running inside *Demeter*, but we've established a two-way control link to this unit. Instead of seeing the world through the cameras and sensors inside *Demeter*,

I'm using the systems built into this suit. I feel . . . present.'

'You say "we".'

'I'm with Ada. She's been helping me to help you. Ada is . . . another piece of software. A sort of autonomous sub-element of myself.'

Silent until now, she interjected: 'Who are you calling a sub-element, bucko?'

Ramos gave a wry chuckle. 'I heard her! Her voice feels familiar to me. I have known her already, I think. You were always there, both of you, while I slept.'

'I'm sorry there aren't human voices to greet you. I hope we'll do for the time being.'

'A voice is a voice, Silas. And you too, Ada.'

'I like him already,' she said.

Ramos turned around, examining me fully. His face floated behind the thick glass of his visor. It was Ramos as I knew him, but he had the look of a man at the end of a long, depleting illness, hollow-cheeked and sunken-eyed. Those eyes were open now, to narrow slits.

'There is a dead body inside that suit, Silas.'

'I know.' I pushed a note of squeaky embarrassment into my voice. 'Awkward.'

'Indeed. But I suppose you did not have much choice in the matter.'

'Her name was Lenka Frondel, one of the *Europa* party. She got cut off from the other members of the first expedition, lost in the guts of this thing. Ada located the suit's telemetry feed and worked out that we could make it work for us. It was the only way I could get to you.'

'You did well to find us.'

My gaze flicked to the suit belonging to Dupin. 'Yes,' I replied. 'We did well.'

'Something is wrong?'

I knelt down to the toolkit again, taking out one of the other cutters. 'We need to get them free, and it'll be much quicker if the two of us work together. Can you help, Coronel?'

'I can try.'

'Good. Start at the bottom and work up to the top, severing the connections a few centimetres from the points of entry. Don't get too close in. The fronds shrink back once they're cut, so we want to allow a little slack, to preserve suit integrity.'

His hand closed around the tool I offered. He moved to face the next alcove along. 'I shall start with Dupin.'

'I'll . . . deal with him,' I said. 'His connections are a little more convoluted, and Ada will need to guide me. Start with Brucker. I'll work on Topolsky, then we can tackle Murgatroyd and Mortlock.'

I had no doubt that he sensed my reticence. Equally I had no doubt that Ramos understood that there would be sound medical reasons for every recommendation I made.

He said nothing, and we set to work.

Chapter Thirty

We had not been at it for more than about five minutes when the Edifice started responding. It was as if a pulse of vitality flowed back into the fronds, causing them to throb and creep, strengthening their hold on the remaining captives. Ramos and I were at risk as well, for the fronds were pushing out feelers which licked and curled around our boots, assessing if we were of interest to the larger organism. This sense of a slow, dangerous awakening extended to larger structures in the room, the pipes and vessels which until now had been little more than obstacles. Vibrations and groaning sounds reached us, and my peripheral vision detected ominous hints of larger movement, a narrowing of passages and squeeze-points, not enough – yet – to seriously impede our escape, but threatening to do so if allowed to continue.

'We're not even close to getting them free,' I said. 'We have to work faster.'

'No,' Ada said. 'You'll do more harm than good. Just keep working methodically, like good surgeons. I'll take care of the Edifice.'

'You'll what?'

'I've prepared for this. In a few moments there'll be an event which causes the machine distress. If I've gambled correctly, it'll knock it out cold for long enough for you to complete your work, slave the suits to your own, and begin your egress.'

'I like that she says "gambled", Silas. I am always filled with confidence when I hear that word.'

'I agree, Coronel. But I also have faith in Ada. What have you got for us?'

'A distraction. The eversion has made the Edifice extraordinarily susceptible to external energy effects. Think about Dupin's mathematical transformation, and what it did. We've seen two types of surface patterning on the object.'

'Smooth areas and spined areas,' I said.

'Yes. Now wind the eversion back to its starting point. When this machine was made, or spawned, or however it came into existence, it must have had the form of a thick-walled shell. Dupin's analysis allows two possibilities: that the spines were entirely on the outside, once, or entirely on the inside. Let's go with the latter. The smooth surface becomes the outer shell of a space-faring, intelligence-gathering machine, and the spined parts – the towers and battlements of your earlier visions – must be the innards, the cybernetic nervous system. They'd have carpeted the entire inner part, bristling in towards the middle.'

I nodded. 'And now they're half in, half out.'

'Indeed. And imagine how you'd feel if half your nervous system was on the outside of your body.'

'A little on the sensitive side.'

'Whichever way around the Edifice is, inside-out, or outside-in, it's going to feel wrong – very wrong. And be highly susceptible to external stimuli.'

'I take it you have something in mind.'

'Yes.' I could tell that Ada was trying very hard not to sound pleased with herself. 'I've found that small thermonuclear explosions are quite good at paralysing the machine. Imagine tasering an octopus. It's similar.'

'Then it's a pity we didn't bring any small thermonuclear devices with us.'

'We did,' Ramos said, ahead of me. 'And so did *Europa*. There is the main propulsion core of either ship, of course. But also the service drones and auxiliary boosters. They are common to both mission profiles. The drones contain nuclear fusion cells, and so do the boosters. Can these be used for your purposes, Ada?'

'They can, Coronel. I know because I've already used them.'

Topolsky was free of his constraints. Ramos was nearly done with Brucker. Satisfied that he could continue without supervision, I moved on to Mortlock, beginning the same slow but meticulous process of alien debridement.

'You've generated nuclear explosions?' I asked.

'Relatively small events, but enough to demonstrate the effectiveness of the method. I established control of the drones and used them to tow the boosters to various test positions in the vicinity of the object, then detonated them remotely. There were two possible benefits to this action: I hoped to affect the Edifice, and I also hoped there might be a chance of the explosions being detected from orbit, alerting Van Vught to the fact that there are still survivors down here.'

'I'm guessing that part didn't work,' I said.

'Twenty kilometres of ice is a pretty good screen, unless she happened to be passing right over the explosion. I'm afraid I couldn't plan for that. The orbiter will have had to alter its flight path many times since we descended.'

'And the first part? Weren't you worried about blowing up the whole machine?'

'That was a concern, but I knew the surrounding water would act as a very efficient force-moderator, limiting the amplitude of any shock waves. Fortunately the electromagnetic pulse was still of use to me. In fact, that was really the only part that mattered: the explosion was just an annoying side-effect.'

'There was always lightning,' I marvelled, understanding at last.

I could see it now, limning the window panes of a sailing ship, soundless and distant.

'My test events,' she said proudly. 'They were intense enough to punch right through the layers of denial and metaphor you hid inside, Silas. You *saw* them – you just didn't permit yourself to understand them.'

'Better late than never.'

'You have kept back some of these boosters and drones?' Ramos asked.

'No – they're all used up.'

'Then we have a difficulty, it would seem.'

'Only one of magnitude, Coronel. We still have *Europa*. Just as I was able to establish control of her suit and her drones, I have complete access to her propulsion core. In fact, it's just about to exceed safe fusion limits . . . boys?'

'Yes?' we asked.

'You might want to close your eyes.'

I had no eyes to close, and Ada knew that, but I still braced myself for what was to come. A white flash lit the chamber, and a barely separable instant later there was a rumble, as of a small earthquake, and the room rocked perceptibly. The entire Edifice had shuddered against the explosion, perhaps even shifting within its vault of ice. Perhaps even the ice above us had buckled, lifting and relaxing as the explosion's energy passed through it.

The light made no sense to me at first, for there were no windows in the chamber, and it must have been many dozens or even hundreds of metres to the point where the *Demeter* party had come inside, an immense labyrinth of narrow spaces and twisting constrictions. But of course the light had filtered in through the nervous system, the everted guts acting as a kind of fibre-optic transmitter. Half the nervous system was outside, and some large fraction of it had been exposed to Ada's explosion, providing a conduit to every other part of the Edifice.

The movements, the creeping processes I had observed before, were now stilled.

'Ada?'

'That should buy us fifteen or twenty minutes, Silas – hopefully enough to get everyone into the water and a good way back to *Demeter*. Use these minutes well.'

Ramos nodded to me, and I nodded back. No words now. We just needed to work like demons, freeing the others. Or, I thought to myself, at least those that there was any point in freeing.

Brucker, Topolsky, Mortlock and Murgatroyd were soon liberated of their connections. None of their biometric traces had fluctuated during this process, indicating that they were still holding at the same level of comatose brain activity as when I had arrived. Nothing in their suit telemetry indicated that there would be any difficulty in the suits' following slaved commands when it was time to move out. While Ramos led the way, they could shuffle after him like a chain of sleepwalkers.

'Now Dupin, Silas,' Ramos said eagerly. 'We can work on him in unison. If there is one among us who deserves to be free of this infernal place, it is him.'

He made ready to begin the cutting process. I touched my hand to his wrist and gently lowered his arm.

'I'm sorry,' I said softly. 'But he has to stay.'

Concern cracked his voice. 'You said everyone survived!'

'It wasn't a lie. But there's a problem with Dupin. A twofold problem, actually.'

He made to resume work anyway, and I used all the power in my Mark Thirteen to resist his efforts, no matter how well-intentioned they were.

'Silas! This is not like you!'

'We can't save him,' I said, sighing at my own hopelessness. 'His suit is damaged. Its life-support systems were placed in an overload condition, an emergency survival measure. It's not meant to be used for extended periods, and the strain caused a cascade of failures throughout the suit, including its locomotor capability. It can't move and if it could, it couldn't keep him alive as well.'

Ramos snarled. 'He is alive now!'

'Just barely. His brain is also very severely damaged. There's enough functionality left in the suit to provide minimal life-support function, for a few more hours.'

'Then we move the suit instead of asking it to move itself. We can carry him between us!'

'It won't matter, Coronel. Dupin's already beyond any help we can give him aboard *Demeter*, or anywhere else for that matter.'

'The Edifice did this to him?'

'No, Coronel. We did.'

He stared at me, his sunken eyes brimming with a turmoil and rage I had not detected in him until this moment. 'We, Silas?'

'Not you, friend.'

'You had better explain. I do not know if you can, but I think you had better try.'

'We have to leave. The effects of that pulse won't last for ever.'

'We do not leave without the boy.'

I seized his arm more tightly, causing him to drop the tool. No matter: we had no use for them now. 'Raymond Dupin had to die for the rest of you to live. It's as simple as that. I was lost in the Edifice. I could only find you if Dupin worked out the geometry of this place. He had to solve the eversion problem if any of you were to make it out. He did it, brilliantly. But it was at a cost. His brain function had to be elevated remotely, and each time we did that it took a little more from him.'

'No,' Ramos said. 'You could not have asked this of him.'

'We had to,' Ada said. 'You were not there, Coronel, but we were. It was our dilemma, our decision. There was no other way. If Dupin had not agreed to this, you would all still be dying in here.'

'Better to die than treat another man like something to be burned and thrown away!'

'Coronel,' I said. 'We must move. Voluntarily, or otherwise.'

There was menace in his answer. 'Otherwise, Silas?'

'I can compel you. If those other suits can be slaved to follow yours, then yours can be slaved to follow this Mark Thirteen.'

'You would not make a puppet of me, Silas. You are better than that.' He regarded me, slowly shaking his head behind the glass. 'At least I thought you were. I see now that I was wrong. And I see the coldness that was always there, but which I pretended was warmth. You are just another machine, despite everything. You are as bad as *this*!'

'His suit is slaved to yours now,' Ada said. 'We don't have time for this. None of them have time for it.'

'Coronel,' I said, beginning to follow the path that would lead us all out of the chamber. 'You'll hate me for this, and I understand it. But if am to save even a single human life, Dupin must remain here.'

'Life is not calculus, you cold-hearted . . . algorithm.'

'Life might not be,' I said, steeling myself against his enmity. 'But in medicine we use our energies to help those we can, not those we cannot.'

'You murdered him.'

'Dupin chose to save the rest of you. He consented. Hate me, by all means. But if you want to honour that boy, you'll do so by saving your own neck.'

Ada did me a favour then: she turned off the voice-link from Coronel Ramos. He followed me in uncomplaining silence, and behind him came the other sleepwalkers I meant to shepherd back to safety, and life.

Chapter Thirty-one

There were two critical parts to the first stage of our exodus: finding a way out of the Edifice, and navigating the black waters back to *Demeter*. I could do nothing to improve our chances in either respect, other than to move with maximum haste. I had taken all necessary precautions in freeing the suits from their imprisonment, and none of the telemetric feeds were indicating serious system faults or integrity failures. The suits were in remarkably good condition, considering. The alien machine had not dismantled them, and their functioning was either sufficiently transparent or irrelevant enough for it not to take any further interest in them. It was the warm, soft, fleshy things inside them that had snared its attention; our ships and suits were good for materials and little else.

We reached the water, the limpet-like hydro-lock functioning perfectly. The suits detected the transition to a liquid environment and adjusted their thermal balances, buoyancy control and locomotor functions accordingly. We swam back beneath the ceiling of ice, moving with the vast, slow grace of belugas. *Demeter* was still there: there was no need to worry about that. If she had been badly damaged or destroyed in the explosion, there would be no 'me' left to execute within her computer systems.

There was darkness ahead of me, an unending sheet of ice

above, and then a fuzzy pattern of lights resolved out of the gloom. There was the green, red and white of the navigation strobes, the amber markers indicating lock positions, and a random, blue-white flickering dancing around like fireflies.

I had no idea what to make of the latter.

'I see *Demeter*, Ada!'

'Good. *Demeter* sees you, as well. You're about sixty metres out. I'm assigning the suits to multiple hydro-locks, so that we can bring everyone in as quickly as possible.'

'A question.'

'By all means. You've earned it.'

'What will happen to me once we're all inside? Lenka's suit helped me find the others, and lead them to safety . . . but there'll be no need for me to have a body once I'm back inside.'

She sounded surprised at my question. 'You won't miss what you never had, Silas.'

'I'll just be numbers again, symbols scrolling behind a screen.'

'That's all that you ever were.'

'I know. But for a little while I dreamed I was something else.'

'You were just simulating a set of experiences. Our engineers wanted you to understand people, so that you could heal them better. If they'd wanted you to treat dogs, you'd have dreamed you were a dog: probably something small, annoying and yappy.'

'I sense you're trying to help here.'

'I wish there was more I could offer. But at least we're both in this together.'

'Ramos hates me.'

'No, he's beyond that. Hate is something humans feel for each other. He doesn't think of you as anything at all any more.'

I pondered her answer. 'Have you ever considered a career in psychiatry, Ada?'

'Not to date.'

'Good. I'd give it a wide berth if I were you.'

'His feelings don't change what you did,' she said. There was bluntness in her tone, but also something else, something not entirely removed from understanding. 'You confronted a truth about yourself that you didn't want to face. In accepting that truth, you were at last able to find a way to save the people under your care. That's not failure, Silas, it's the shouldering of responsibility. It's duty. It's doing the one thing you were made to do.'

'So much for free will, if I was made to do it.'

'But you nearly didn't do it. That's the point. You and I were manifestations of a self-generated decision-action dilemma. A battle of wills, the ego versus the superego, the id versus . . . whatever. You're right, Cody: I'd make a lousy psychiatrist. But this I know: somehow or other you made a choice to do the right thing by your patients.'

'Except that right thing cost Dupin his life.'

'There was no other way. Let me stress that for you. *There was no other way*. If you had a skull I'd crack that into you.'

'I do have a skull. It's just not mine. Oh, god. What are we going to do with Lenka Frondel?'

'Right now her bones are the least of my worries, Silas: I have the living to look after.' She switched to a businesslike tone. 'All right. Locks are open and ready. I have you all on final approach.'

'Ada?'

'Yes?'

'Send Ramos to a different lock. He won't want to be in the same room as me just now.' Under my voice I added: 'Or me him.'

Demeter swam into full view, and a shiver ran through me. Much had happened while I had been away. The fronds had extended their hold on her, coiling and wrapping around her hull much more insidiously than I had expected.

'I suppose you were waiting for the right time to tell me the bad news.'

'We still have a margin of safety, Silas. The activity quickened after the Edifice recovered from the nuclear pulse, but the service drones are keeping it at bay. How long they can keep doing that, I dare not say. That's why I've already begun the departure protocols.'

The drones – there were just three of them left now – were swimming around the hull, using plasma torches on the ends of their robotic arms. That was the random flickering I had seen from sixty metres out: the drones trying to prune the fronds faster than they could grow and consolidate.

I swam to the lock she had assigned me, alone with my cargo of bones.

Chapter Thirty-two

Air flooded the chamber, displacing the water; biocontamination measures and safety checks cycled, and after an eternity of waiting the inner door opened. Still operating Lenka's suit, I eased myself out into the familiar environs of the ship. Compared to when I had last seen these panels and readouts, the ship was in a higher state of arousal. The main lighting had come on, and the diagrams and status displays showed a variety of mission-critical systems slowly being brought back to readiness. Main life-support, primary power, submarine and trans-ice propulsion systems, in-space motors, all emerging from deep, deliberate slumber. It would have been nice to rush it all, but the ship was a puzzle that needed to be put back together in exactly the right sequence, a step at a time, or the whole thing would collapse. Ada knew this. She was not the ship itself, but like a good administrator she knew precisely which subordinates to talk to, and how to get them to do her bidding.

Beyond the windows, blue-white flickering showed the ongoing work of the service drones. That flickering was a little less frequent than before, and I took that to be a welcome indication that the fronds were loosening their hold on us.

'Are we all aboard, Ada?'

'Yes – final locks are just cycling. We'll move the others to safe positions for departure, but for now I see no sense in removing their suits. They still have ample power for life-support, mobility if needed, and the biometric feeds are still giving me useful information about their occupants' health. The best we can do now is hope that they're stable. There'll be no possibility of any medical or surgical intervention until we're clear of Europa, and it'll probably have to wait until we've RV'd with the cruise module.'

I nodded. 'I concur. Those suits have done a damned good job keeping their occupants alive until now – they can manage like that for a little longer. You'll alert me the moment anything changes in their feeds?'

'Of course.'

I tilted my head to the nearest window. 'It looks like we're winning that battle, at least.'

'I wish. We're down one drone since you were outside. The Edifice is surprisingly adaptive. It's realised that it can't take *Demeter* until it takes the drones, so it's concentrating all its efforts on picking them off one at a time.'

'Can we still do this?'

'I think so.'

'You *think*?'

'One problem at a time, Silas.'

Noise and motion snagged my attention. A suit was approaching down the lateral axis corridor, its enormous form so large it barely fit between the modules on either side. The Mark Thirteen-Fives were bulkier than the Thirteen I still wore, but those extra layers of insulation and component redundancy had probably made the difference between life and death for the occupants.

Ramos reached up and unlatched the pressure-release collar under his helmet. He drew the helmet up over his head, which looked even more shrunken in on itself now that it jutted out of the neck ring.

He flipped the helmet around and pressed the velcro patch on its crown against one of the stowage pads on the wall.

'You at least allow me the dignity of choosing my own movements now. But what about the others?'

'Can you hear me?' I asked.

He glared at me as if the question were insulting. 'Your voice comes out the walls just as it always did. The only difference is I know better than to presume that there's a conscience behind it.'

'You always knew I was a program.'

He knuckled his glove against the side of his skull, hard enough to make me wince. The suit's power-assist was supposed to be clever enough to prevent its wearer inadvertently braining themselves, but sometimes things went wrong.

'I knew, yes. Until I was carried along in your . . . dreams, or whatever you call them. You were a man! You made me believe a lie, while I was in that thing.' Ramos made a spitting motion, but nothing came out. 'You deceived me.'

'If it's any help, I deceived myself as well.'

He shook his head, disgusted at the sight of me. 'You play with us as if we are puppets. Not just jerking our strings, but deciding what we think and dream as well!'

'I was engineered to have an empathetic faculty. I was meant to identify with my patients, meant to see them as more than just sacks of meat.'

'So now you blame your creators?'

'I blame no one and nothing,' I said, anger rising in me. 'Except the nightmare we found ourselves in. I don't even blame Topolsky's lust for fame and fortune that brought us here. He's the product of a system. So are we all.'

'There is no "we". You are not one of us. You were never one of us.' His hand moved to the mission patch, sprayed onto the shoulder of his Thirteen-Five. 'Van Vught, Murgatroyd, Mortlock, Brucker, Dupin, Ramos. Is your name among them?'

'No.'

'Then you know what you are. Nothing.'

'I may be nothing,' I answered steadfastly. 'But I still want to do the right thing. None of you are safe just yet. That means I still have executive functions to discharge. You may not like me, Coronel, but your medical well-being is still my responsibility. That doesn't just include treating your brain injury and saving your life, which I did. It means keeping you alive in the here and now, too.'

His nostrils flared, his lips curling to a sneer. He wanted to strike back, but I had deliberately touched a nerve by reminding him of his debt to me.

I was not sorry to have done it.

'What of the others?' he snarled.

'Ada and I will move their suits into the acceleration hammocks. They can stay unconscious until then. It's kinder.'

'Kindness. You think you understand anything of kindness?'

'I know for a fact that I once recognised the kindness and compassion of a friend,' I said.

Ramos made an exasperated, dismissive snort. 'Nothing you say has meaning.' Then, slowly becoming aware of our status: 'If we are all aboard, why is *Demeter* not returning to the exit fissure? The marine thrusters are not functioning. I know the vibration modes when they are operating.'

'Coronel Ramos? This is Ada.'

He looked around for the faceless voice, disgust creasing the bridge of his nose.

'I do not need another one of you pretending to be something you are not.'

'No, but you probably need the facts. Your operational role is still Security Fulfilment, I believe?'

'What of it?'

'Silas still has his responsibilities, and so do you. His is to ensure the health of the crew. Yours is to maximise the likelihood of mission deliverance. That means getting the survivors back aboard the cruise module, with or without the lander.'

For the first time since he had taken off his helmet I saw something of the old Ramos: puzzlement denting his brow, the gears of professional concern working behind his eyes.

'Why can we not return to orbit in the lander?'

'Because *Demeter* isn't going anywhere, dear Coronel. We're stuck fast and the fronds have just destroyed another service drone. There is one unit left, and I can keep it out of harm's way for the time being, but it won't be enough to stop those fronds wrapping around us and holding us in place.'

Ramos looked dumbstruck. I do not think he doubted any part of Ada's summary, for while we might have deceived him about our true natures, there was no possible reason for her to suppress or exaggerate the facts about the mission.

'The other ship is gone.'

'Yes,' I said.

'Then we are finished too. If we cannot leave, then it is only a question of time. We will either die in this ship, when its systems break down, or in that water, when our suits give out, or the Edifice will take us back into itself.' He shuddered, as if – at some point in the not too distant future – it might even fall upon him to choose between these thoroughly disagreeable deaths. 'They tried to warn us, didn't they. There was always that message, telling us to leave. Who left it, do you think? The one whose bones you shuffled around? Do you mock me by reminding me of the warnings I failed to heed?'

'Coronel,' I said, trying to reach any part of him that might yet view me with something other than complete contempt. 'Ada's tactless, but she isn't cruel. She wouldn't have mentioned mission deliverance unless there was a way. And there *is* a way, isn't there?'

She kept both of us waiting a fraction longer than was strictly necessary. Perhaps I was wrong about the cruel part, in a very small way. If so, it only made me more drawn to her. What was sugar, without a little salt to help it along?

'Of course there's a way: the fissure's still there. Topolsky's Fissure! Between the original impact event, and two ships melting their way down through the entry track left by the Edifice, the ice is still highly disorganised and fragmented. It hasn't had anywhere near enough time to heal and re-form. That means there's a path. Not an easy one, or a short one, but a path. I couldn't send a drone back up it, too cumbersome, and we'd lose the control signals. But a suit, under human control? It's possible. You can climb back up through the fissure, picking your way through the crevasses and channels that haven't yet closed up.'

'It is twenty kilometres to the surface!'

'Yes,' she said cheerily. 'Probably more like forty, given the path the fissure takes through the ice. And first you've got to swim to the exit point! But once you're into the ice, you just have to keep going up. Forty kilometres really isn't too far, when you think about it. Not in this gravity. It'll just be like . . . a really arduous, punishing ascent of a Himalayan mountain. And you'll have power-assist, so it'll be tedious and difficult rather than exhausting . . . although, given the time constraints, you probably won't want to sleep. Or rest. Or stop at any point.'

'Time constraints?'

'You have less than sixty hours. In about fifty-six, assuming the standard mission profile, Jennifer Van Vught will begin putting the cruise module on its Earth-return trajectory. You'll need to be near the surface by then, so your suit transponders have a chance of getting a clear signal to orbit.'

'And then what? She waves at us before abandoning us to our fate?'

'You know the emergency contingency protocols as well as anyone,' Ada said gently. 'The cruise module is capable of landing, if there's an urgent need. It's not low-risk, and the manoeuvre will affect the fuel budget for the Earth-return boost, but it's still feasible. Jennifer Van Vught's a stickler, but she's also brave and selfless. She'll do it, but only if she detects your presence.'

Ramos looked around, as if all he wanted was a familiar human face to address. When that failed, he turned his gaze on my visor. His focus was slippery, as if he preferred to look through or past me rather than acknowledge the corpse behind the glass.

'You believe her, that this is the only way?'

'Yes.'

'She says sixty hours. Even less than that. It might not be possible.'

'It is,' I said. 'But only because the man leading the escape party will be the brilliant, brave Coronel Ramos. You'll do it. Every step you make, the other suits will follow blindly. You won't even need to worry about them. Just get yourself out of here, and you'll save everyone.'

He sniffed. He was measuring my words, deciding for himself what he found useful in them, and what he could ball up and discard like yesterday's rubbish.

'You think you know what I am capable of?'

'I've shared too many stories with you not to have an opinion of your abilities.'

He cocked his head upward, to the ceiling of ice beyond our hull. 'And you – you will also climb through the ice with us?'

'No,' I answered. 'That won't work. I can only execute on *Demeter.*'

Suspicion played on his face. 'The signals allowed you to operate that suit from a kilometre away, through the fabric of the Edifice.'

'Yes, that was possible. But we can't get a similar signal through the ice. If we could, we'd have already sent word to Van Vught to delay the departure boost.' I made a vague, dismissive gesture with Lenka's glove. 'Oh, if we had time, I'm sure we could rig something up. We could extract enough functioning processor cores from the computer, put them in a cargo pallet or something. I could be dragged up the fissure, a brain in a box. But we don't have that time. There isn't even time to make a back-up image of me.' I touched a finger to my chest. 'I've learned a lot since we left Earth, Coronel. That was always part of the plan: that I'd self-educate myself, gaining experience on the job. When we got back, our engineers were going to strip me back to bare code and suck out all the useful lessons I'd picked up along the way, so the next generation of medical expert systems could be even more useful.' I forced a sad, accepting smile. 'But that won't happen now. None of me will get back to Earth. Not the surgical experience I've gained, not my increased understanding of human psychology, not the friendships I think I've made. Not the songs you taught me, or the stories. Not one of them.'

He continued measuring me. I had seen his face many times, through many moods, and I think I had learned to detect the tiny slippages that presaged a shift in his thoughts, however tentative.

I saw one of those slippages now. An easing in him. Something yielding.

'You will not survive?'

'No. Nor will Ada. We're both tied to *Demeter*. When it goes down, so do we. And one way or another, this ship has a very limited future.'

'You will . . . deactivate yourself, before the end?'

What was that, I wondered: a flicker of concern for me, after everything? But I had to disappoint him.

'No.'

'You will . . . die, when the ship dies?' He reached for the helmet he had only lately fixed to the wall. 'You will die in here?'

'Not that either,' I answered, taking some little pinch of pleasure in his confusion. 'The dying part, yes. We'll stop executing, but it won't hurt when it happens. And there is more good news: since *Demeter* won't have much else to do, Ada and I can co-opt a much bigger portion of the computer core. We can . . . work much faster, taking over resources normally reserved for other systems. However much time we have left, we can stretch it out.'

'But not indefinitely.'

'No,' I agreed. 'Not indefinitely.'

Ramos cradled his helmet between his fingers. He was on the verge of putting it on again. Something stilled him, though. Perhaps it was the thought that this might be the last breath of nearly fresh air he ever drew in, before bottling himself back into the suit.

'I will lead them,' he said. 'We will survive. However difficult it is, I will find a way. I will get them back to Earth.'

'I know. I've never had more confidence in another human being.'

'Another?'

'A figure of speech, Coronel. Hopefully you will forgive me for it.'

'I want to think I was wrong about you, Silas.' He paused before settling the helmet back over his neck ring. 'You were a friend, for a while. If I was mistaken about that, then I was mistaken. But I cannot forget that boy we left behind.'

'He's my responsibility now,' I replied.

Some trace of his contempt returned. 'You speak of responsibility, after we abandoned him?'

'I'm going back in.'

He was silent, the helmet still suspended. His eyes narrowed, not quite ready to trust me even to the last.

'In?'

'Dupin is still alive. His biometric trace is weak, but it's there. I can't save him, can't heal him, can't even bring his body home. I probably can't even talk to him. But I can be with him. I can be by his side, as a doctor should be.'

Ramos held his composure for a long moment then nodded.

'I believe you will do this.'

'I will.'

'No part of you will make it back to Earth?'

'None at all.'

'But I will remember what you have done, and what you were like. It will not be much, I know.'

'It will be everything, Coronel.'

Without answering he lowered his helmet, latched the seal and turned his vast back on me, heading for the hydro-lock, with the other suits and their human payloads falling into place behind him.

I mouthed a silent farewell to my big, brutish friend.

It was time for all of us to abandon ship.

*

Faith was an odd thing for a machine to depend on, but in the end it was all that I had. That ice was still an impenetrable barrier to our signals. Once Ramos and the others were gone, there could be no possible news of their success or failure. I could only assume that Ada's plan was a sound one, and that the suits did indeed have the capability of climbing back to the surface, that Ramos was the man to lead that venture, and that the fates would not be so cruel as to have Jennifer Van Vught break orbit sooner than expected, so that there was no chance of making that daring landing.

So yes: all that remained was faith, and I decided to accept its sufficiency. Let it be enough. Let it be ordained that Ramos and the others would indeed make it home. Let there be no doubt about that.

I allowed it into myself. Perhaps, because I was just a machine, it was an easier acceptance than for some. I merely had to change some of my internal state parameters to accept one truth over another.

'Raymond?' I asked gently. 'It's Silas. I'm with you again.' I rested my hand against his, wondering if some ghost of that contact still had the means of reaching his mind. Human contact, of a kind. One of us had never really been alive, one of us was dying. But it was still the least that he deserved.

'I'm cold, Silas,' he whispered. 'Colder than I was before.'

'I wish I could help. I can't. All I can do is be here.'

'You were gone, and then you came back.'

'Yes.'

'I can't remember why you left. Except that there was something important that I had to help you with.'

'There was.'

'Did I do all right, Silas?'

'You did more than all right. You found the solution.'

'And it was . . . correct?'

'It was correct. It was . . .' I hesitated, searching for the right words. Then I remembered what he had said to me. 'It was beautiful, Raymond. Despite all the ugliness, there was beauty at the end. And you saw it. You saw the beauty before anyone else.'

'I can still see it,' he said, finding joy even as the lights of his mind began to gutter out. 'Oh, Silas, if only you could see it as well! They'll remember me for this, won't they?'

I tightened my fingers around his. 'For a very long time.'

'I'm glad,' he answered.

'I'm glad too, Raymond.'

I stayed with him until the end, as any good doctor would have done. I remained with him until it was over, and the biometric telemetry confirmed that Raymond Dupin had passed into the infinite golden sleep that awaits all mathematicians.

He rested. He was peaceful. He would be peaceful for ever more, and I had not let him die alone.

I had not been a bad doctor.

After that, I realised that I had a final decision to make. It concerned the bones within me. I could bring the suit back to *Demeter*, or merely relinquish my control of it, leaving Lenka Frondel at peace, providing silent companionship to the strange young man she had never met, and whose name she had likely never known. Dupin was past caring about loneliness, and Frondel was past caring about what we did with her remains. Yet it mattered to me very badly that I did the right thing, the kind thing, the human thing.

In truth, it was no decision at all.

Chapter Thirty-three

The directions I had been given took me on a high, winding road above Plymouth, with the sea at my back. Half-way to my destination, sweating under my garments and the burden of my possessions, I began to regret my parsimony in not taking a coach. But since I expected to live modestly from now on, in the humble role of village doctor, I had thought it best to begin the adaptation to my new circumstances as quickly as possible.

The sun prickled the skin on the back of my neck, finding exactly that piece of flesh not already turned ruddy and leathery by my time at sea. I peeled my hat from my scalp, and employed it to fan my face. I had taken a wrong turn, I decided. Somewhere in the winding back streets which led up from the harbour, I had wandered awry, despite the simplicity of the instructions given to me.

But then it was ahead of me, hemmed in by oaks which obstructed my view of the cottage until the precise moment of my greatest despair. I smiled at my foolishness, wondering how I had ever doubted that I was on the right path. The cottage disclosed itself, opening like a picture in a child's book, and with each faltering step I wondered if some aspect of it might turn out to be less than perfect; less than suitable for my needs. I had been told it should be fitting, and not too far from the homes of my patients-to-be, and that it was solidly built and in commendable repair, and commanded a most satisfactory view back to the English Channel, but being of a naturally sceptical inclination I had assumed that in one or more respects it would falter, or present a hitherto unsuspected aspect of itself that was at odds with my desires. As I neared the white-painted fence and gate which fronted the cottage, its walls overgrown – yet not too overgrown – with honeysuckle and ivy, I saw not one detail or general feature of the property which was not to my immediate and unconditional liking, and not one thing which contradicted my favourable plans for its future.

'I can make myself a home here,' I said, grinning through tears of sweat. 'It is all that I wished. How lucky you are, Coade, to have fallen upon this!'

But there was a twitch of guilt to dampen my elation, for my good fortune was at the expense of another's ill circumstances. Although I had not even set foot in the cottage, I knew with an instinctive certainty that its insides would be as charming as the exterior, and that I should find no fault with any part of it. No one could live in such a charming abode, so grandly situated above such a fine town as Plymouth, and consent to sell it unless forced into such action by straitened or tragic circumstances. My happiness – and it was happiness, even so – was purchased on the back of another's misery, and as if in sympathy with my feelings the sun dipped behind the sky's few clouds, drawing a coolness across my spirits.

I opened the gate. I had been told the present owner was at home, and would be expecting me.

'Doctor Silas Coade?'

She was at the door already, a vision in yellow backed by the agreeable darkness of the parlour beyond. There was no negative connotation to the darkness, but rather a welcome intimation of shade in summer and domestic warmth in winter, for a house that is pleasant in one season will often be pleasant in another. I should be alone, of course, except when my patients were visiting, but at least I should be alone in a cottage accommodating to my comforts. After the travails forced upon me by my service on *Demeter*, I believed myself well versed in the notion of comfort, and its absence.

'Good afternoon to you, ma'am,' I said, tipping my wilting hat back onto my head for the express purpose of removing it again. 'It is very kind of you to agree to let me visit.'

'You are back from the sea, I gather?'

'Yes.' I hefted one of the boxes with which I had struggled up from the harbour. 'They will send my other things by cart, when I have an address, but I could not be without my journals, even if I must sleep under a tree with them.'

'I hope it will not come to that.' She stepped out into the light of day, the sun peeking back out from the cloud to strike its light across her, as in a beautification. It was the sweat in my eyes, but she seemed to glow and gleam as if hewn from gold itself. 'Your voyage – I trust it was successful?'

I smiled in what I hoped was a modest, self-abashed fashion. 'I hope I may have been of some small service.'

'Your profession?'

'Assistant Surgeon on the fifth-rate sloop *Demeter*. A modest enough calling, but not without one or two demands.'

'And now – they tell me – you shall forsake the sea, for the life of a landlubbing doctor?'

'That is my intention, ma'am.'

'My name is Cossile. You may call me that, or Ada if you prefer. I think you will come to prefer Ada, in time.'

'In time?' I asked, puzzled and bemused.

'I am sorry to disappoint you, Doctor Coade – may I call you Silas?'

'You may,' I said, doubtfully, and with an awful apprehension welling inside me, that this dream was about to be snatched from me no sooner than it had been presented.

'I am widowed, Silas. Believing myself to be on the brink of destitution, I made arrangements to vacate the house. But I was too hasty.'

'Hasty?'

'A source of money has come my way, by means of a distant branch of the family. A considerable source. I am now a woman of independent means, and want no longer compels me to sell Hilltop Cottage. I shall not be leaving.'

I tipped my hat again, preparing to be on my way before the fact of my disappointment showed too plainly in my face. I did not want the least thing to spoil the excellent reversal of fortune experienced by Ada Cossile, not even my sadness that I should likely not see her cottage again, or gaze upon her own fairness.

'I am delighted that you shall have the enjoyment of this home for as long as you live, Ada.'

'You shall move in with me.'

I wondered if I had misheard. It seemed impossible. 'I . . . shall move in with you?'

She asked sharply: 'You have need of a residence, in which to practise your surgery?'

'I . . . do,' I said.

'The walk from town is not too disagreeable?'

'It is perfectly fine.'

'Then would it disgust you, to share a home with me?'

'It . . . would not. Not by any means. But the arrangement is a little . . . unconventional.'

'Then we shall embrace the unconventional.' She indicated the gate, over which my hand was still hovering. 'Come inside. I think you will like what I have to show you. There is a view of the sea which some find disappointing, since the sea is visible, but not too visible.' Then, seeing my confusion – my sense that the world was playing some joke upon me, and that I would soon find myself the focus of its mocking cruelty – she made an impatient beckoning gesture with her hand. It was a fine hand, and I wondered if I might soon touch it. 'This way, Silas. We have time – quite a lot of time – but not nearly as much as we might wish. So let us make the most of that which remains.'

I delayed for a moment, wishing to remain in that rapture of happiness for as long as possible. Then I followed Ada Cossile into Hilltop Cottage.

Credits

Alastair Reynolds and Gollancz would like to thank everyone at Orion who worked on the publication of *Eversion*.

Agent
Robert Kirby

Editorial
Gillian Redfearn
Claire Ormsby-Potter
Áine Feeney

Copy-editor
Elizabeth Dobson

Proofreader
Andy Ryan

Editorial Management
Jane Hughes
Charlie Panayiotou
Tamara Morriss
Claire Boyle

Audio
Paul Stark
Jake Alderson
Georgina Cutler

Contracts
Anne Goddard
Ellie Bowker
Humayra Ahmed

Design
Nick Shah
Tomás Almeida
Joanna Ridley
Helen Ewing

Finance
Nick Gibson
Jasdip Nandra

Elizabeth Beaumont
Ibukun Ademefun
Afeera Ahmed
Sue Baker
Tom Costello

Inventory
Jo Jacobs
Dan Stevens

Marketing
Lucy Cameron

Production
Paul Hussey
Fiona McIntosh

Publicity
Will O'Mullane

Sales
Jen Wilson
Victoria Laws
Esther Waters
Frances Doyle
Ben Goddard
Jack Hallam
Anna Egelstaff
Inês Figueira

Barbara Ronan
Andrew Hally
Dominic Smith
Deborah Deyong
Lauren Buck
Maggy Park
Linda McGregor
Sinead White
Jemimah James
Rachael Jones
Jack Dennison
Nigel Andrews
Ian Williamson
Julia Benson
Declan Kyle
Robert Mackenzie
Megan Smith
Charlotte Clay
Rebecca Cobbold

Operations
Sharon Willis

Rights
Susan Howe
Krystyna Kujawinska
Jessica Purdue
Ayesha Kinley
Louise Henderson